Writer: *Paul Tobin*
Penciler: *Alvin Lee*
Inker: *Terry Pallot*
Colorists: *Val Staples with Emily Warren (Issue #1)*
Letterer: *Blambot's Nate Piekos*
Cover Art: *Roger Cruz with Guru eFX, Christina Strain & Val Staples*
Assistant Editor: *Nathan Cosby*
Editor: *Mark Paniccia*

Collection Editor: *Jennifer Grünwald*
Editorial Assistant: *Alex Starbuck*
Assistant Editors: *Cory Levine & John Denning*
Editor, Special Projects: *Mark D. Beazley*
Senior Editor, Special Projects: *Jeff Youngquist*
Senior Vice President of Sales: *David Gabriel*
Book Designer: *Spring Hoteling*
Vice President of Creative: *Tom Marvelli*

Editor in Chief: *Joe Quesada*
Publisher: *Dan Buckley*

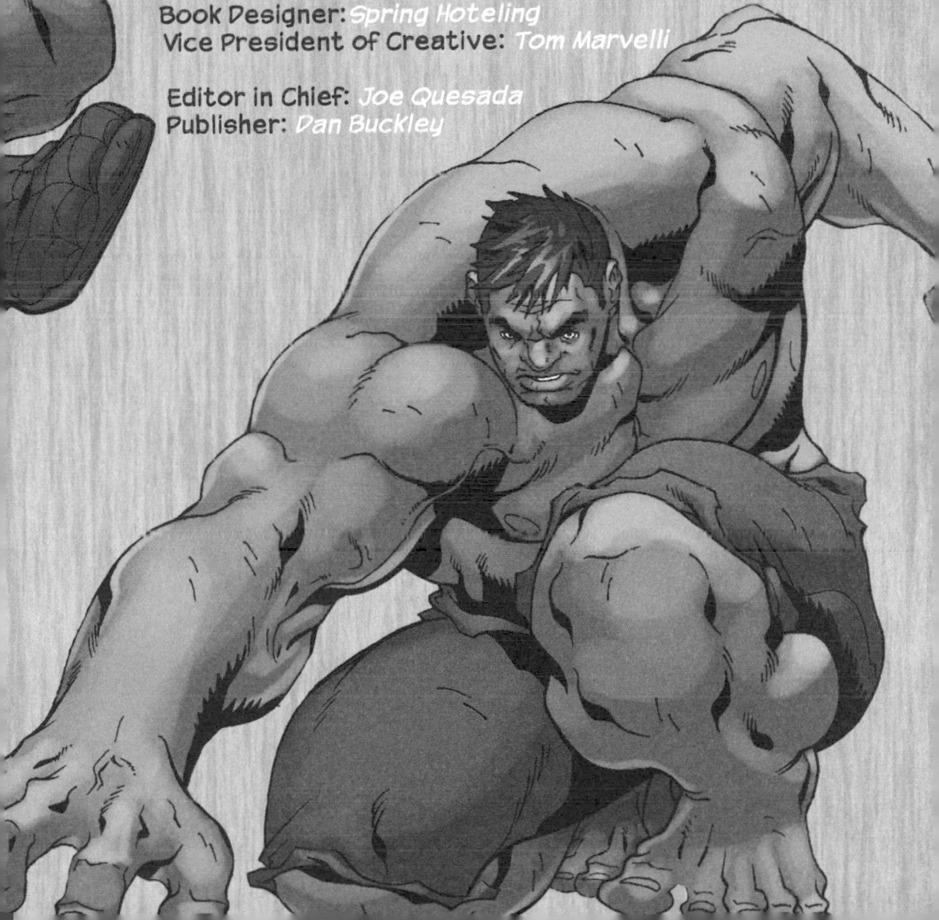

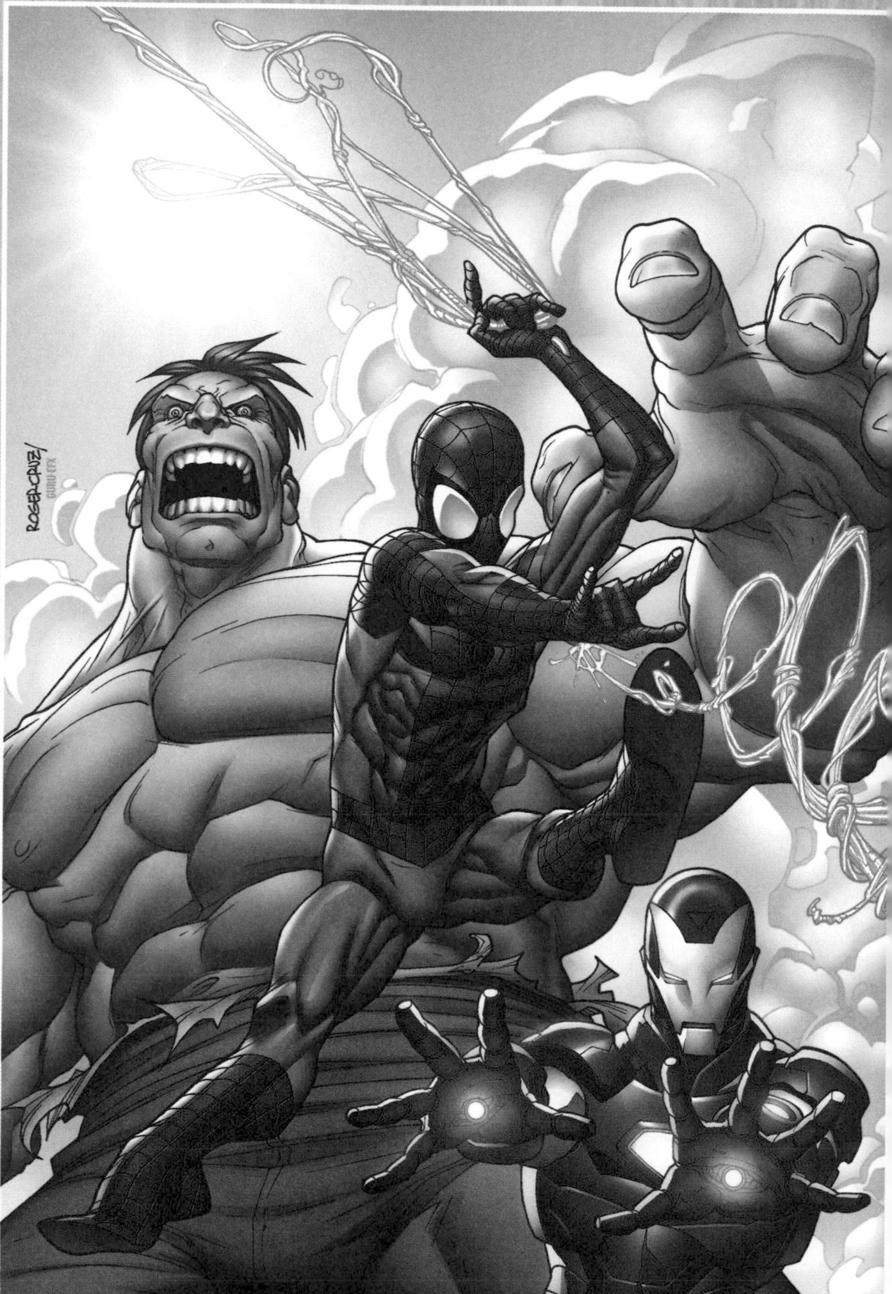
ROGER CRUZ/
GURU-EFX

#1

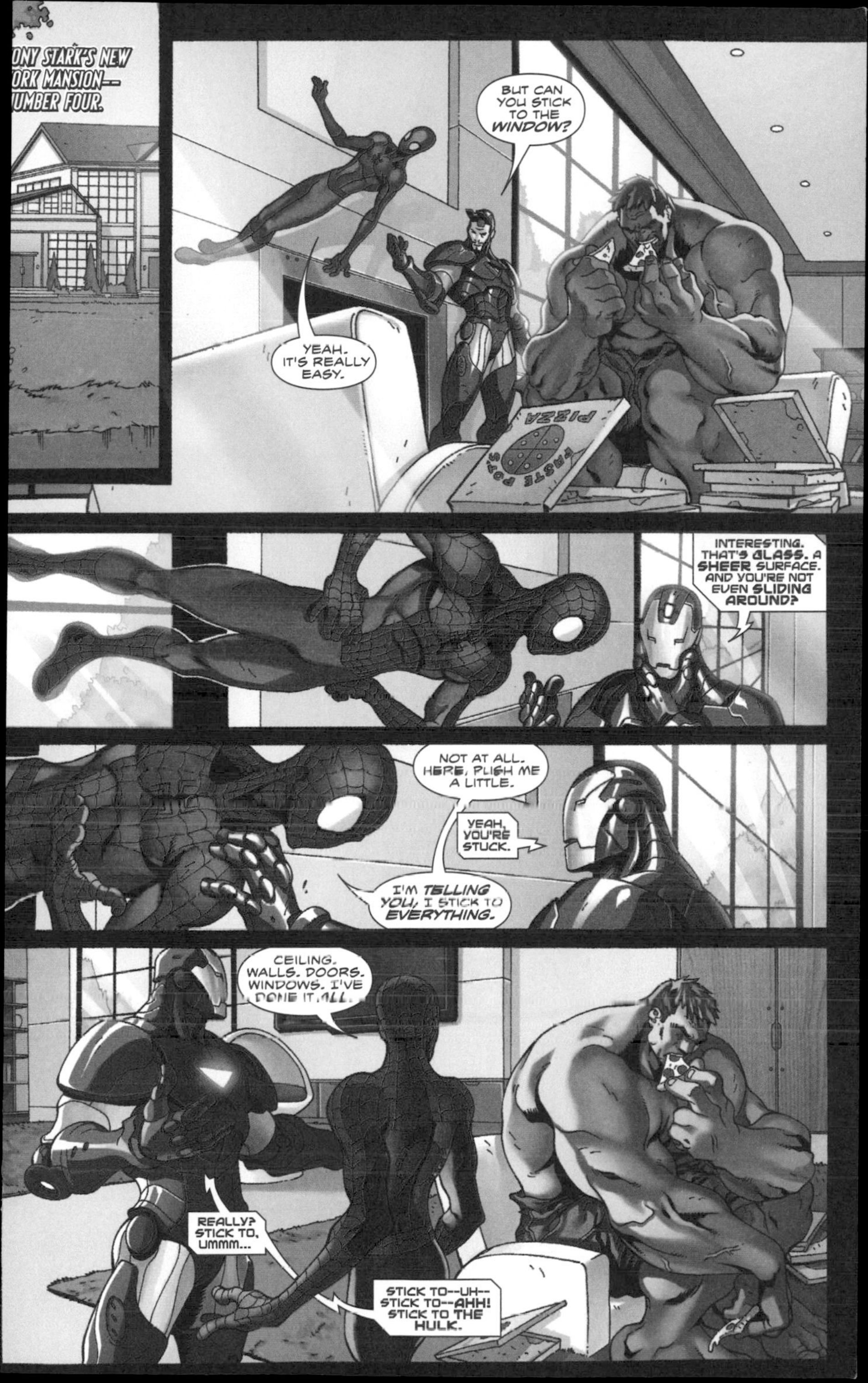
ONY STARK'S NEW
ORK MANSION--
UMBER FOUR.
BUT CAN YOU STICK TO THE WINDOW?
YEAH. IT'S REALLY EASY.
PIZZA
TASTE POT'S
INTERESTING. THAT'S GLASS. A SHEER SURFACE. AND YOU'RE NOT EVEN SLIDING AROUND?
NOT AT ALL. HERE, PUSH ME A LITTLE.
YEAH, YOU'RE STUCK.
I'M TELLING YOU, I STICK TO EVERYTHING.
CEILING. WALLS. DOORS. WINDOWS. I'VE DONE IT ALL.
REALLY? STICK TO, UMMM...
STICK TO--UH-- STICK TO--AHH! STICK TO THE HULK.

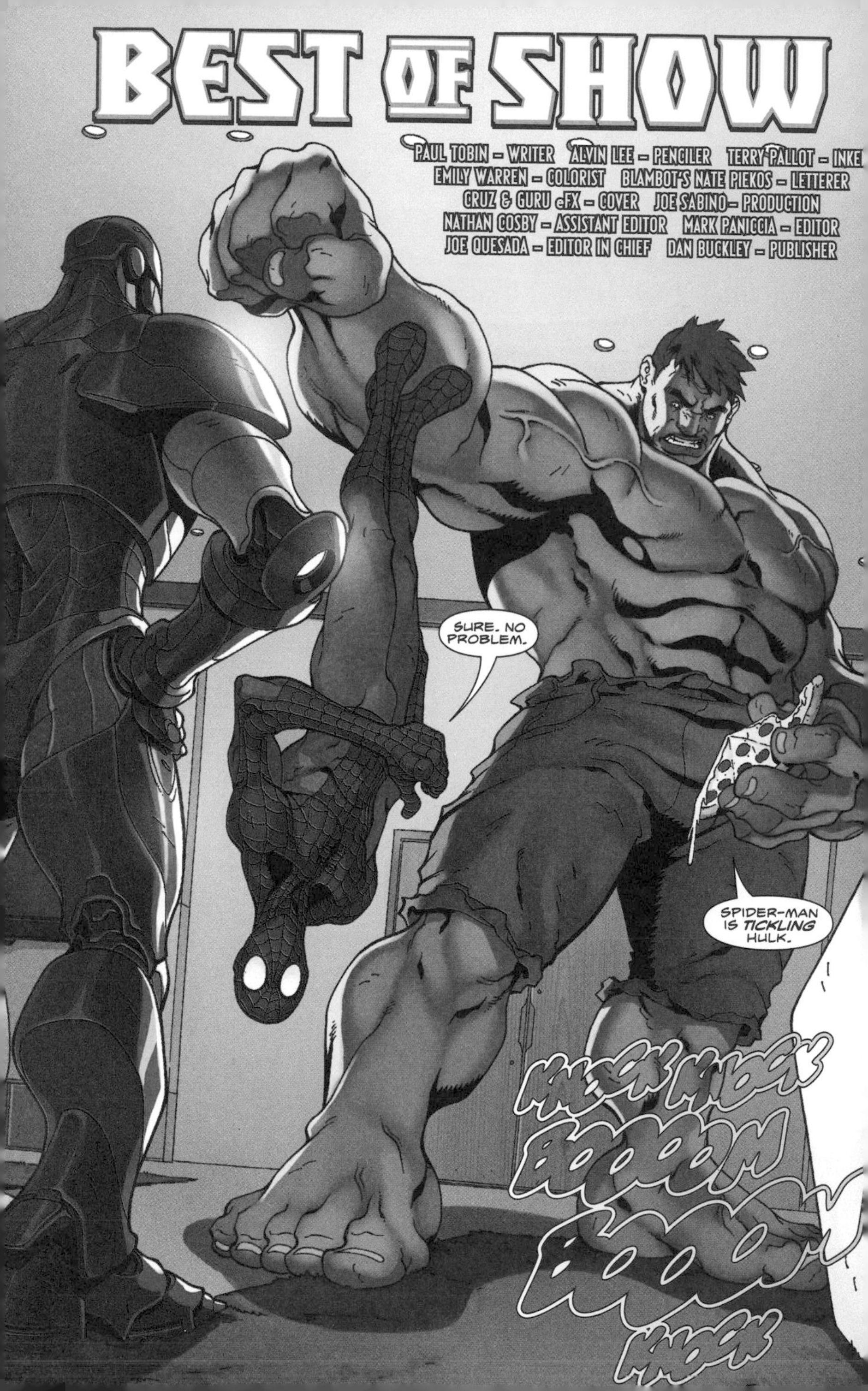
BEST OF SHOW
PAUL TOBIN – WRITER ALVIN LEE – PENCILER TERRY PALLOT – INKE
EMILY WARREN – COLORIST BLAMBOT'S NATE PIEKOS – LETTERER
CRUZ & GURU eFX – COVER JOE SABINO – PRODUCTION
NATHAN COSBY – ASSISTANT EDITOR MARK PANICCIA – EDITOR
JOE QUESADA – EDITOR IN CHIEF DAN BUCKLEY – PUBLISHER
SURE. NO PROBLEM.
SPIDER-MAN IS TICKLING HULK.

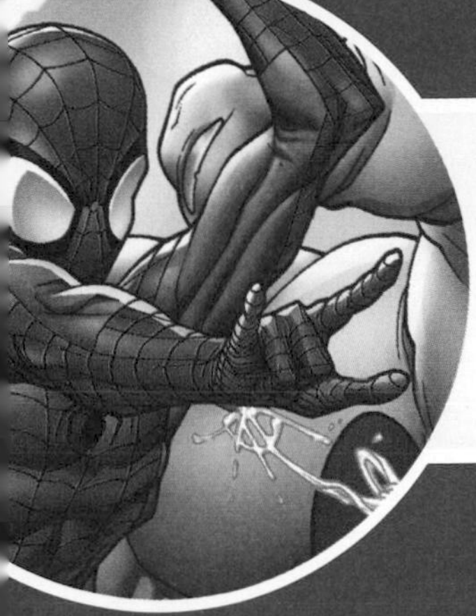

BITTEN BY AN IRRADIATED SPIDER, WHICH GRANTED HIM INCREDIBLE ABILITIES, PETER PARKER LEARNED THE ALL-IMPORTANT LESSON, THAT WITH GREAT POWER THERE MUST ALSO COME GREAT RESPONSIBILITY. AND SO HE BECAME THE AMAZING

SPIDER-MAN

CAUGHT IN A BLAST OF GAMMA-IRRADIATION, BRILLIANT SCIENTIST BRUCE BANNER HAS BEEN TRANSFORMED INTO THE LIVING ENGINE OF DESTRUCTION KNOWN AS THE

HULK

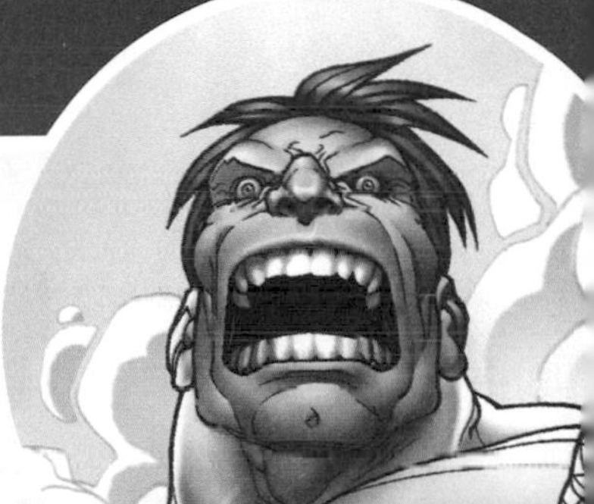

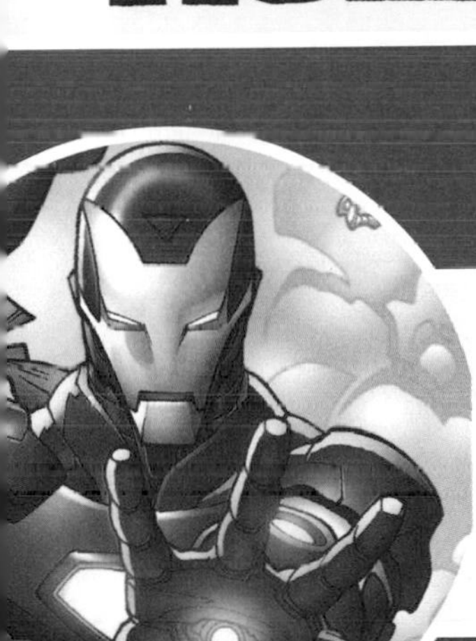

BILLIONAIRE INVENTOR TONY STARK BUILT A SUIT OF ARMOR THAT SAVED HIS LIFE. HE NOW FIGHTS AGAINST THE FORCES OF EVIL AS THE INVINCIBLE

IRON MAN

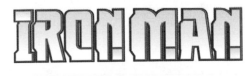

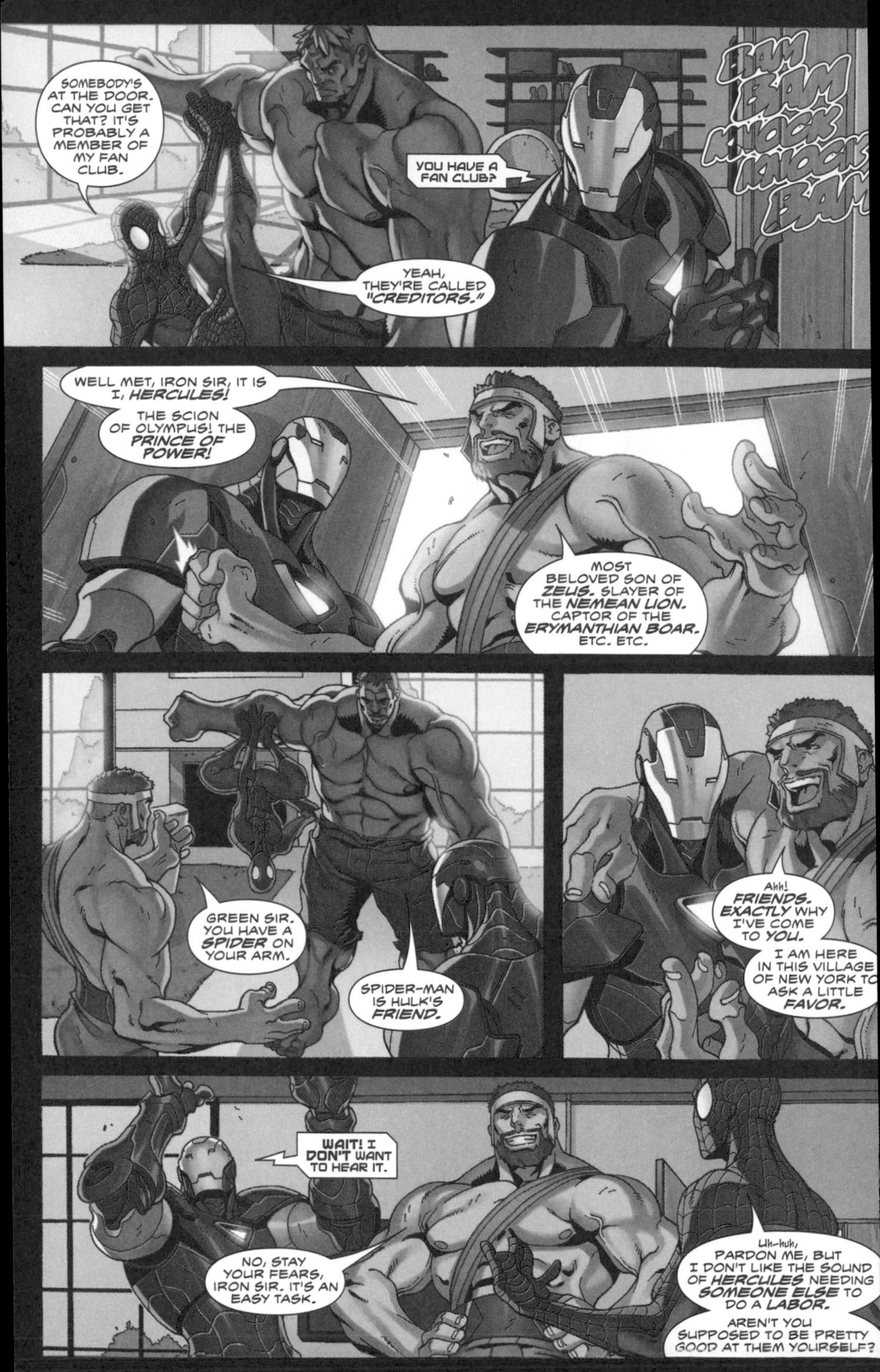
BAM BAM KNOCK KNOCK BAM
SOMEBODY'S AT THE DOOR. CAN YOU GET THAT? IT'S PROBABLY A MEMBER OF MY FAN CLUB.
YOU HAVE A FAN CLUB?
YEAH, THEY'RE CALLED "CREDITORS."
WELL MET, IRON SIR, IT IS I, HERCULES!
THE SCION OF OLYMPUS! THE PRINCE OF POWER!
MOST BELOVED SON OF ZEUS. SLAYER OF THE NEMEAN LION. CAPTOR OF THE ERYMANTHIAN BOAR. ETC. ETC.
GREEN SIR. YOU HAVE A SPIDER ON YOUR ARM.
SPIDER-MAN IS HULK'S FRIEND.
Ahh! FRIENDS. EXACTLY WHY I'VE COME TO YOU.
I AM HERE IN THIS VILLAGE OF NEW YORK TO ASK A LITTLE FAVOR.
WAIT! I DON'T WANT TO HEAR IT.
NO, STAY YOUR FEARS, IRON SIR. IT'S AN EASY TASK.
Uh-huh, PARDON ME, BUT I DON'T LIKE THE SOUND OF HERCULES NEEDING SOMEONE ELSE TO DO A LABOR.
AREN'T YOU SUPPOSED TO BE PRETTY GOOD AT THEM YOURSELF?

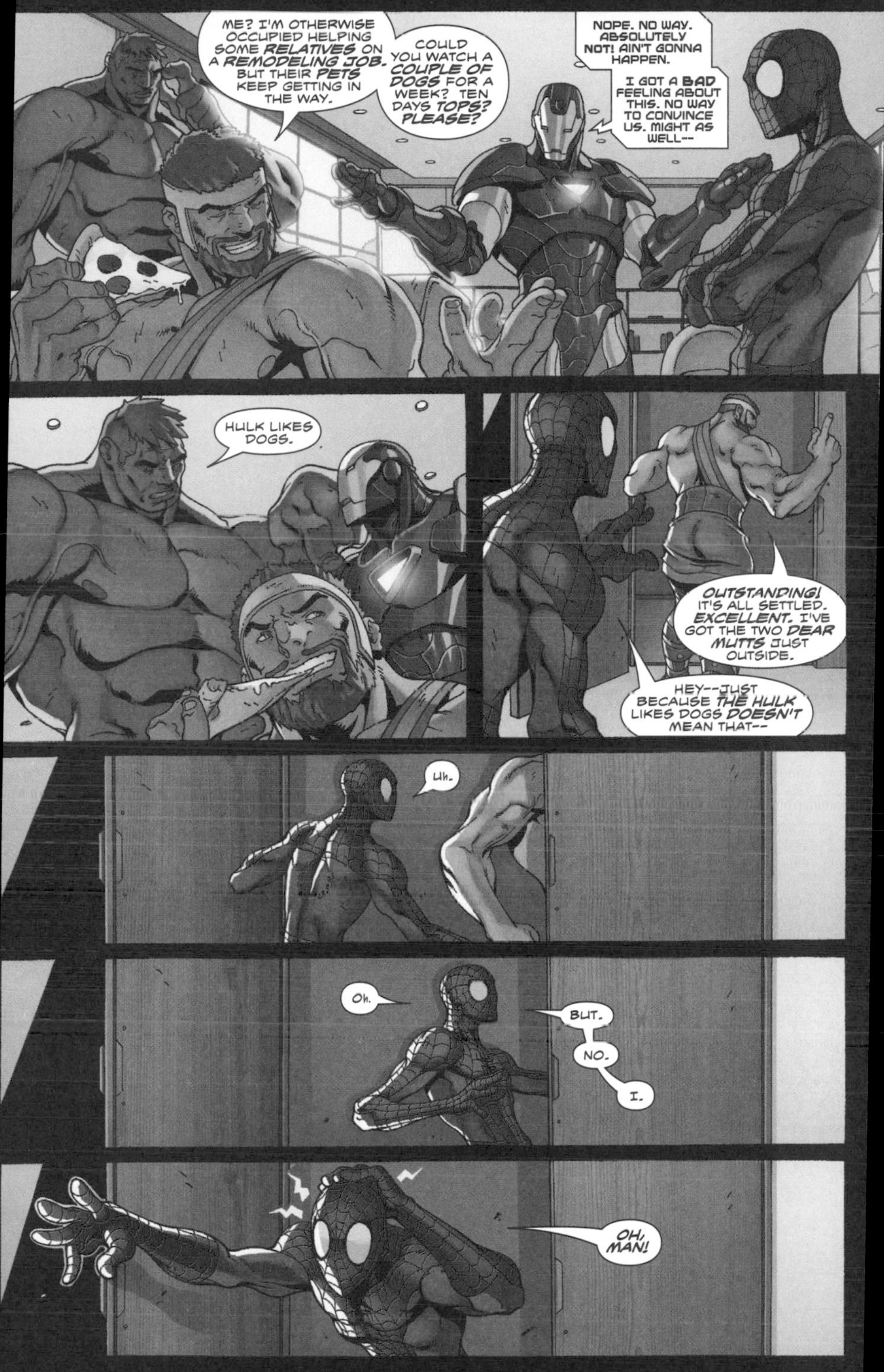

ME? I'M OTHERWISE OCCUPIED HELPING SOME RELATIVES ON A REMODELING JOB. BUT THEIR PETS KEEP GETTING IN THE WAY.
COULD YOU WATCH A COUPLE OF DOGS FOR A WEEK? TEN DAYS TOPS? PLEASE?
NOPE. NO WAY. ABSOLUTELY NOT! AIN'T GONNA HAPPEN.
I GOT A BAD FEELING ABOUT THIS. NO WAY TO CONVINCE US. MIGHT AS WELL--
HULK LIKES DOGS.
OUTSTANDING! IT'S ALL SETTLED. EXCELLENT. I'VE GOT THE TWO DEAR MUTTS JUST OUTSIDE.
HEY--JUST BECAUSE THE HULK LIKES DOGS DOESN'T MEAN THAT--
Uh.
Oh.
BUT.
NO.
I.
OH, MAN!

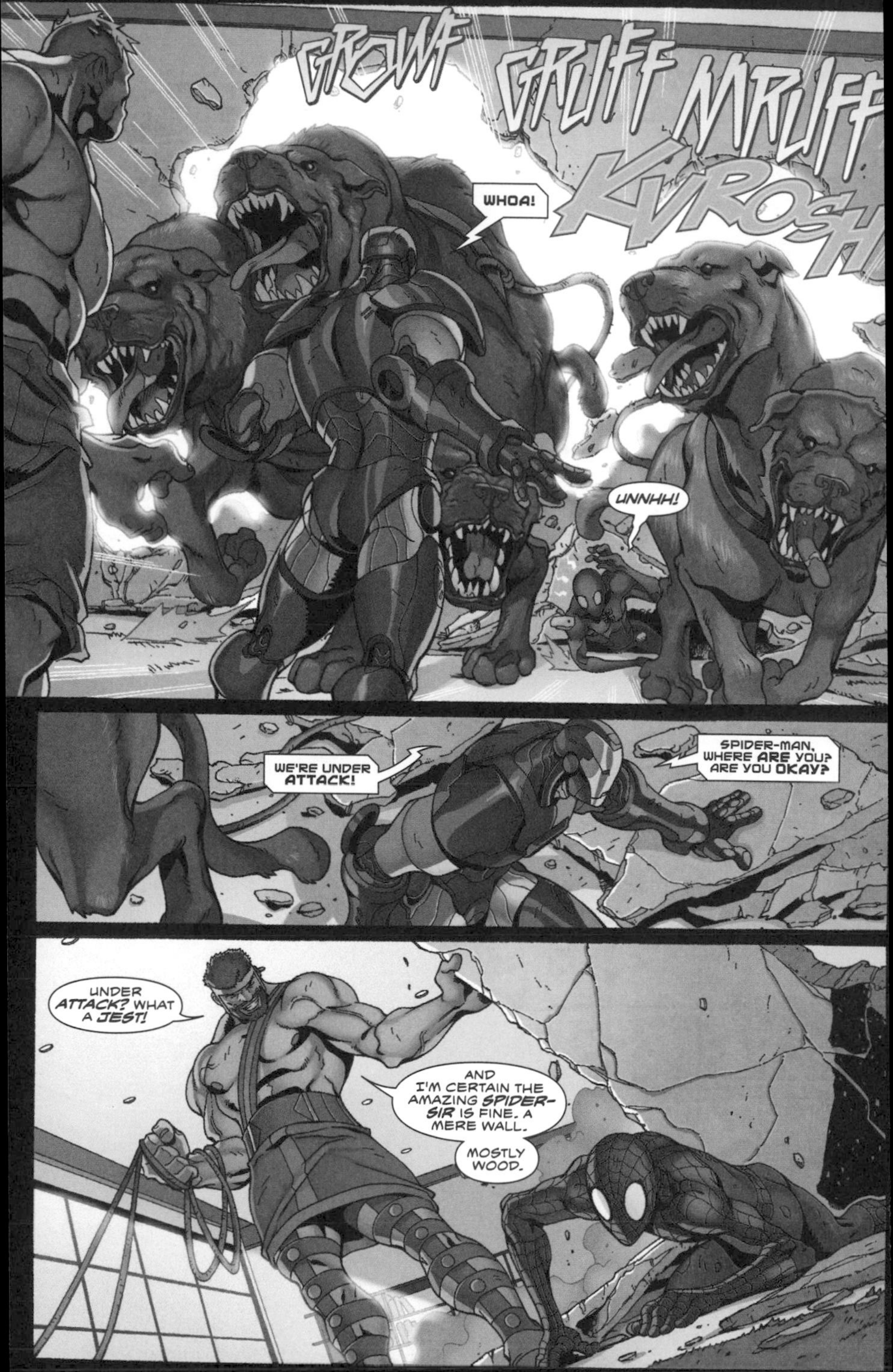
GROWF
GRUFF MRUFF
KVROSH
WHOA!
UNNHH!
WE'RE UNDER ATTACK!
SPIDER-MAN, WHERE ARE YOU? ARE YOU OKAY?
UNDER ATTACK? WHAT A JEST!
AND I'M CERTAIN THE AMAZING SPIDER-SIR IS FINE. A MERE WALL.
MOSTLY WOOD.

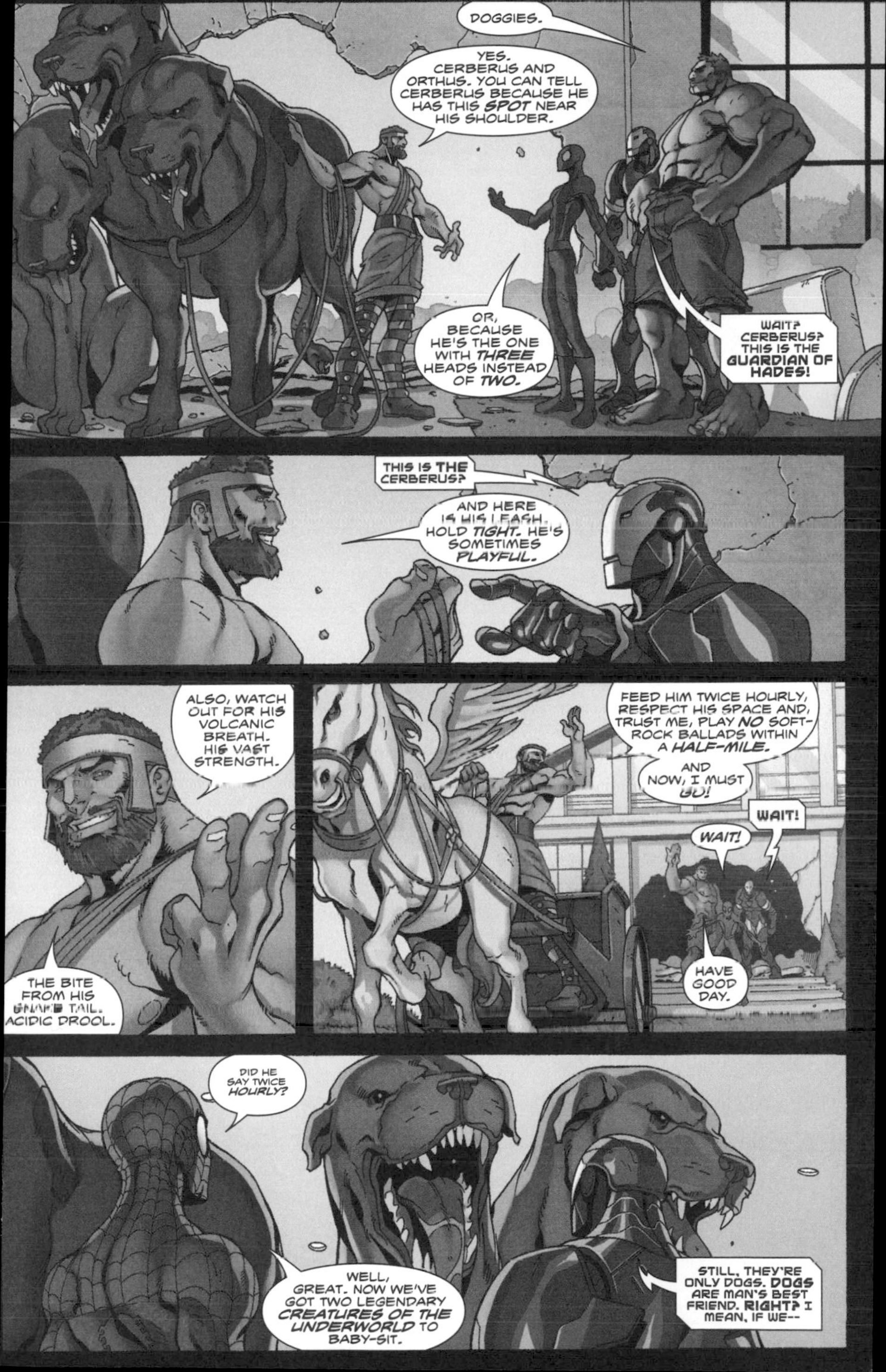
DOGGIES.
YES. CERBERUS AND ORTHUS. YOU CAN TELL CERBERUS BECAUSE HE HAS THIS SPOT NEAR HIS SHOULDER.
OR, BECAUSE HE'S THE ONE WITH THREE HEADS INSTEAD OF TWO.
WAIT? CERBERUS? THIS IS THE GUARDIAN OF HADES!
THIS IS THE CERBERUS?
AND HERE IS HIS LEASH. HOLD TIGHT. HE'S SOMETIMES PLAYFUL.
ALSO, WATCH OUT FOR HIS VOLCANIC BREATH. HIS VAST STRENGTH.
THE BITE FROM HIS SNAKE TAIL. ACIDIC DROOL.
FEED HIM TWICE HOURLY, RESPECT HIS SPACE AND, TRUST ME, PLAY NO SOFT-ROCK BALLADS WITHIN A HALF-MILE.
AND NOW, I MUST GO!
WAIT!
WAIT!
HAVE GOOD DAY.
DID HE SAY TWICE HOURLY?
WELL, GREAT. NOW WE'VE GOT TWO LEGENDARY CREATURES OF THE UNDERWORLD TO BABY-SIT.
STILL, THEY'RE ONLY DOGS. DOGS ARE MAN'S BEST FRIEND. RIGHT? I MEAN, IF WE--

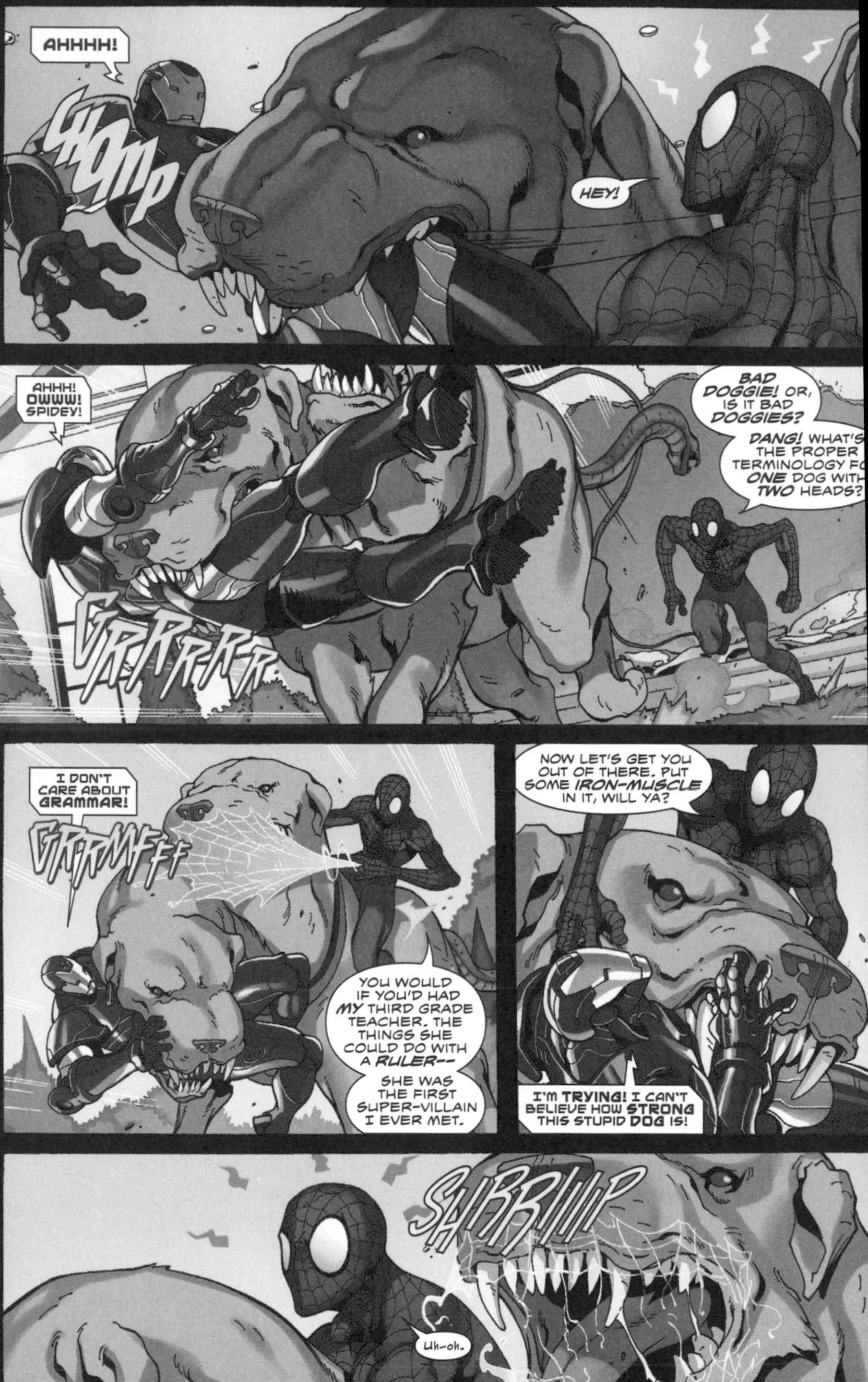
AHHHH!
CHOMP
HEY!
AHHH! OWWW! SPIDEY!
BAD DOGGIE! OR, IS IT BAD DOGGIES?
DANG! WHAT'S THE PROPER TERMINOLOGY FOR ONE DOG WITH TWO HEADS?
GRRRRRR
I DON'T CARE ABOUT GRAMMAR!
GRRMFFF
YOU WOULD IF YOU'D HAD MY THIRD GRADE TEACHER. THE THINGS SHE COULD DO WITH A RULER--
SHE WAS THE FIRST SUPER-VILLAIN I EVER MET.
NOW LET'S GET YOU OUT OF THERE. PUT SOME IRON-MUSCLE IN IT, WILL YA?
I'M TRYING! I CAN'T BELIEVE HOW STRONG THIS STUPID DOG IS!
SHRIIIP
Uh-oh.

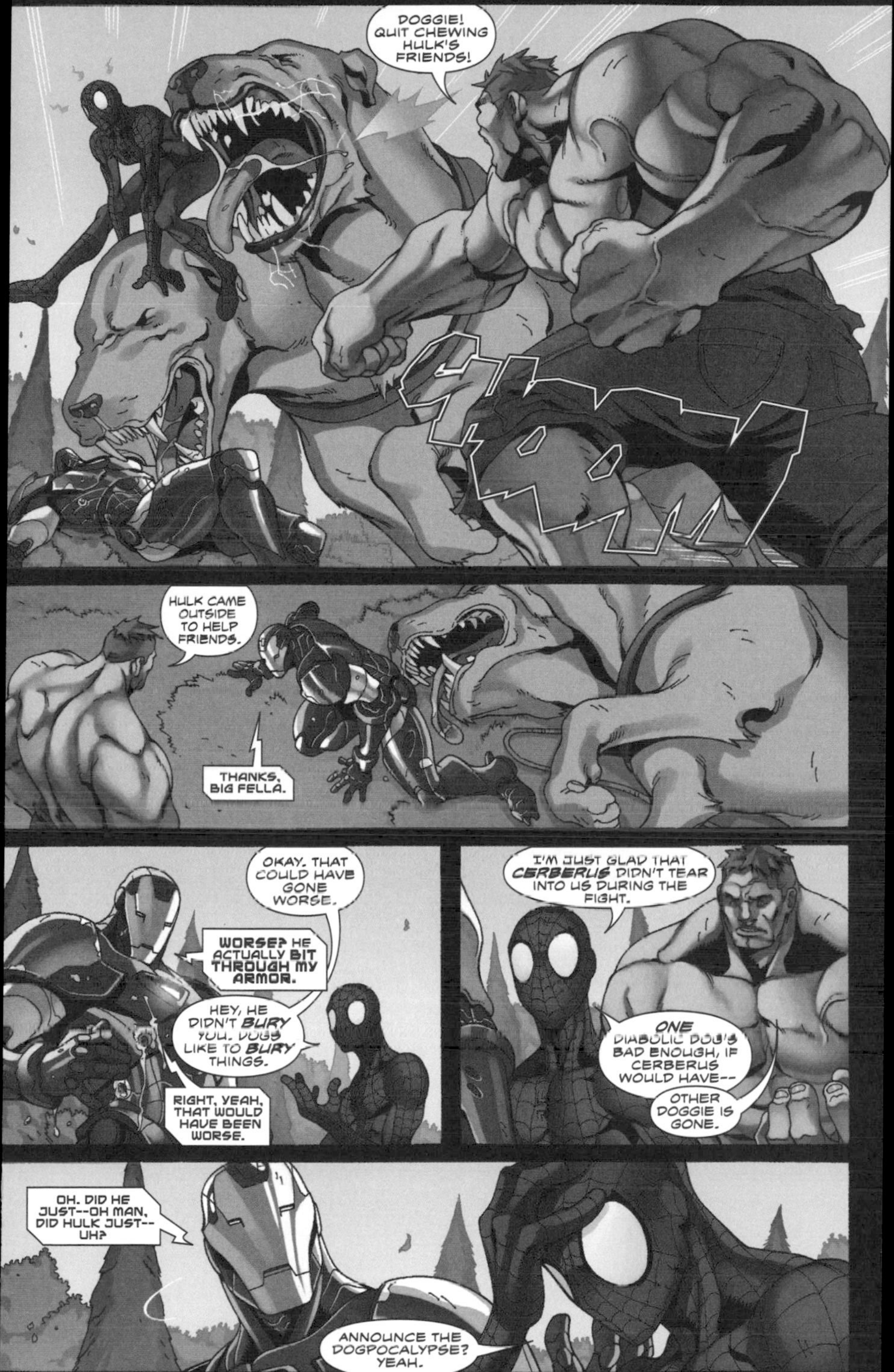
DOGGIE! QUIT CHEWING HULK'S FRIENDS!
HULK CAME OUTSIDE TO HELP FRIENDS.
THANKS, BIG FELLA.
OKAY. THAT COULD HAVE GONE WORSE.
WORSE? HE ACTUALLY BIT THROUGH MY ARMOR.
HEY, HE DIDN'T BURY YOU. DOGS LIKE TO BURY THINGS.
RIGHT, YEAH, THAT WOULD HAVE BEEN WORSE.
I'M JUST GLAD THAT CERBERUS DIDN'T TEAR INTO US DURING THE FIGHT.
ONE DIABOLIC DOG'S BAD ENOUGH, IF CERBERUS WOULD HAVE--
OTHER DOGGIE IS GONE.
OH. DID HE JUST--OH MAN. DID HULK JUST-- UH?
ANNOUNCE THE DOGPOCALYPSE? YEAH.

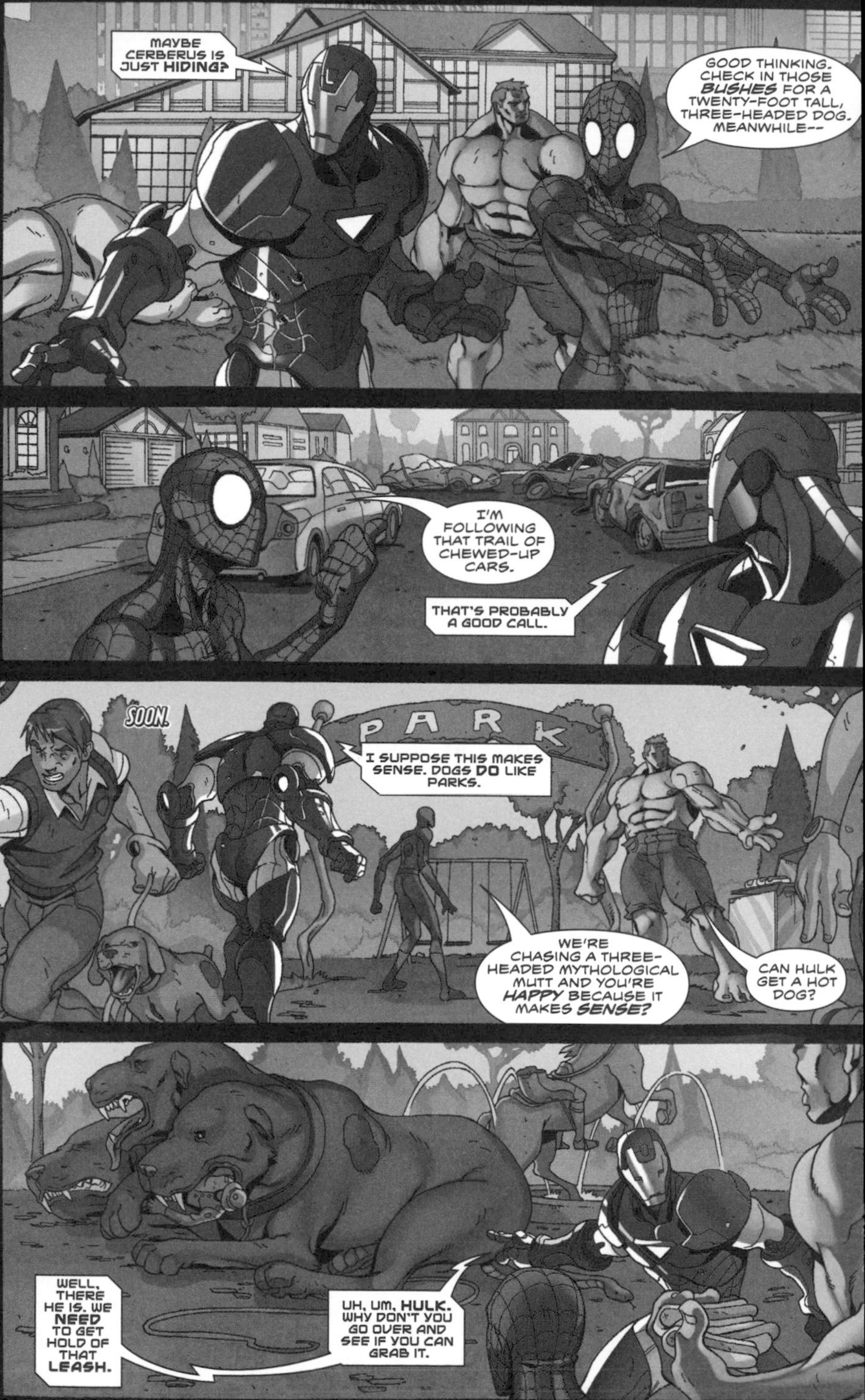
MAYBE CERBERUS IS JUST HIDING?
GOOD THINKING. CHECK IN THOSE BUSHES FOR A TWENTY-FOOT TALL, THREE-HEADED DOG. MEANWHILE--
I'M FOLLOWING THAT TRAIL OF CHEWED-UP CARS.
THAT'S PROBABLY A GOOD CALL.
SOON.
PARK
I SUPPOSE THIS MAKES SENSE. DOGS DO LIKE PARKS.
WE'RE CHASING A THREE-HEADED MYTHOLOGICAL MUTT AND YOU'RE HAPPY BECAUSE IT MAKES SENSE?
CAN HULK GET A HOT DOG?
WELL, THERE HE IS. WE NEED TO GET HOLD OF THAT LEASH.
UH, UM, HULK. WHY DON'T YOU GO OVER AND SEE IF YOU CAN GRAB IT.

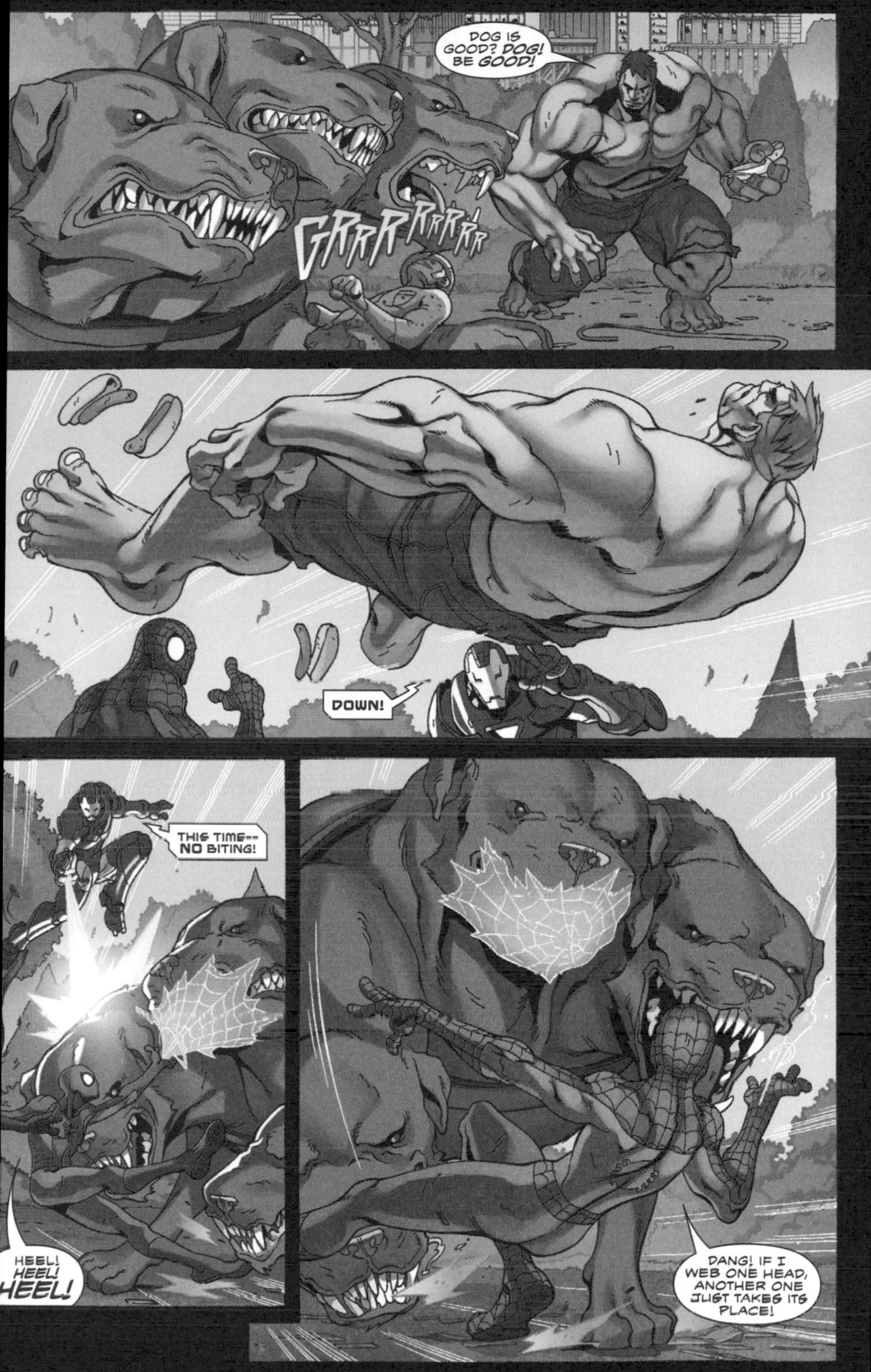
DOG IS GOOD? DOG! BE GOOD!
GRRRRRRRR
DOWN!
THIS TIME-- NO BITING!
HEEL! HEEL! HEEL!
DANG! IF I WEB ONE HEAD, ANOTHER ONE JUST TAKES ITS PLACE!

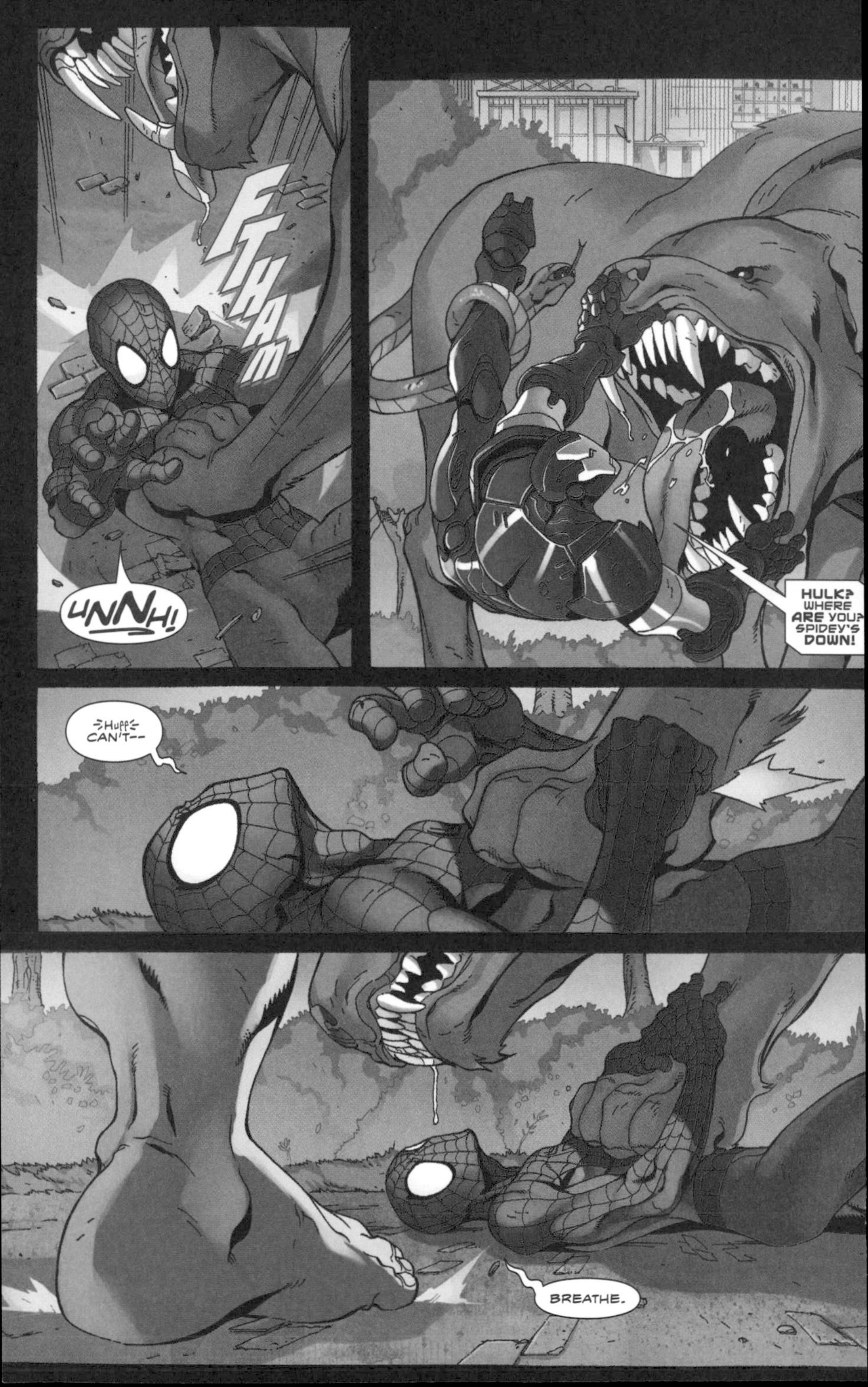
FTHAM
UNNH!
HULK? WHERE ARE YOU? SPIDEY'S DOWN!
Huff CAN'T--
BREATHE.

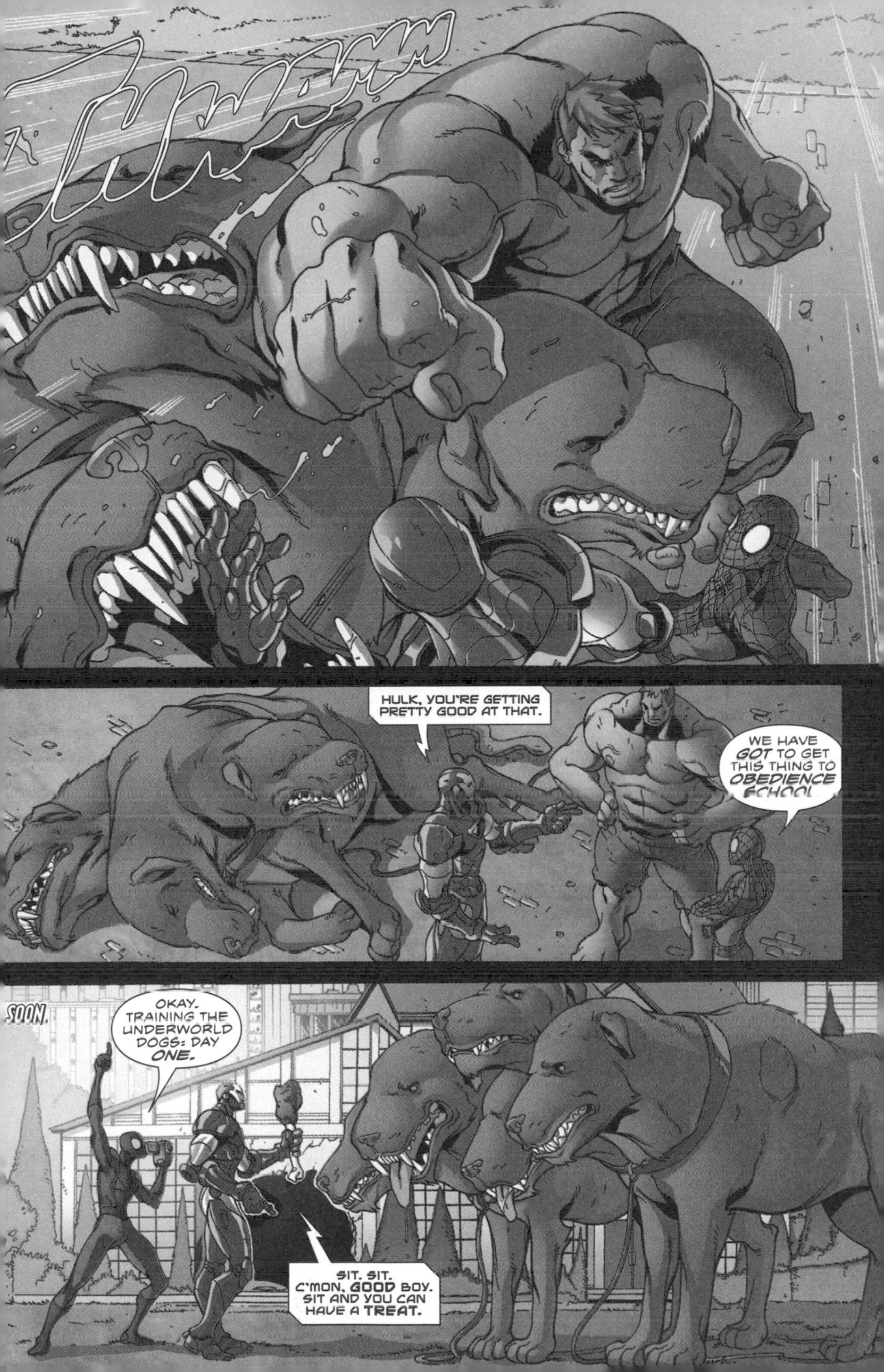
HULK, YOU'RE GETTING PRETTY GOOD AT THAT.
WE HAVE GOT TO GET THIS THING TO OBEDIENCE SCHOOL.
SOON.
OKAY. TRAINING THE UNDERWORLD DOGS: DAY ONE.
SIT. SIT. C'MON, GOOD BOY. SIT AND YOU CAN HAVE A TREAT.

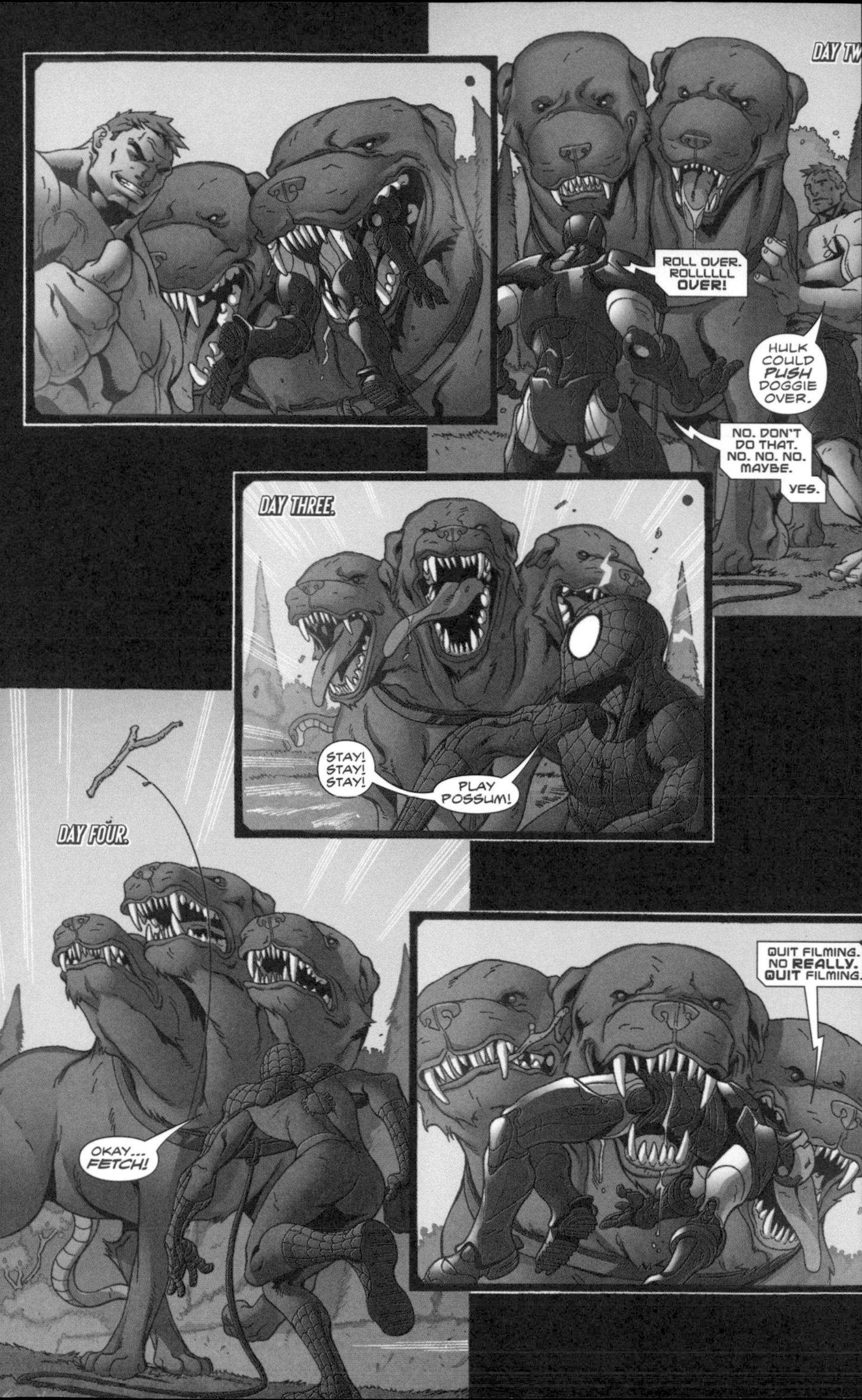
DAY TW
ROLL OVER. ROLLLLLLL OVER!
HULK COULD PUSH DOGGIE OVER.
NO. DON'T DO THAT. NO. NO. NO. MAYBE.
YES.
DAY THREE.
STAY! STAY! STAY!
PLAY POSSUM!
DAY FOUR.
OKAY... FETCH!
QUIT FILMING. NO REALLY. QUIT FILMING.

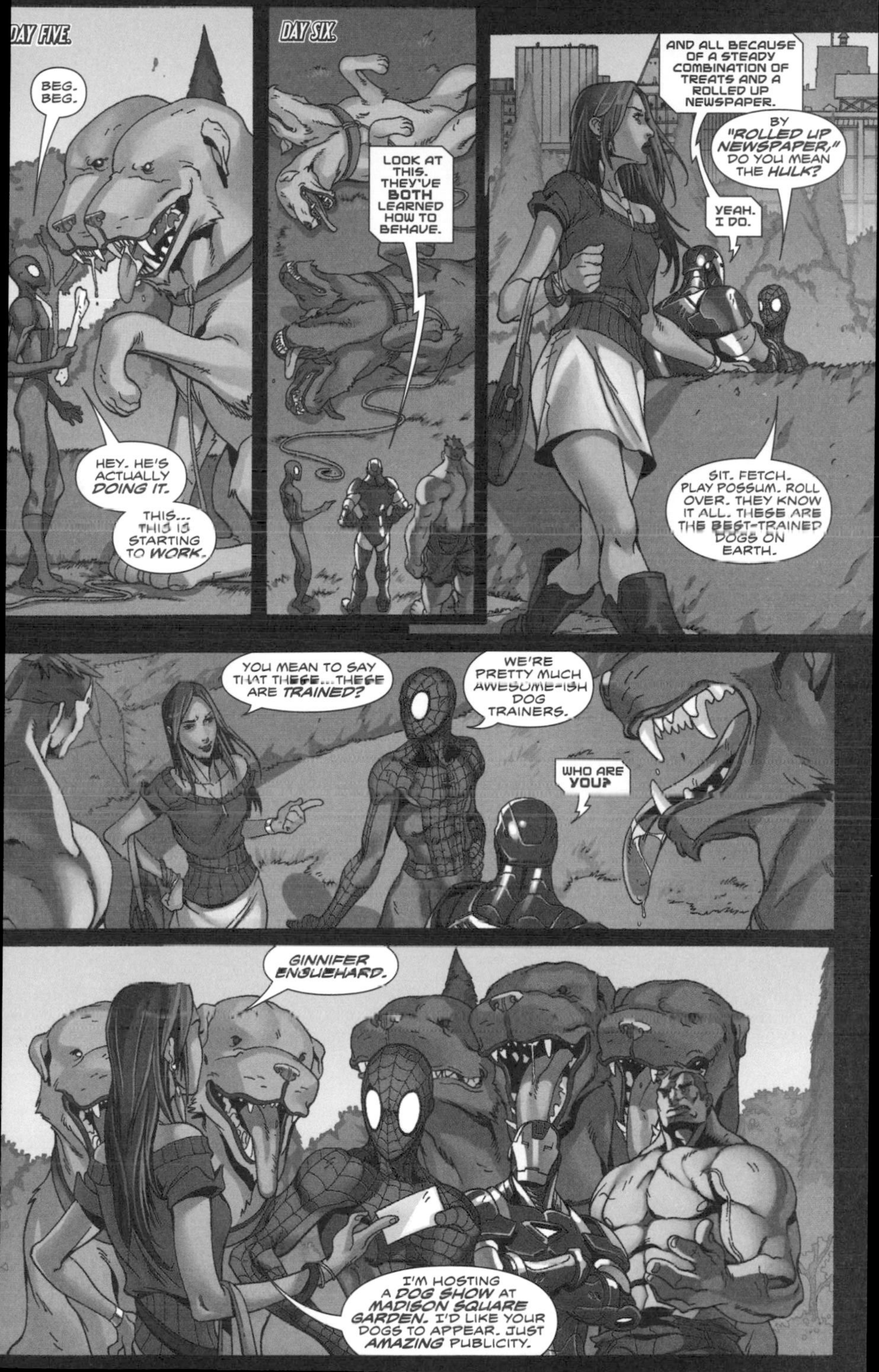
DAY FIVE.
BEG. BEG.
HEY. HE'S ACTUALLY DOING IT.
THIS... THIS IS STARTING TO WORK.
DAY SIX.
LOOK AT THIS. THEY'VE BOTH LEARNED HOW TO BEHAVE.
AND ALL BECAUSE OF A STEADY COMBINATION OF TREATS AND A ROLLED UP NEWSPAPER.
BY "ROLLED UP NEWSPAPER," DO YOU MEAN THE HULK?
YEAH. I DO.
SIT. FETCH. PLAY POSSUM. ROLL OVER. THEY KNOW IT ALL. THESE ARE THE BEST-TRAINED DOGS ON EARTH.
YOU MEAN TO SAY THAT THESE...THESE ARE TRAINED?
WE'RE PRETTY MUCH AWESOME-ISH DOG TRAINERS.
WHO ARE YOU?
GINNIFER ENGUEHARD.
I'M HOSTING A DOG SHOW AT MADISON SQUARE GARDEN. I'D LIKE YOUR DOGS TO APPEAR. JUST AMAZING PUBLICITY.

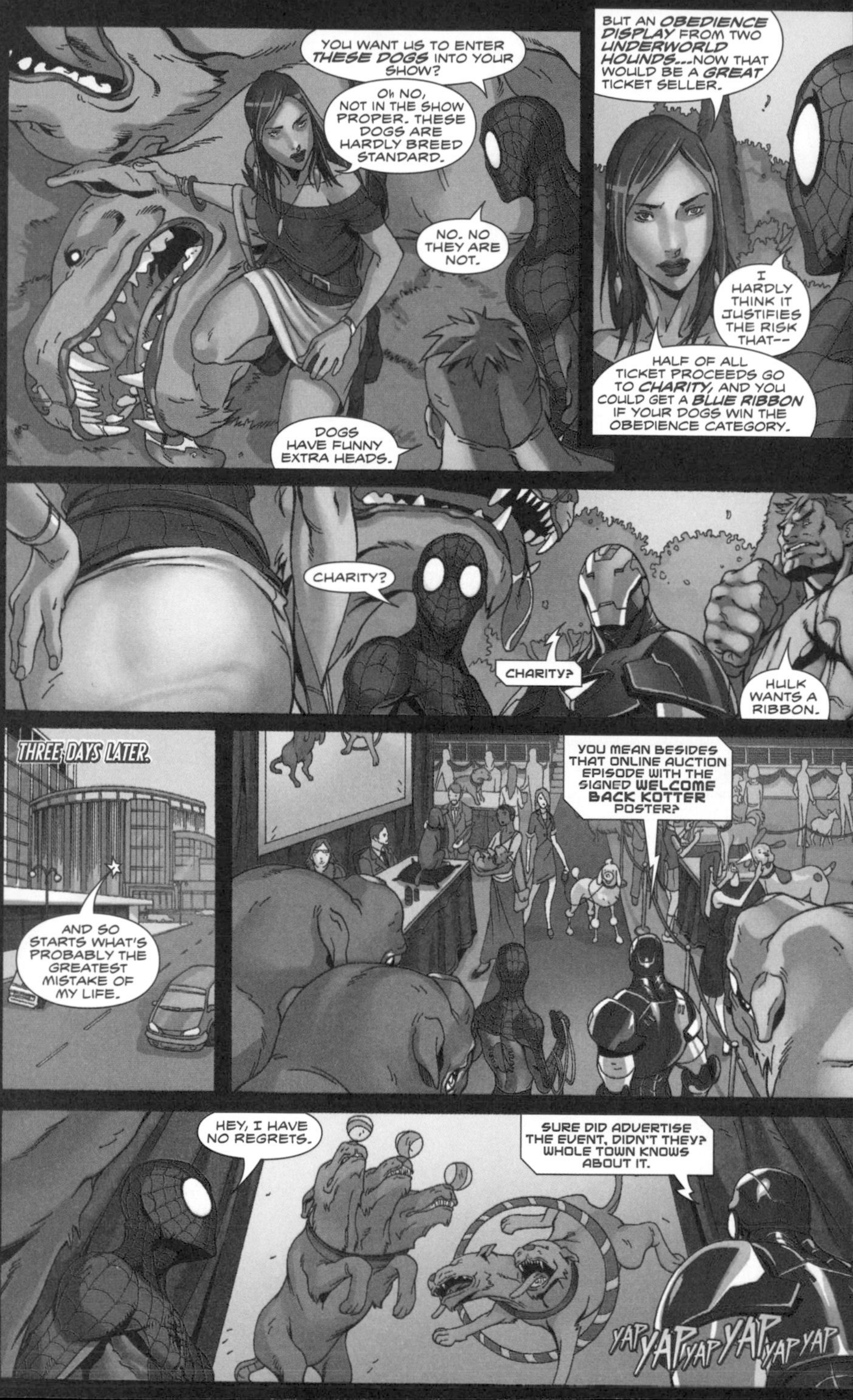
YOU WANT US TO ENTER THESE DOGS INTO YOUR SHOW?
OH NO, NOT IN THE SHOW PROPER. THESE DOGS ARE HARDLY BREED STANDARD.
NO. NO THEY ARE NOT.
DOGS HAVE FUNNY EXTRA HEADS.
BUT AN OBEDIENCE DISPLAY FROM TWO UNDERWORLD HOUNDS...NOW THAT WOULD BE A GREAT TICKET SELLER.
I HARDLY THINK IT JUSTIFIES THE RISK THAT--
HALF OF ALL TICKET PROCEEDS GO TO CHARITY, AND YOU COULD GET A BLUE RIBBON IF YOUR DOGS WIN THE OBEDIENCE CATEGORY.
CHARITY?
CHARITY?
HULK WANTS A RIBBON.
THREE DAYS LATER.
AND SO STARTS WHAT'S PROBABLY THE GREATEST MISTAKE OF MY LIFE.
YOU MEAN BESIDES THAT ONLINE AUCTION EPISODE WITH THE SIGNED WELCOME BACK KOTTER POSTER?
HEY, I HAVE NO REGRETS.
SURE DID ADVERTISE THE EVENT, DIDN'T THEY? WHOLE TOWN KNOWS ABOUT IT.
YAP YAP YAP YAP YAP YAP YAP

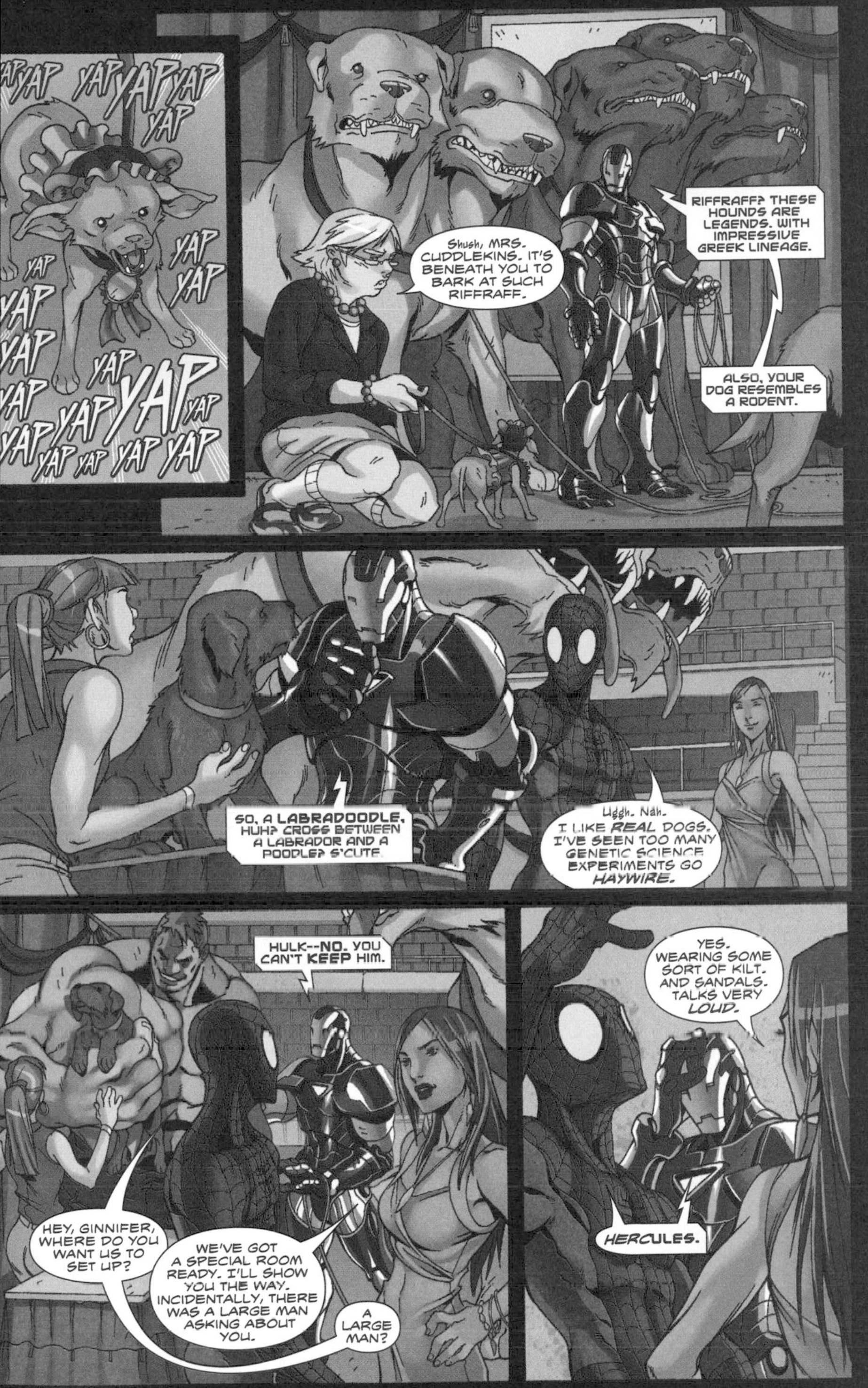
YAP YAP YAP YAP YAP YAP
YAP YAP YAP YAP YAP YAP YAP YAP YAP YAP YAP YAP YAP YAP YAP YAP
Shush, MRS. CUDDLEKINS. IT'S BENEATH YOU TO BARK AT SUCH RIFFRAFF.
RIFFRAFF? THESE HOUNDS ARE LEGENDS. WITH IMPRESSIVE GREEK LINEAGE.
ALSO, YOUR DOG RESEMBLES A RODENT.
SO, A LABRADOODLE, HUH? CROSS BETWEEN A LABRADOR AND A POODLE? S'CUTE.
Uggh. Nah. I LIKE REAL DOGS. I'VE SEEN TOO MANY GENETIC SCIENCE EXPERIMENTS GO HAYWIRE.
HULK--NO. YOU CAN'T KEEP HIM.
HEY, GINNIFER, WHERE DO YOU WANT US TO SET UP?
WE'VE GOT A SPECIAL ROOM READY. I'LL SHOW YOU THE WAY. INCIDENTALLY, THERE WAS A LARGE MAN ASKING ABOUT YOU.
A LARGE MAN?
YES. WEARING SOME SORT OF KILT. AND SANDALS. TALKS VERY LOUD.
HERCULES.

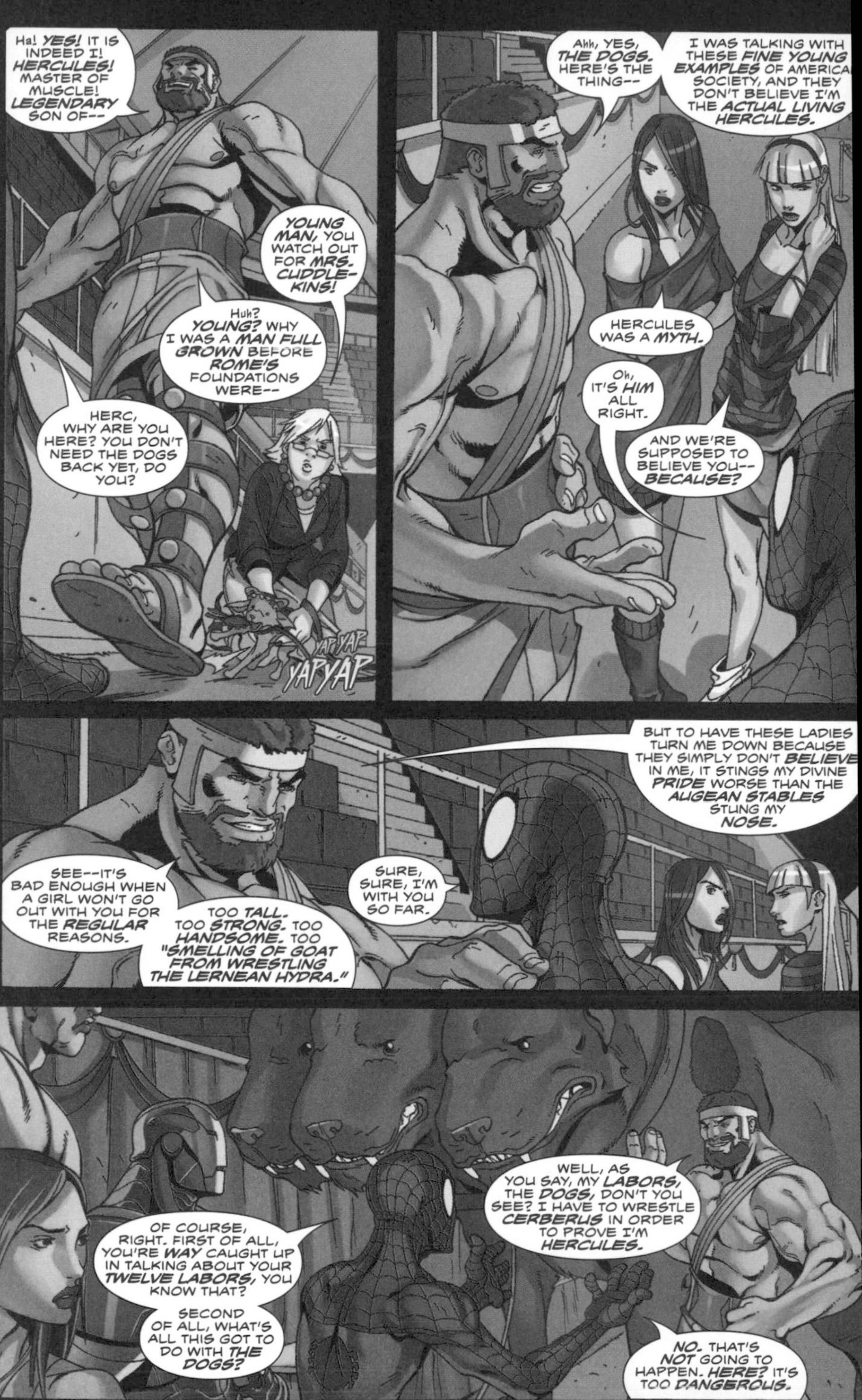

Ha! YES! IT IS INDEED I! HERCULES! MASTER OF MUSCLE! LEGENDARY SON OF--
YOUNG MAN, YOU WATCH OUT FOR MRS. CUDDLE-KINS!
Huh? YOUNG? WHY I WAS A MAN FULL GROWN BEFORE ROME'S FOUNDATIONS WERE--
HERC, WHY ARE YOU HERE? YOU DON'T NEED THE DOGS BACK YET, DO YOU?
YAP YAP
YAPYAP
Ahh, YES, THE DOGS. HERE'S THE THING--
I WAS TALKING WITH THESE FINE YOUNG EXAMPLES OF AMERICA SOCIETY, AND THEY DON'T BELIEVE I'M THE ACTUAL LIVING HERCULES.
HERCULES WAS A MYTH.
Oh, IT'S HIM ALL RIGHT.
AND WE'RE SUPPOSED TO BELIEVE YOU-- BECAUSE?
BUT TO HAVE THESE LADIES TURN ME DOWN BECAUSE THEY SIMPLY DON'T BELIEVE IN ME, IT STINGS MY DIVINE PRIDE WORSE THAN THE AUGEAN STABLES STUNG MY NOSE.
SEE--IT'S BAD ENOUGH WHEN A GIRL WON'T GO OUT WITH YOU FOR THE REGULAR REASONS.
TOO TALL. TOO STRONG. TOO HANDSOME. TOO "SMELLING OF GOAT FROM WRESTLING THE LERNEAN HYDRA."
SURE, SURE, I'M WITH YOU SO FAR.
WELL, AS YOU SAY, MY LABORS, THE DOGS, DON'T YOU SEE? I HAVE TO WRESTLE CERBERUS IN ORDER TO PROVE I'M HERCULES.
OF COURSE, RIGHT. FIRST OF ALL, YOU'RE WAY CAUGHT UP IN TALKING ABOUT YOUR TWELVE LABORS, YOU KNOW THAT?
SECOND OF ALL, WHAT'S ALL THIS GOT TO DO WITH THE DOGS?
NO. THAT'S NOT GOING TO HAPPEN. HERE? IT'S TOO DANGEROUS.

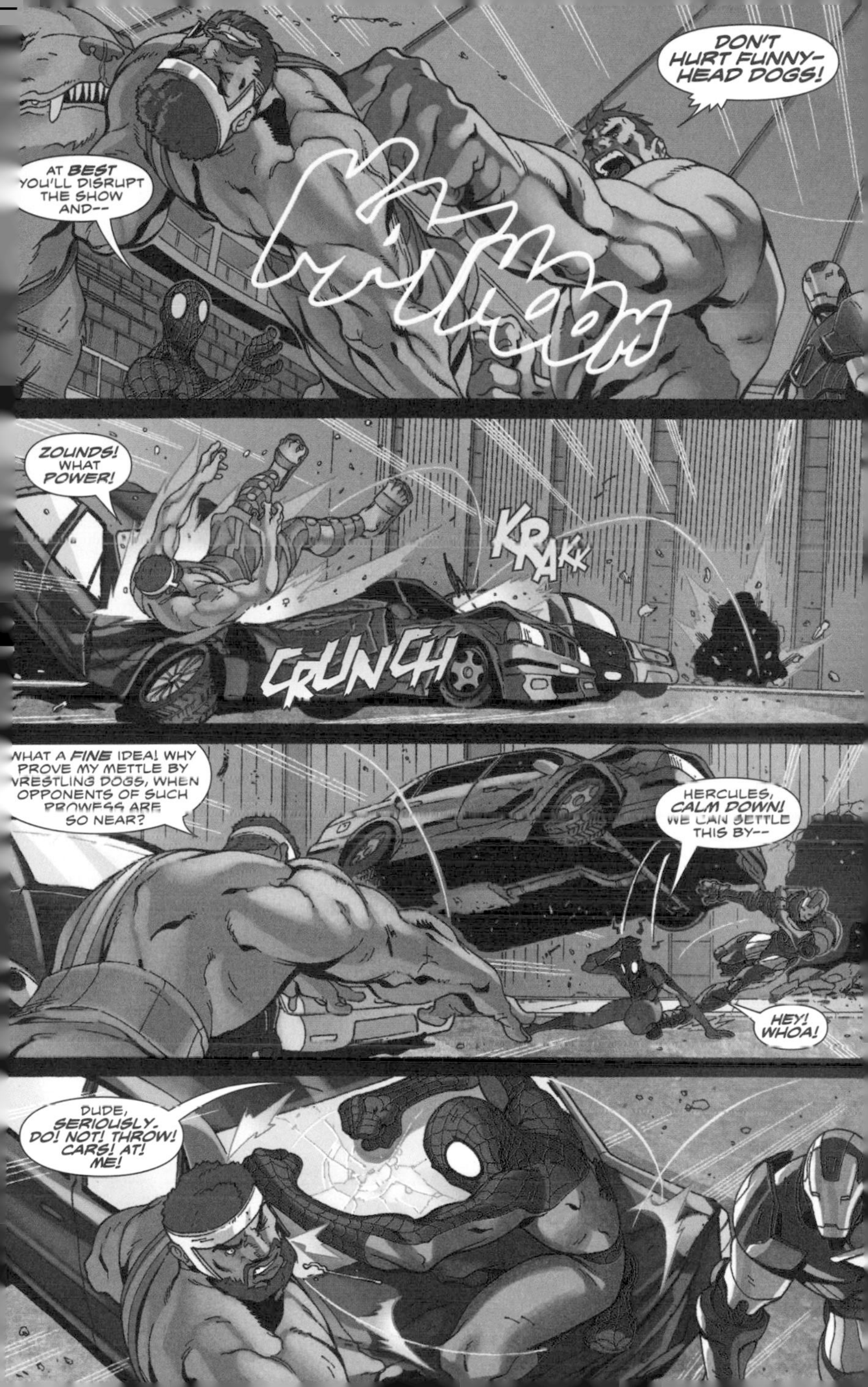
DON'T HURT FUNNY-HEAD DOGS!
AT BEST YOU'LL DISRUPT THE SHOW AND--
ZOUNDS! WHAT POWER!
KRAKK
CRUNCH
WHAT A FINE IDEA! WHY PROVE MY METTLE BY WRESTLING DOGS, WHEN OPPONENTS OF SUCH PROWESS ARE SO NEAR?
HERCULES, CALM DOWN! WE CAN SETTLE THIS BY--
HEY! WHOA!
DUDE, SERIOUSLY. DO! NOT! THROW! CARS! AT! ME!

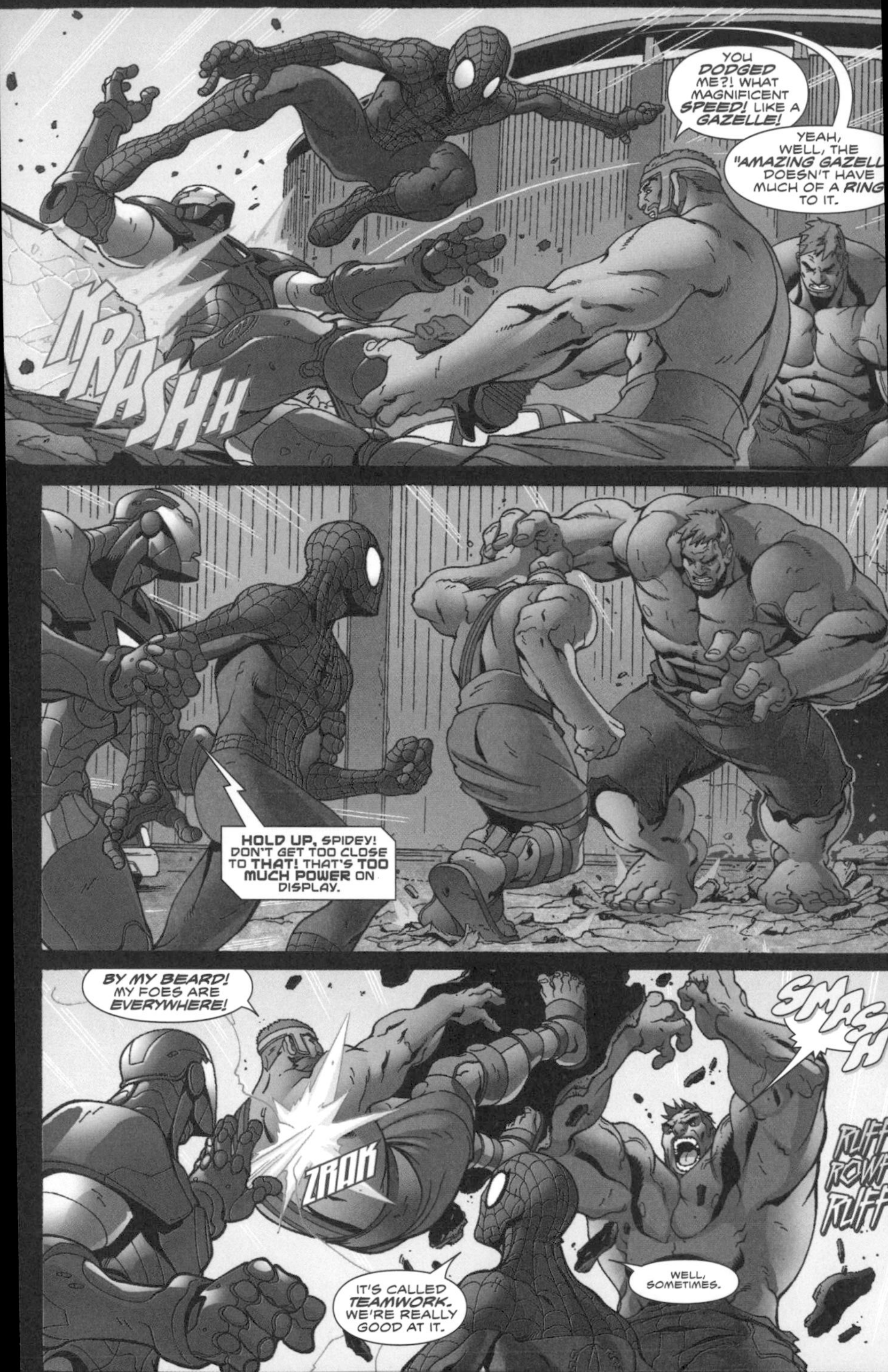
YOU DODGED ME?! WHAT MAGNIFICENT SPEED! LIKE A GAZELLE!
YEAH, WELL, THE "AMAZING GAZELL DOESN'T HAVE MUCH OF A RING TO IT.
KRASHH
HOLD UP, SPIDEY! DON'T GET TOO CLOSE TO THAT! THAT'S TOO MUCH POWER ON DISPLAY.
BY MY BEARD! MY FOES ARE EVERYWHERE!
SMASH
ZRAK
RUFF ROWF RUFF
IT'S CALLED TEAMWORK. WE'RE REALLY GOOD AT IT.
WELL, SOMETIMES.

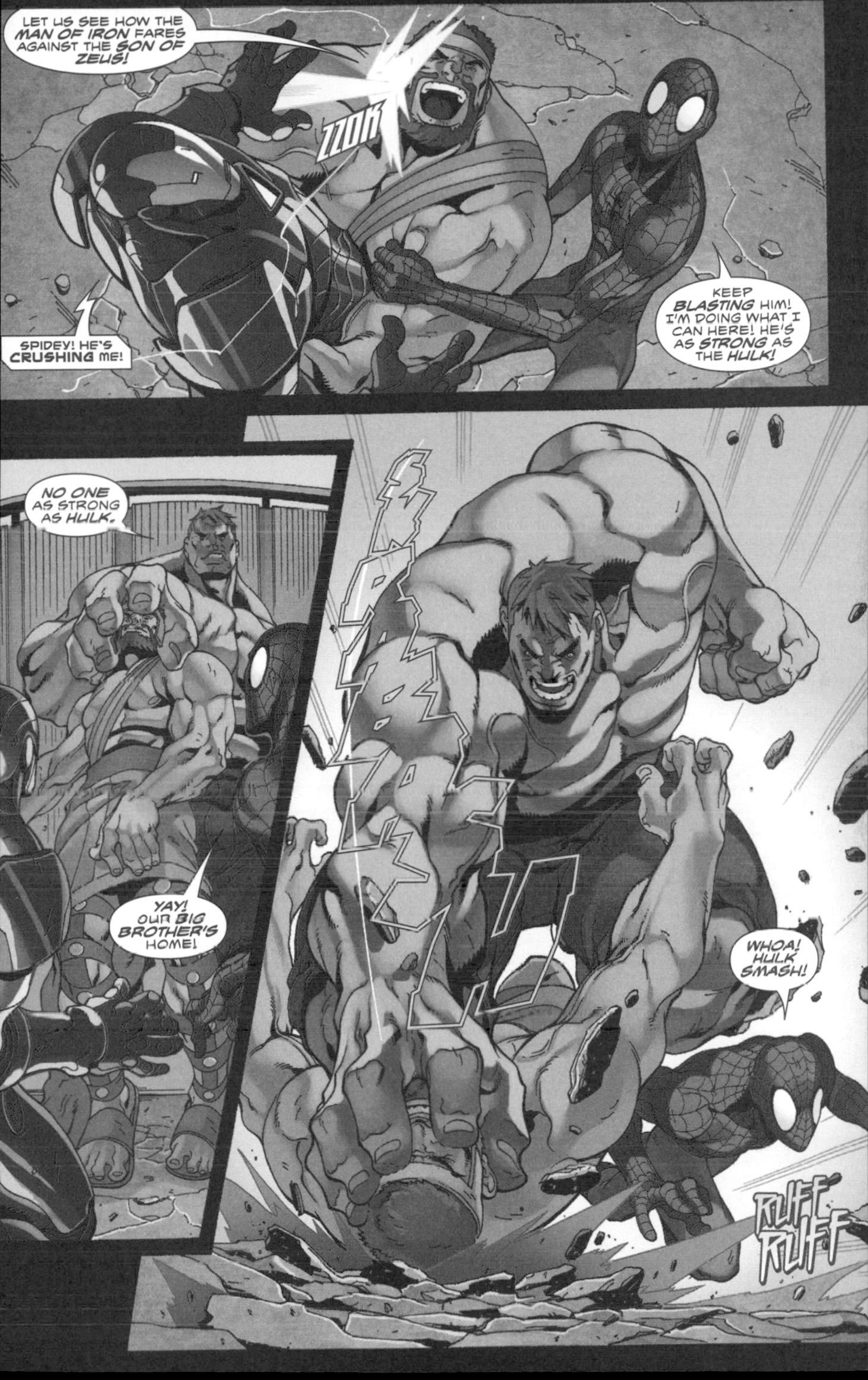
LET US SEE HOW THE MAN OF IRON FARES AGAINST THE SON OF ZEUS!
ZZOK
SPIDEY! HE'S CRUSHING ME!
KEEP BLASTING HIM! I'M DOING WHAT I CAN HERE! HE'S AS STRONG AS THE HULK!
NO ONE AS STRONG AS HULK.
YAY! OUR BIG BROTHER'S HOME!
WHOA! HULK SMASH!
RUFF RUFF

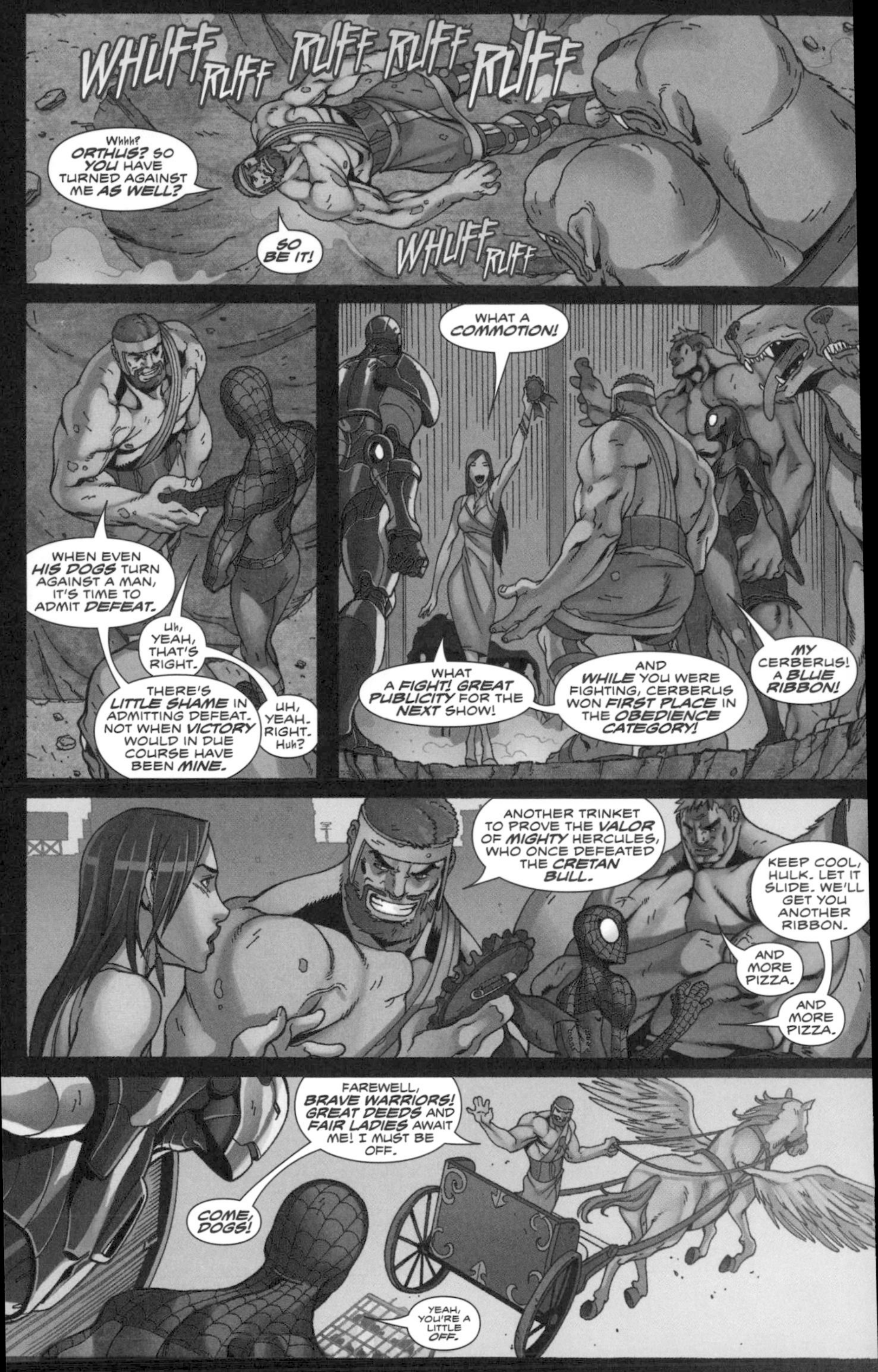
WHUFF RUFF RUFF RUFF RUFF
Whhh? ORTHUS? SO YOU HAVE TURNED AGAINST ME AS WELL?
SO BE IT!
WHUFF RUFF
WHEN EVEN HIS DOGS TURN AGAINST A MAN, IT'S TIME TO ADMIT DEFEAT.
UH, YEAH, THAT'S RIGHT.
THERE'S LITTLE SHAME IN ADMITTING DEFEAT. NOT WHEN VICTORY WOULD IN DUE COURSE HAVE BEEN MINE.
UH, YEAH. RIGHT. Huh?
WHAT A COMMOTION!
WHAT A FIGHT! GREAT PUBLICITY FOR THE NEXT SHOW!
AND WHILE YOU WERE FIGHTING, CERBERUS WON FIRST PLACE IN THE OBEDIENCE CATEGORY!
MY CERBERUS! A BLUE RIBBON!
ANOTHER TRINKET TO PROVE THE VALOR OF MIGHTY HERCULES, WHO ONCE DEFEATED THE CRETAN BULL.
KEEP COOL, HULK. LET IT SLIDE. WE'LL GET YOU ANOTHER RIBBON.
AND MORE PIZZA.
AND MORE PIZZA.
FAREWELL, BRAVE WARRIORS! GREAT DEEDS AND FAIR LADIES AWAIT ME! I MUST BE OFF.
COME, DOGS!
YEAH, YOU'RE A LITTLE OFF.

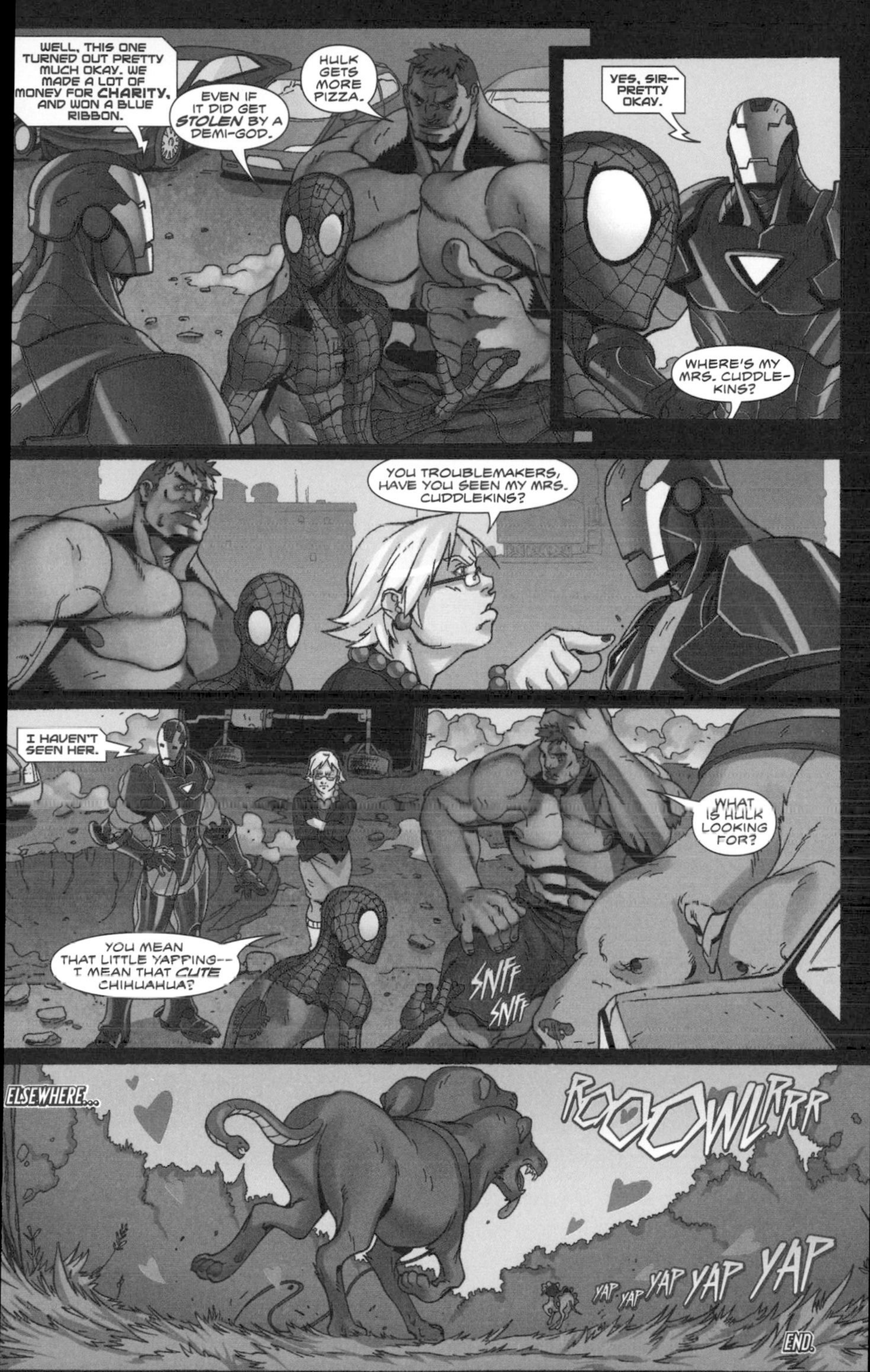

WELL, THIS ONE TURNED OUT PRETTY MUCH OKAY. WE MADE A LOT OF MONEY FOR CHARITY, AND WON A BLUE RIBBON.
EVEN IF IT DID GET STOLEN BY A DEMI-GOD.
HULK GETS MORE PIZZA.
YES, SIR-- PRETTY OKAY.
WHERE'S MY MRS. CUDDLE-KINS?
YOU TROUBLEMAKERS, HAVE YOU SEEN MY MRS. CUDDLEKINS?
I HAVEN'T SEEN HER.
WHAT IS HULK LOOKING FOR?
YOU MEAN THAT LITTLE YAPPING-- I MEAN THAT CUTE CHIHUAHUA?
SNFF SNFF
ELSEWHERE...
ROOOWLRRR
YAP YAP YAP YAP YAP
END.

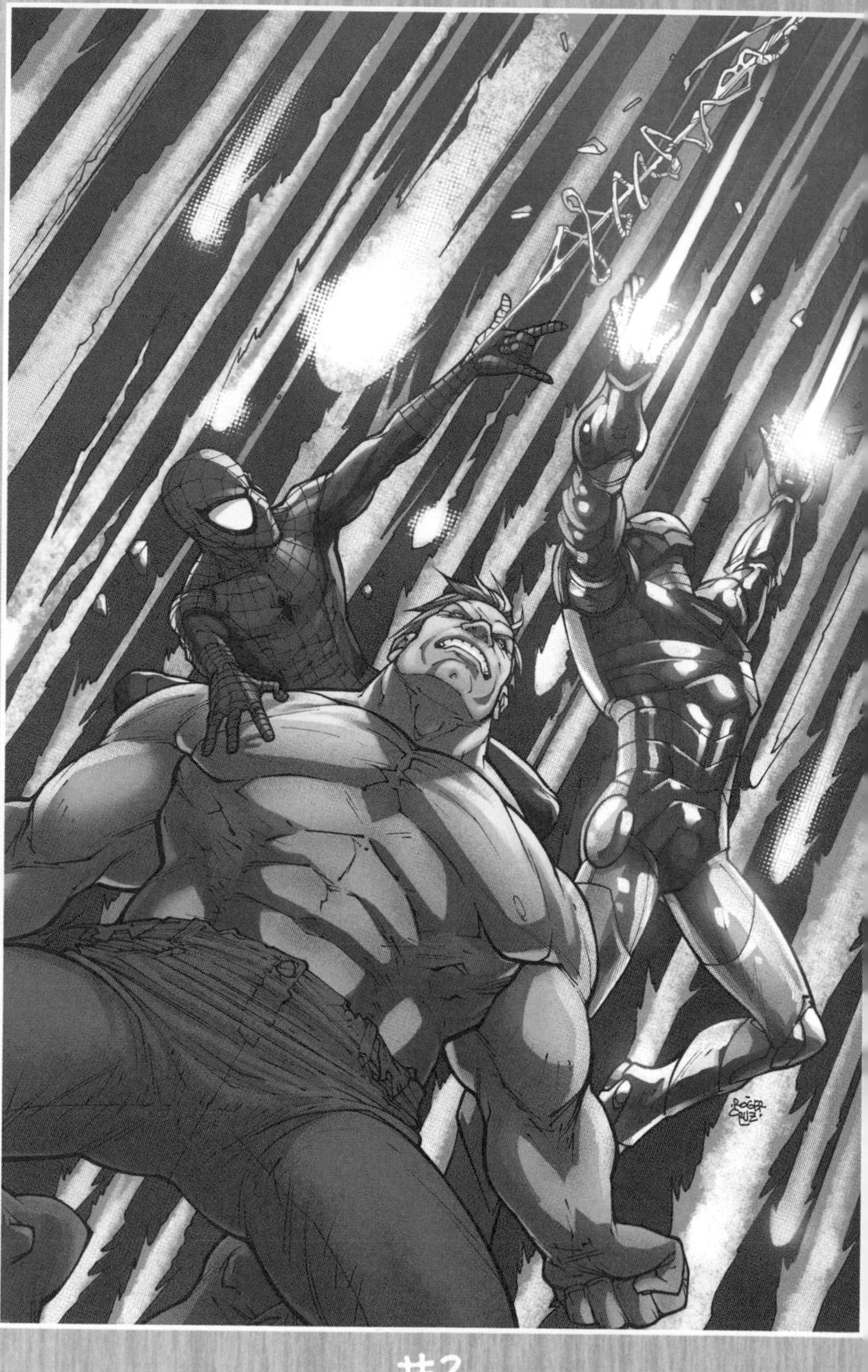

#2

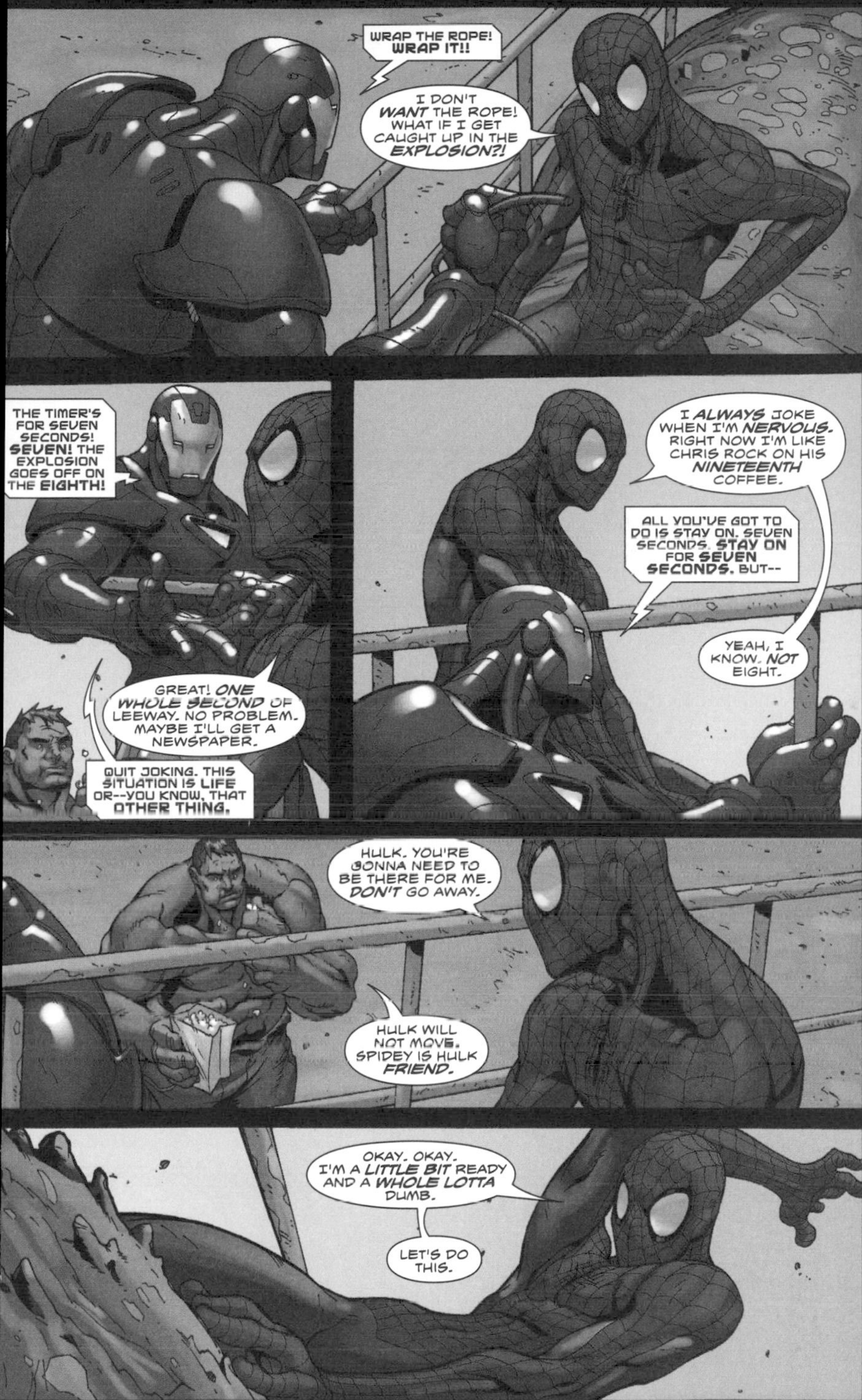
WRAP THE ROPE! WRAP IT!!
I DON'T WANT THE ROPE! WHAT IF I GET CAUGHT UP IN THE EXPLOSION?!
THE TIMER'S FOR SEVEN SECONDS! SEVEN! THE EXPLOSION GOES OFF ON THE EIGHTH!
GREAT! ONE WHOLE SECOND OF LEEWAY. NO PROBLEM. MAYBE I'LL GET A NEWSPAPER.
QUIT JOKING. THIS SITUATION IS LIFE OR--YOU KNOW, THAT OTHER THING.
I ALWAYS JOKE WHEN I'M NERVOUS. RIGHT NOW I'M LIKE CHRIS ROCK ON HIS NINETEENTH COFFEE.
ALL YOU'VE GOT TO DO IS STAY ON. SEVEN SECONDS. STAY ON FOR SEVEN SECONDS. BUT--
YEAH, I KNOW. NOT EIGHT.
HULK. YOU'RE GONNA NEED TO BE THERE FOR ME. DON'T GO AWAY.
HULK WILL NOT MOVE. SPIDEY IS HULK FRIEND.
OKAY. OKAY. I'M A LITTLE BIT READY AND A WHOLE LOTTA DUMB.
LET'S DO THIS.

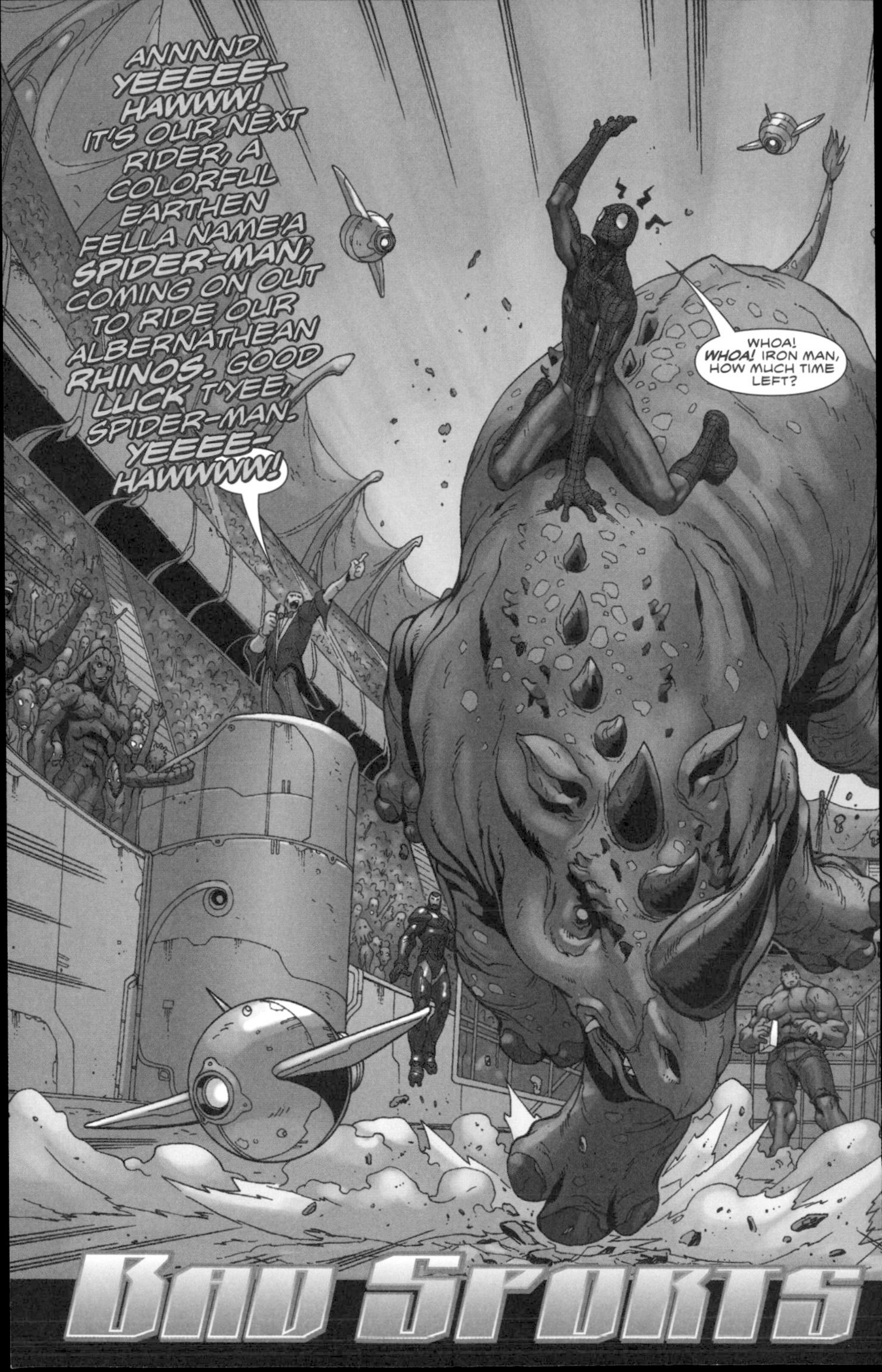
ANNNND YEEEEE-HAWWW! IT'S OUR NEXT RIDER, A COLORFUL EARTHEN FELLA NAME'A SPIDER-MAN, COMING ON OUT TO RIDE OUR ALBERNATHEAN RHINOS. GOOD LUCK T'YEE, SPIDER-MAN. YEEEE-HAWWWW!
WHOA! WHOA! IRON MAN, HOW MUCH TIME LEFT?
BAD SPORTS

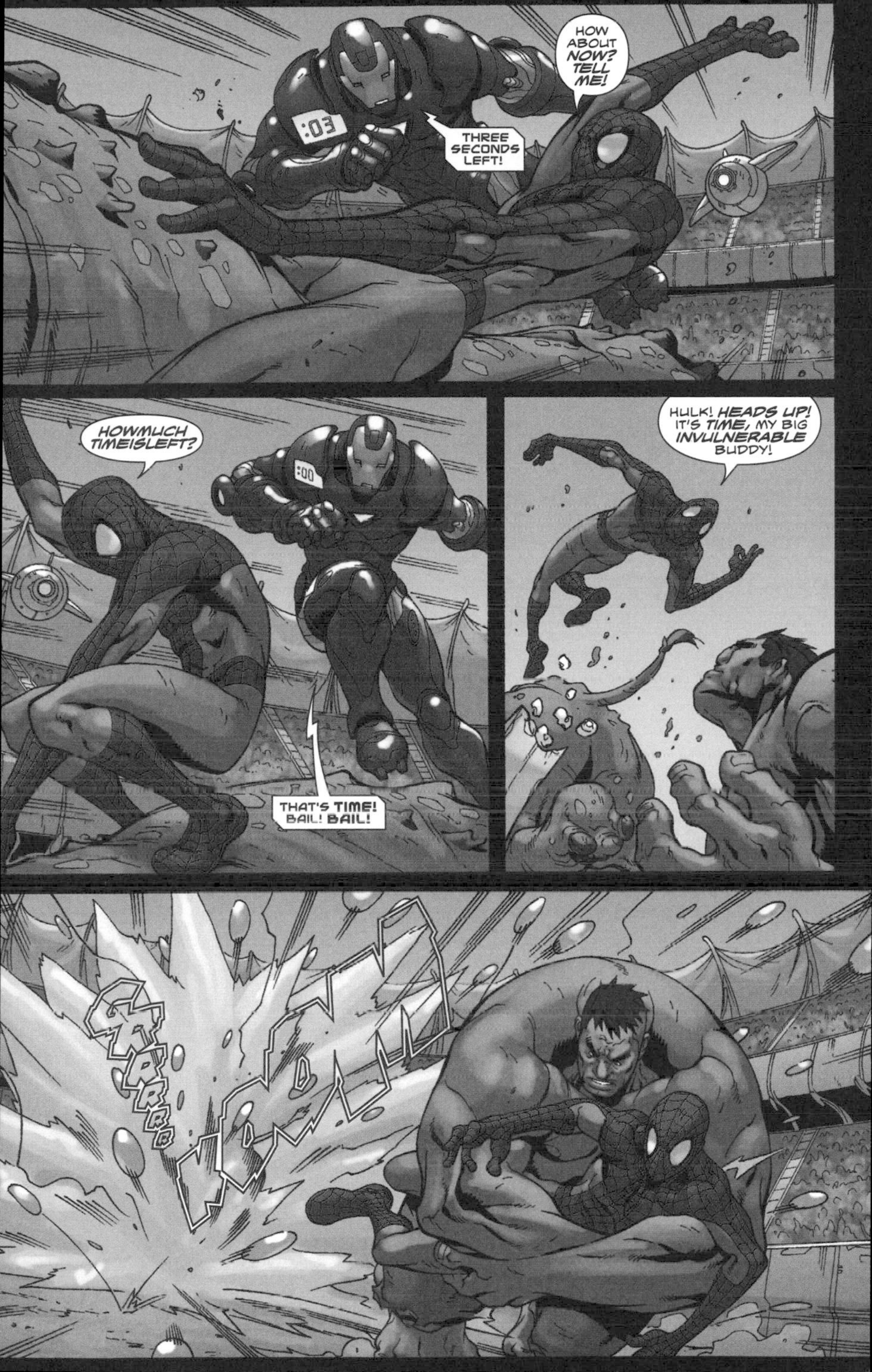
:03
HOW ABOUT NOW? TELL ME!
THREE SECONDS LEFT!
HOWMUCH TIMEISLEFT?
:00
THAT'S TIME! BAIL! BAIL!
HULK! HEADS UP! IT'S TIME, MY BIG INVULNERABLE BUDDY!

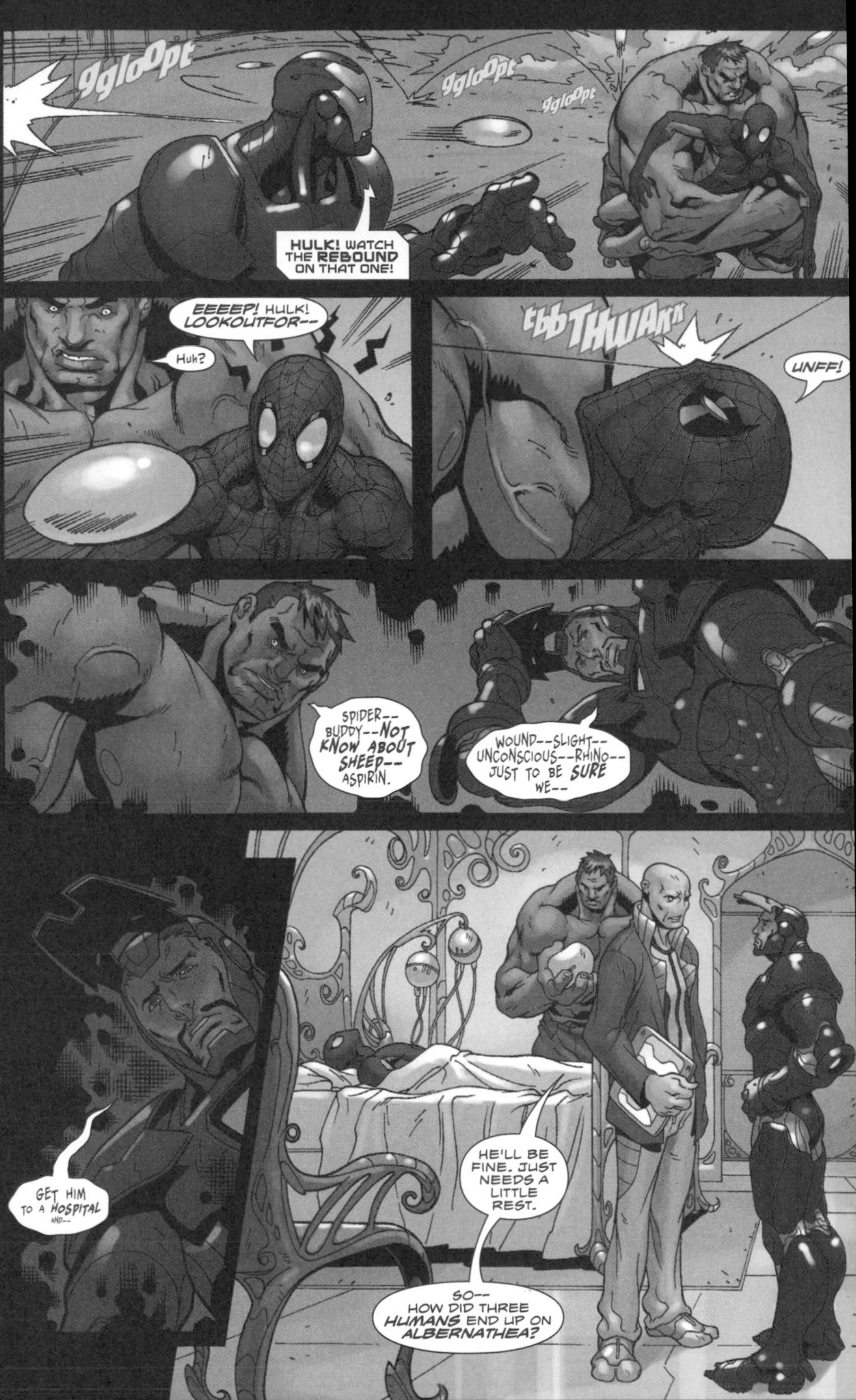

ggloOpt
ggloOpt
ggloOpt
HULK! WATCH THE REBOUND ON THAT ONE!
EEEEP! HULK! LOOKOUTFOR--
Huh?
tbbTHWAKk
UNFF!
SPIDER--BUDDY--NOT KNOW ABOUT SHEEP--ASPIRIN.
WOUND--SLIGHT--UNCONSCIOUS--RHINO--JUST TO BE SURE WE--
GET HIM TO A HOSPITAL AND--
HE'LL BE FINE. JUST NEEDS A LITTLE REST.
SO--HOW DID THREE HUMANS END UP ON ALBERNATHEA?

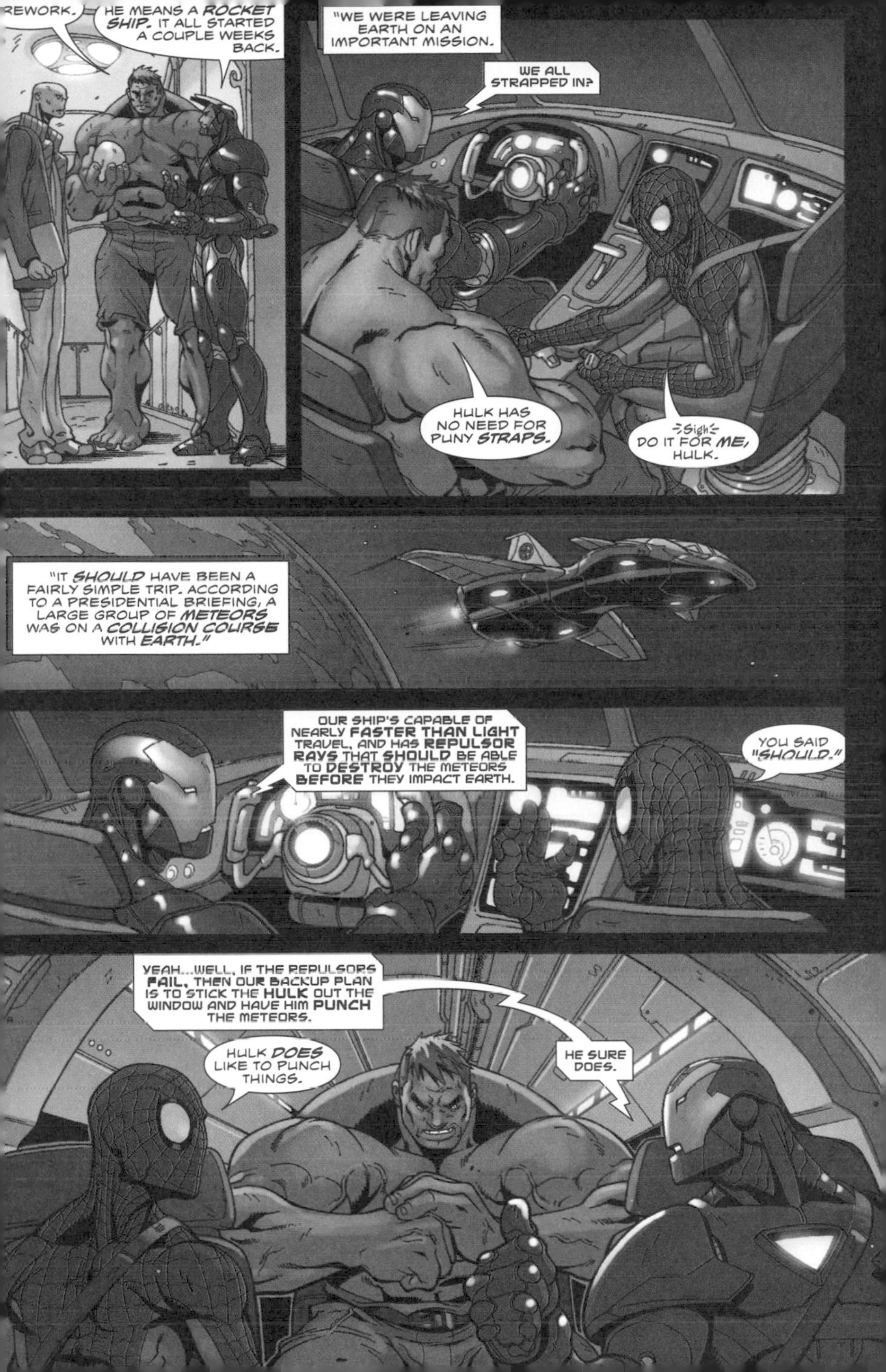
REWORK.
HE MEANS A ROCKET SHIP. IT ALL STARTED A COUPLE WEEKS BACK.
"WE WERE LEAVING EARTH ON AN IMPORTANT MISSION.
WE ALL STRAPPED IN?
HULK HAS NO NEED FOR PUNY STRAPS.
SIGH
DO IT FOR ME, HULK.
"IT SHOULD HAVE BEEN A FAIRLY SIMPLE TRIP. ACCORDING TO A PRESIDENTIAL BRIEFING, A LARGE GROUP OF METEORS WAS ON A COLLISION COURSE WITH EARTH."
OUR SHIP'S CAPABLE OF NEARLY FASTER THAN LIGHT TRAVEL, AND HAS REPULSOR RAYS THAT SHOULD BE ABLE TO DESTROY THE METEORS BEFORE THEY IMPACT EARTH.
YOU SAID "SHOULD."
YEAH...WELL, IF THE REPULSORS FAIL, THEN OUR BACKUP PLAN IS TO STICK THE HULK OUT THE WINDOW AND HAVE HIM PUNCH THE METEORS.
HULK DOES LIKE TO PUNCH THINGS.
HE SURE DOES.

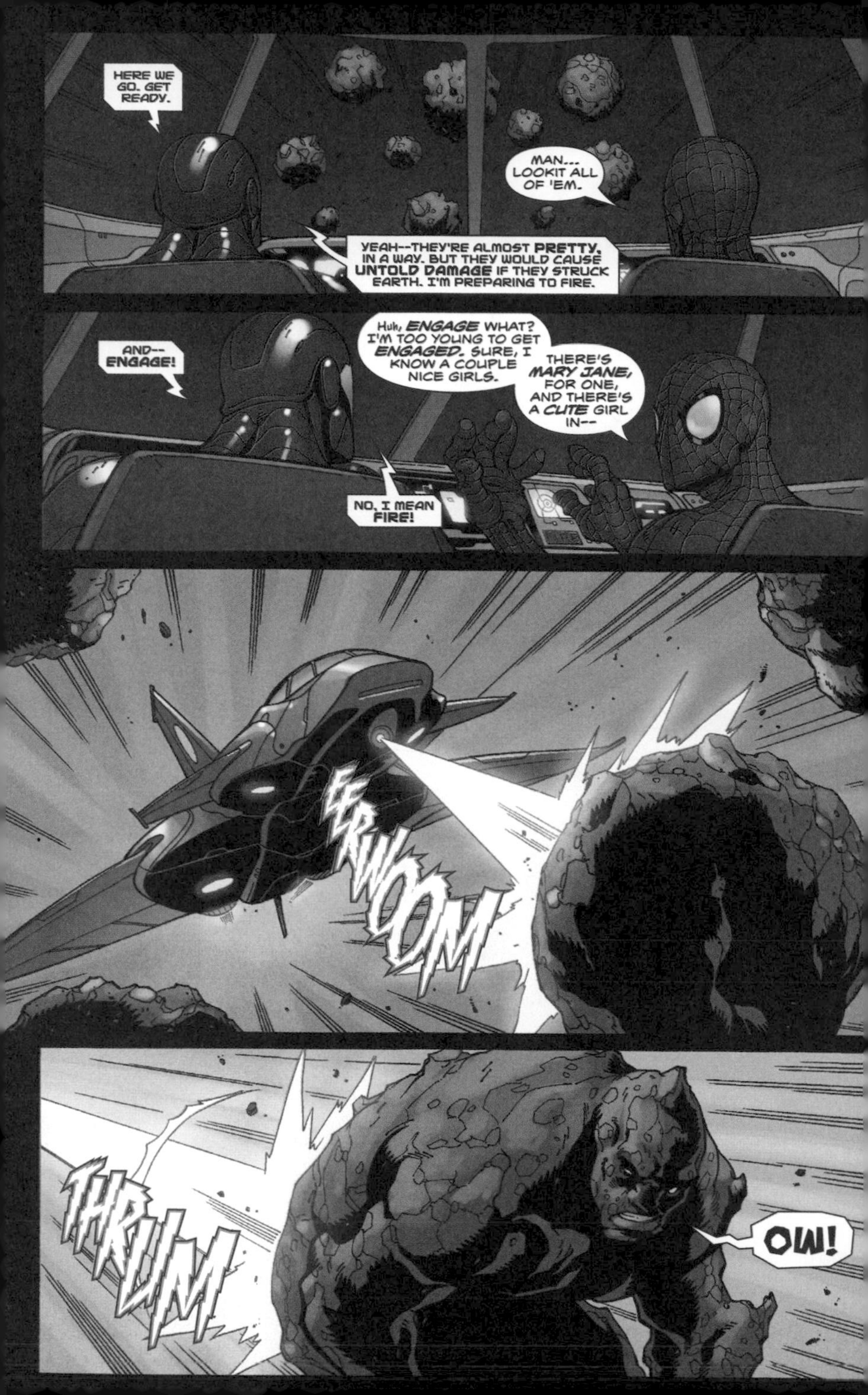
HERE WE GO. GET READY.
MAN... LOOKIT ALL OF 'EM.
YEAH--THEY'RE ALMOST PRETTY, IN A WAY. BUT THEY WOULD CAUSE UNTOLD DAMAGE IF THEY STRUCK EARTH. I'M PREPARING TO FIRE.
AND-- ENGAGE!
Huh, ENGAGE WHAT? I'M TOO YOUNG TO GET ENGAGED. SURE, I KNOW A COUPLE NICE GIRLS.
THERE'S MARY JANE, FOR ONE, AND THERE'S A CUTE GIRL IN--
NO, I MEAN FIRE!
EERWOOM
THRUM
OW!

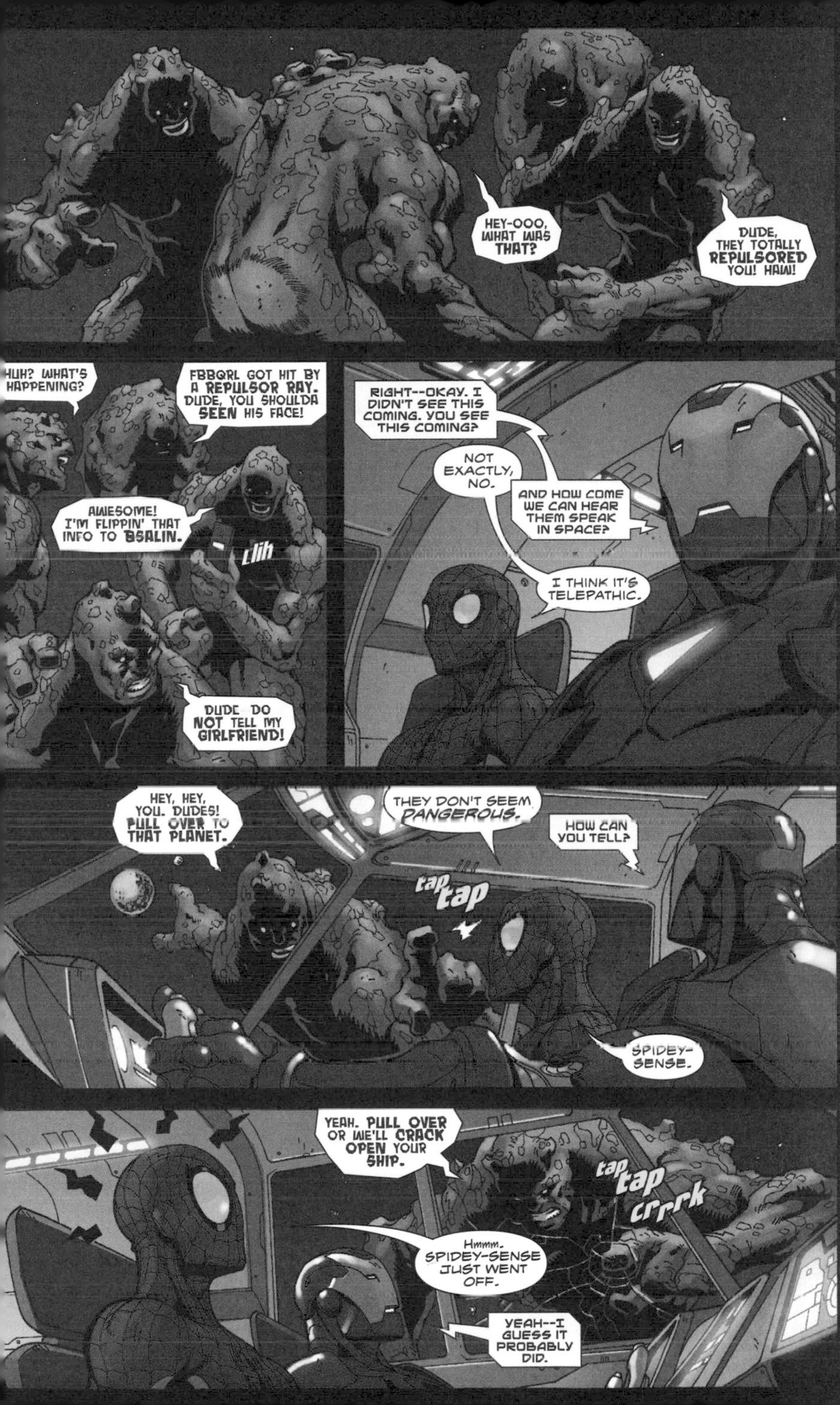
HEY-OOO, WHAT WAS THAT?
DUDE, THEY TOTALLY REPULSORED YOU! HAW!
HUH? WHAT'S HAPPENING?
FBBQRL GOT HIT BY A REPULSOR RAY. DUDE, YOU SHOULDA SEEN HIS FACE!
AWESOME! I'M FLIPPIN' THAT INFO TO BSALIN.
DUDE DO NOT TELL MY GIRLFRIEND!
RIGHT--OKAY. I DIDN'T SEE THIS COMING. YOU SEE THIS COMING?
NOT EXACTLY, NO.
AND HOW COME WE CAN HEAR THEM SPEAK IN SPACE?
I THINK IT'S TELEPATHIC.
HEY, HEY, YOU. DUDES! PULL OVER TO THAT PLANET.
THEY DON'T SEEM DANGEROUS.
HOW CAN YOU TELL?
tap tap
SPIDEY-SENSE.
YEAH. PULL OVER OR WE'LL CRACK OPEN YOUR SHIP.
tap tap crrrk
Hmmm. SPIDEY-SENSE JUST WENT OFF.
YEAH--I GUESS IT PROBABLY DID.

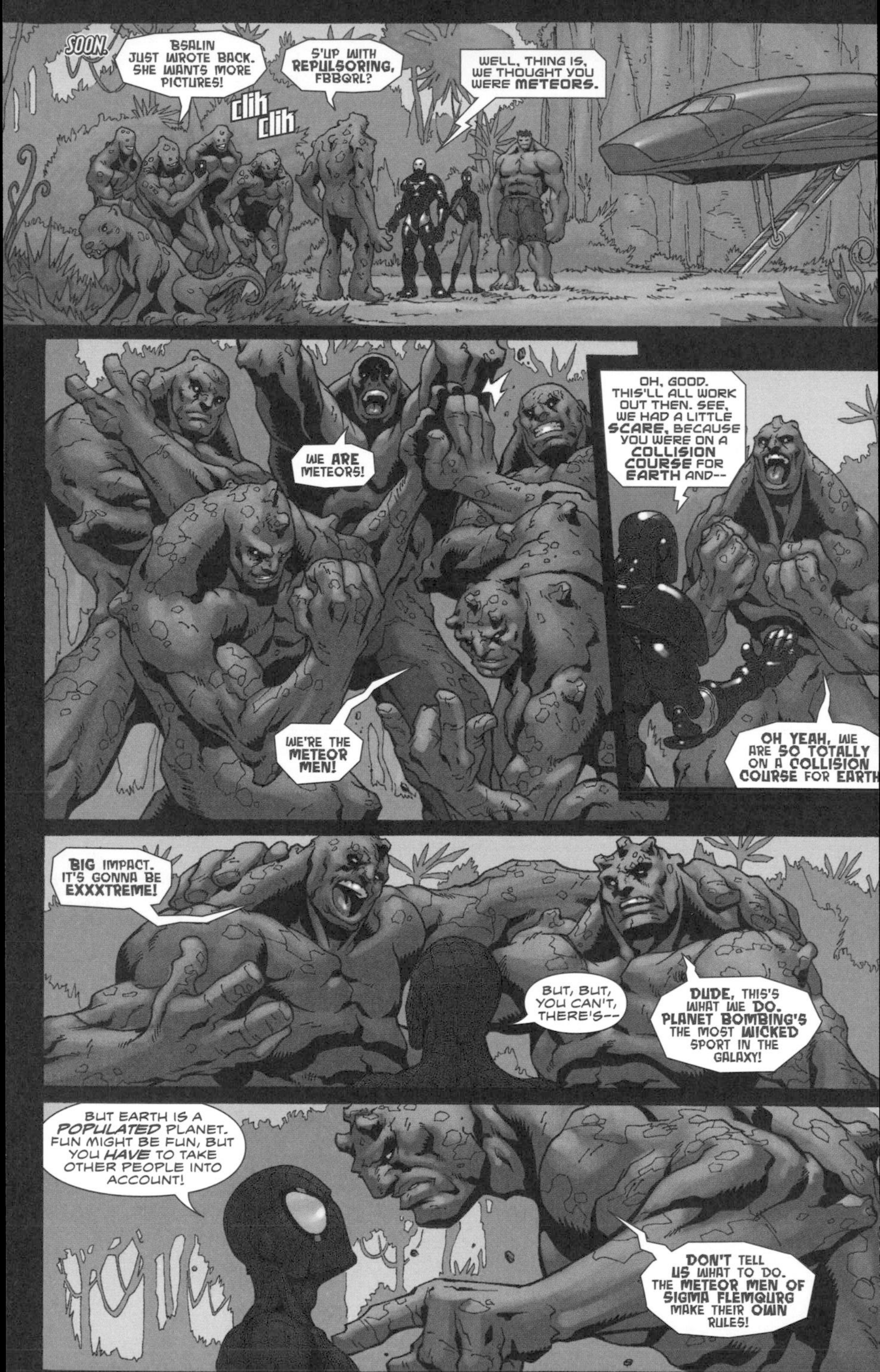
SOON.
BSALIN JUST WROTE BACK. SHE WANTS MORE PICTURES!
clik clik
S'UP WITH REPULSORING, FBBQRL?
WELL, THING IS, WE THOUGHT YOU WERE METEORS.
WE ARE METEORS!
WE'RE THE METEOR MEN!
OH, GOOD. THIS'LL ALL WORK OUT THEN. SEE, WE HAD A LITTLE SCARE, BECAUSE YOU WERE ON A COLLISION COURSE FOR EARTH AND--
OH YEAH, WE ARE SO TOTALLY ON A COLLISION COURSE FOR EARTH
BIG IMPACT. IT'S GONNA BE EXXXTREME!
BUT, BUT, YOU CAN'T, THERE'S--
DUDE, THIS'S WHAT WE DO. PLANET BOMBING'S THE MOST WICKED SPORT IN THE GALAXY!
BUT EARTH IS A POPULATED PLANET. FUN MIGHT BE FUN, BUT YOU HAVE TO TAKE OTHER PEOPLE INTO ACCOUNT!
DON'T TELL US WHAT TO DO. THE METEOR MEN OF SIGMA FLEMQURG MAKE THEIR OWN RULES!

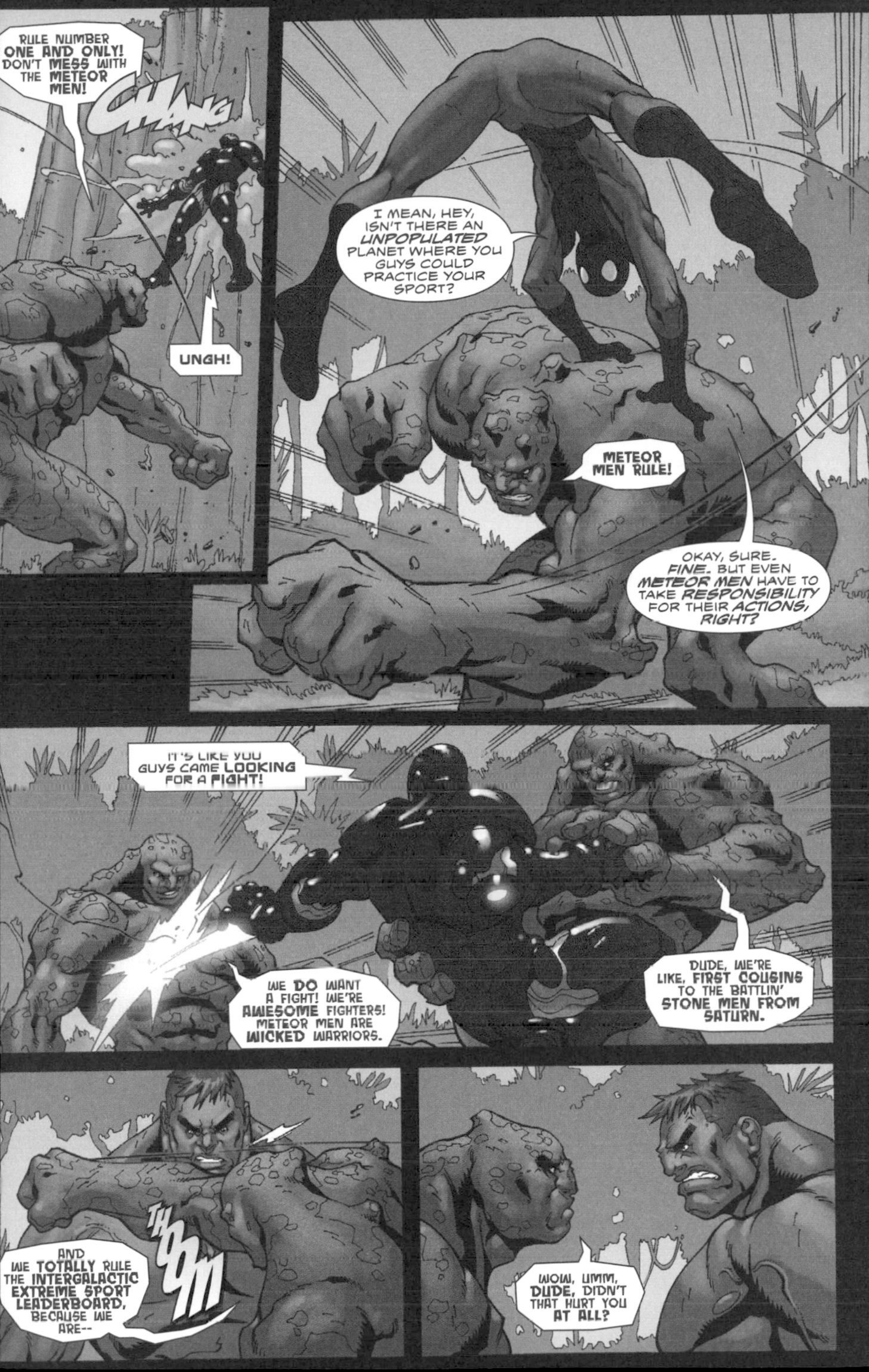
RULE NUMBER ONE AND ONLY! DON'T MESS WITH THE METEOR MEN!
CHANG
UNGH!
I MEAN, HEY, ISN'T THERE AN UNPOPULATED PLANET WHERE YOU GUYS COULD PRACTICE YOUR SPORT?
METEOR MEN RULE!
OKAY, SURE. FINE. BUT EVEN METEOR MEN HAVE TO TAKE RESPONSIBILITY FOR THEIR ACTIONS, RIGHT?
IT'S LIKE YOU GUYS CAME LOOKING FOR A FIGHT!
WE DO WANT A FIGHT! WE'RE AWESOME FIGHTERS! METEOR MEN ARE WICKED WARRIORS.
DUDE, WE'RE LIKE, FIRST COUSINS TO THE BATTLIN' STONE MEN FROM SATURN.
AND WE TOTALLY RULE THE INTERGALACTIC EXTREME SPORT LEADERBOARD, BECAUSE WE ARE--
THOOM
WOW, UMM, DUDE, DIDN'T THAT HURT YOU AT ALL?

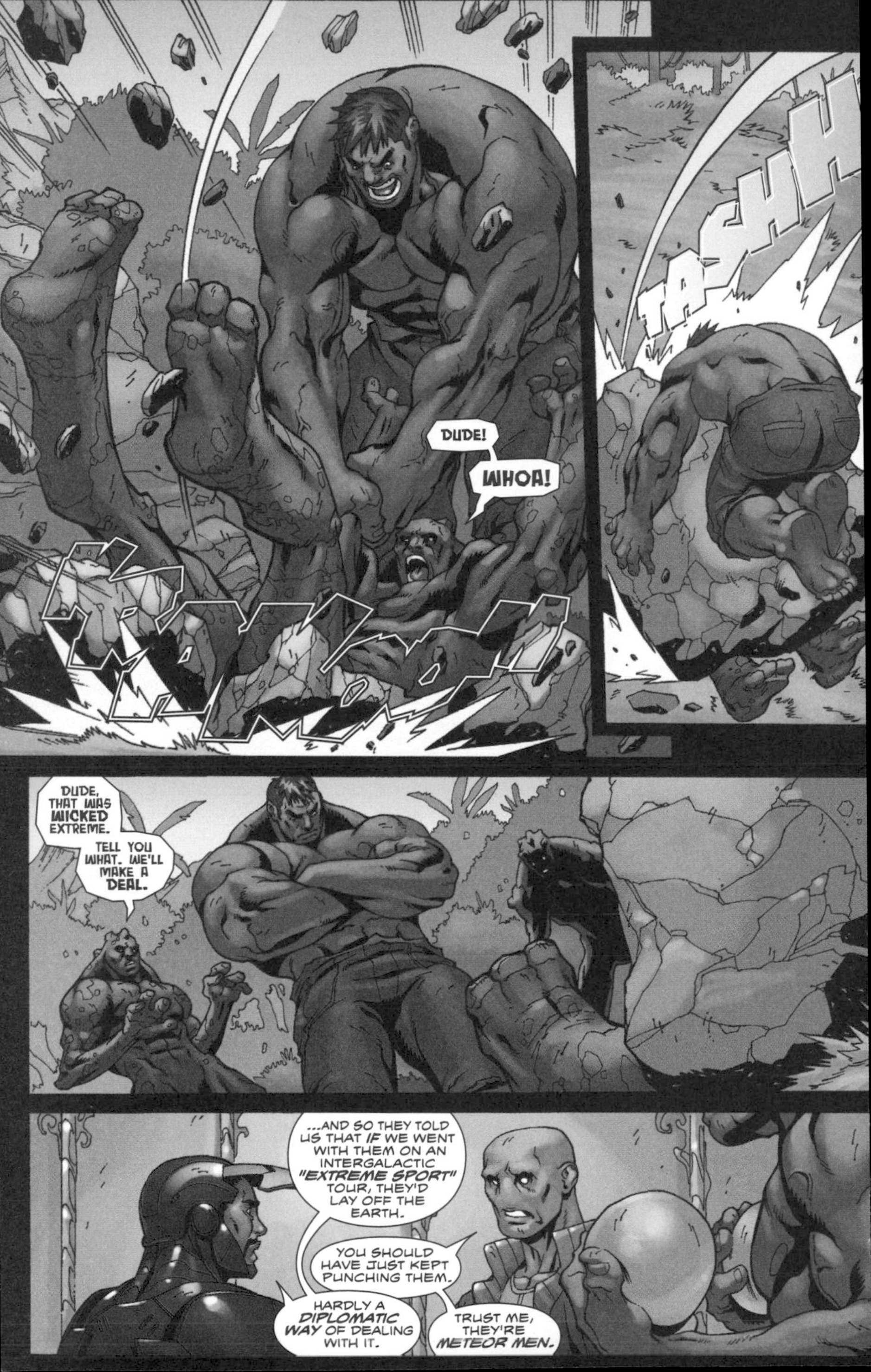
DUDE!
WHOA!
DUDE, THAT WAS WICKED EXTREME.
TELL YOU WHAT. WE'LL MAKE A DEAL.
...AND SO THEY TOLD US THAT IF WE WENT WITH THEM ON AN INTERGALACTIC "EXTREME SPORT" TOUR, THEY'D LAY OFF THE EARTH.
YOU SHOULD HAVE JUST KEPT PUNCHING THEM.
HARDLY A DIPLOMATIC WAY OF DEALING WITH IT.
TRUST ME, THEY'RE METEOR MEN.

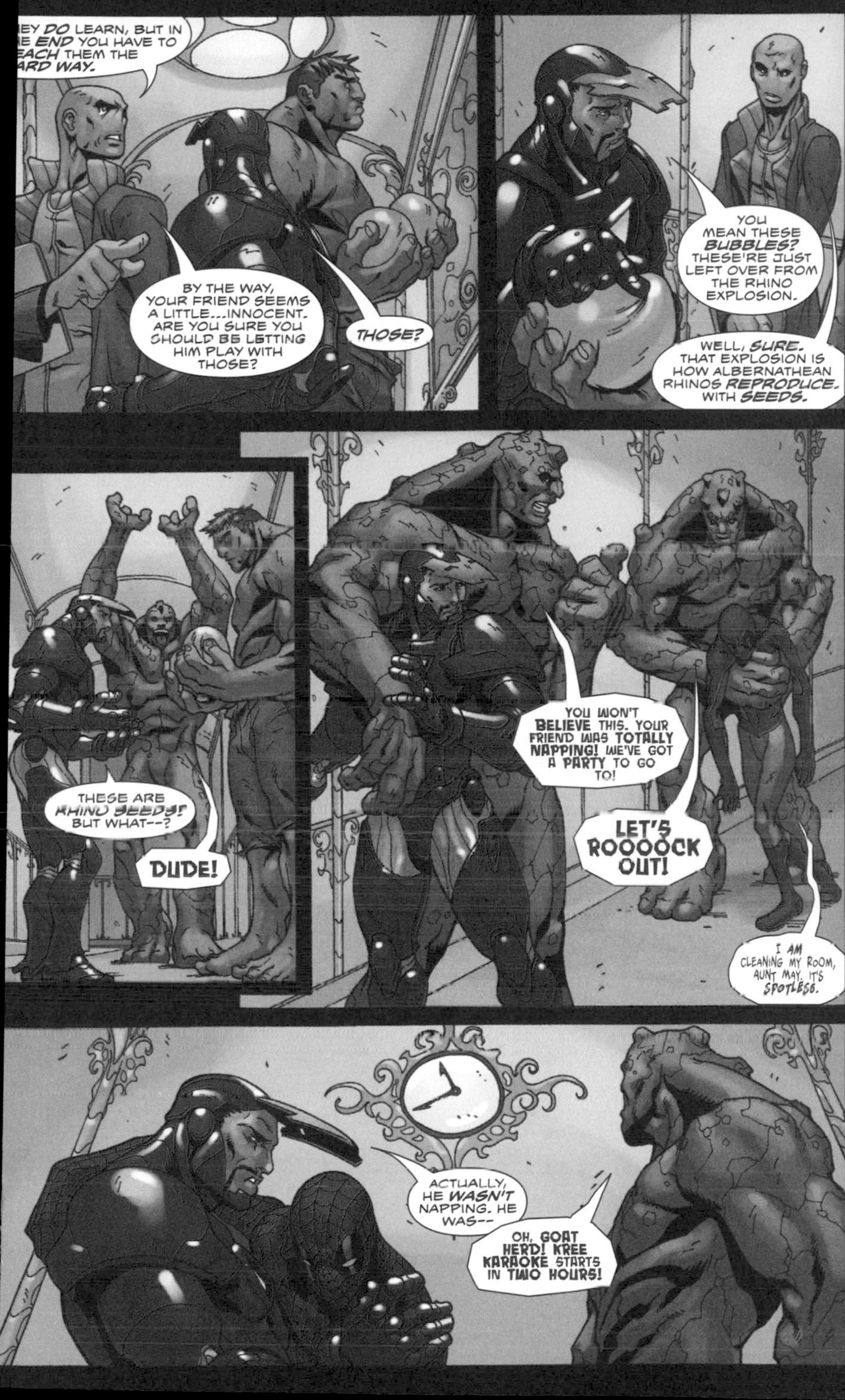

EY DO LEARN, BUT IN
E END YOU HAVE TO
EACH THEM THE
ARD WAY.
BY THE WAY, YOUR FRIEND SEEMS A LITTLE...INNOCENT. ARE YOU SURE YOU SHOULD BE LETTING HIM PLAY WITH THOSE?
THOSE?
YOU MEAN THESE BUBBLES? THESE'RE JUST LEFT OVER FROM THE RHINO EXPLOSION.
WELL, SURE. THAT EXPLOSION IS HOW ALBERNATHEAN RHINOS REPRODUCE. WITH SEEDS.
THESE ARE RHINO SEEDS! BUT WHAT--?
DUDE!
YOU WON'T BELIEVE THIS. YOUR FRIEND WAS TOTALLY NAPPING! WE'VE GOT A PARTY TO GO TO!
LET'S ROOOOCK OUT!
I AM CLEANING MY ROOM, AUNT MAY. IT'S SPOTLESS.
ACTUALLY, HE WASN'T NAPPING. HE WAS--
OH, GOAT HERD! KREE KARAOKE STARTS IN TWO HOURS!

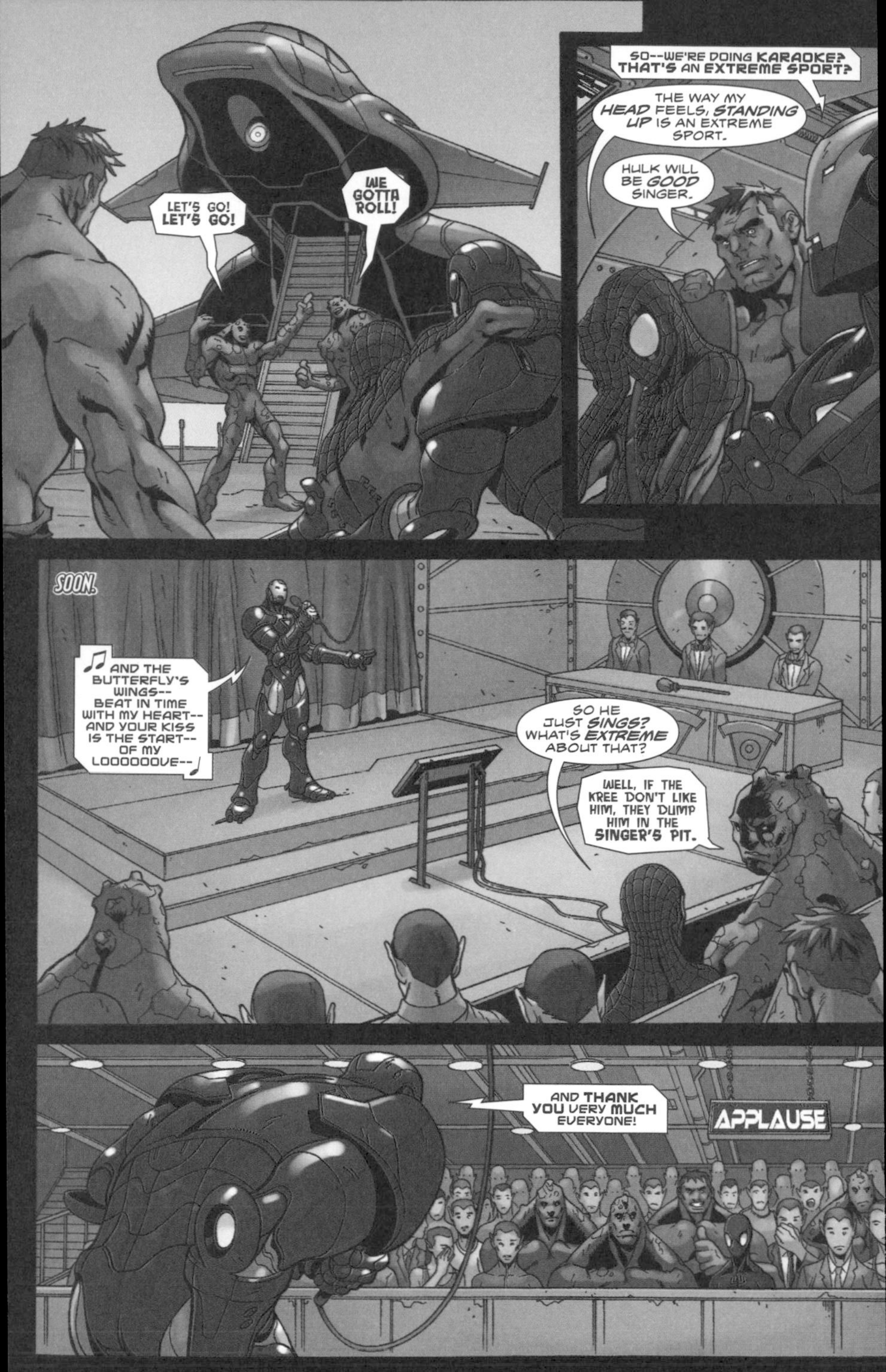

LET'S GO! LET'S GO!
WE GOTTA ROLL!
SO--WE'RE DOING KARAOKE? THAT'S AN EXTREME SPORT?
THE WAY MY HEAD FEELS, STANDING UP IS AN EXTREME SPORT.
HULK WILL BE GOOD SINGER.
SOON.
♫ AND THE BUTTERFLY'S WINGS-- BEAT IN TIME WITH MY HEART-- AND YOUR KISS IS THE START-- OF MY LOOOOOOVE-- ♩
SO HE JUST SINGS? WHAT'S EXTREME ABOUT THAT?
WELL, IF THE KREE DON'T LIKE HIM, THEY DUMP HIM IN THE SINGER'S PIT.
AND THANK YOU VERY MUCH EVERYONE!
APPLAUSE

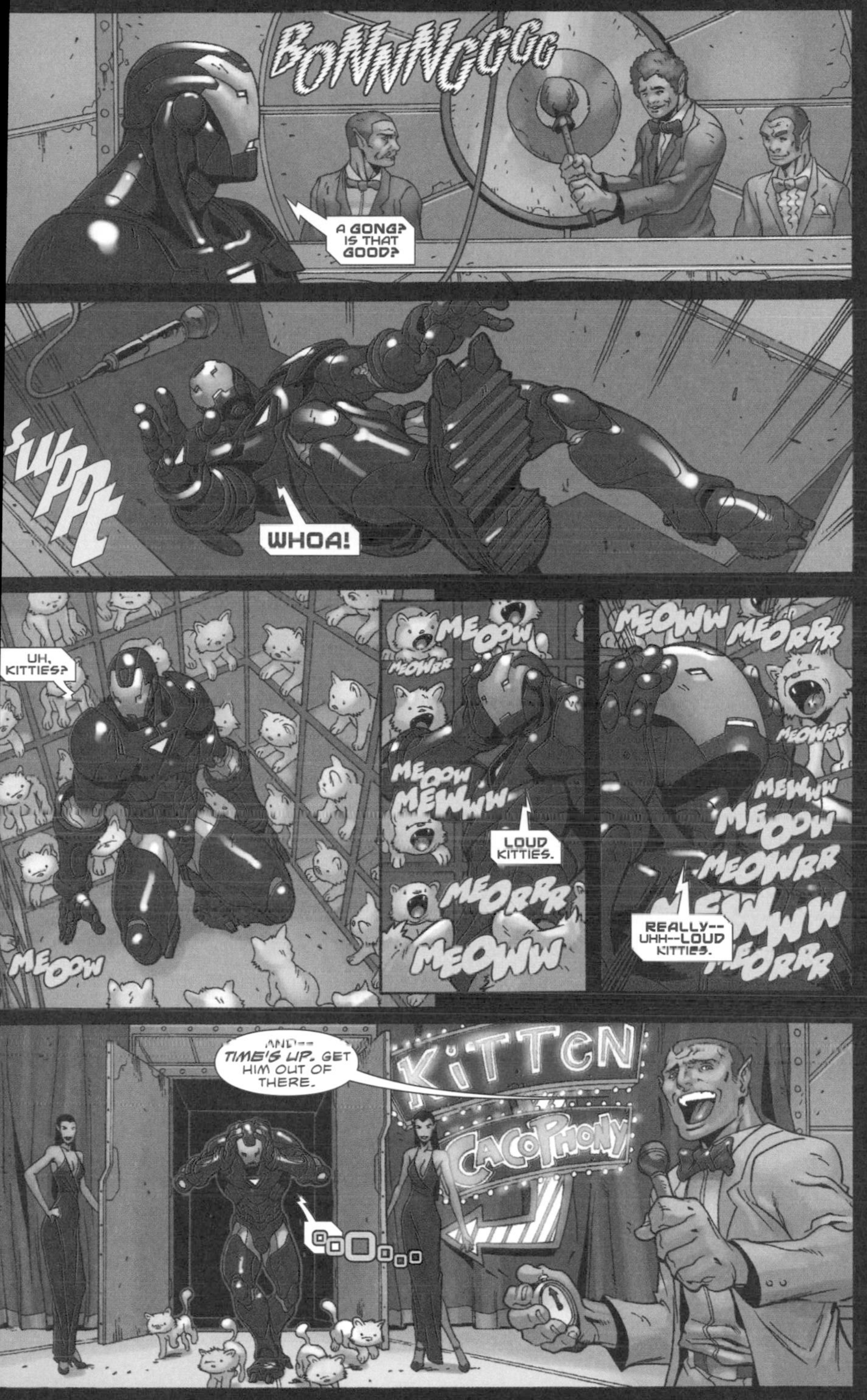
BONNNGGGG
A GONG? IS THAT GOOD?
FUPPT
WHOA!
UH, KITTIES?
MEOOW
MEOOW
MEOWRR
MEOOW
MEWWW
LOUD KITTIES.
MEORRR
MEOWW
MEOWW
MEORRR
MEOWRR
MEWWW
MEOOW
MEOWRR
REALLY-- UHH--LOUD KITTIES.
MEWWW
MEORRR
AND-- TIME'S UP. GET HIM OUT OF THERE.
KITTEN CACOPHONY
OoOOoo

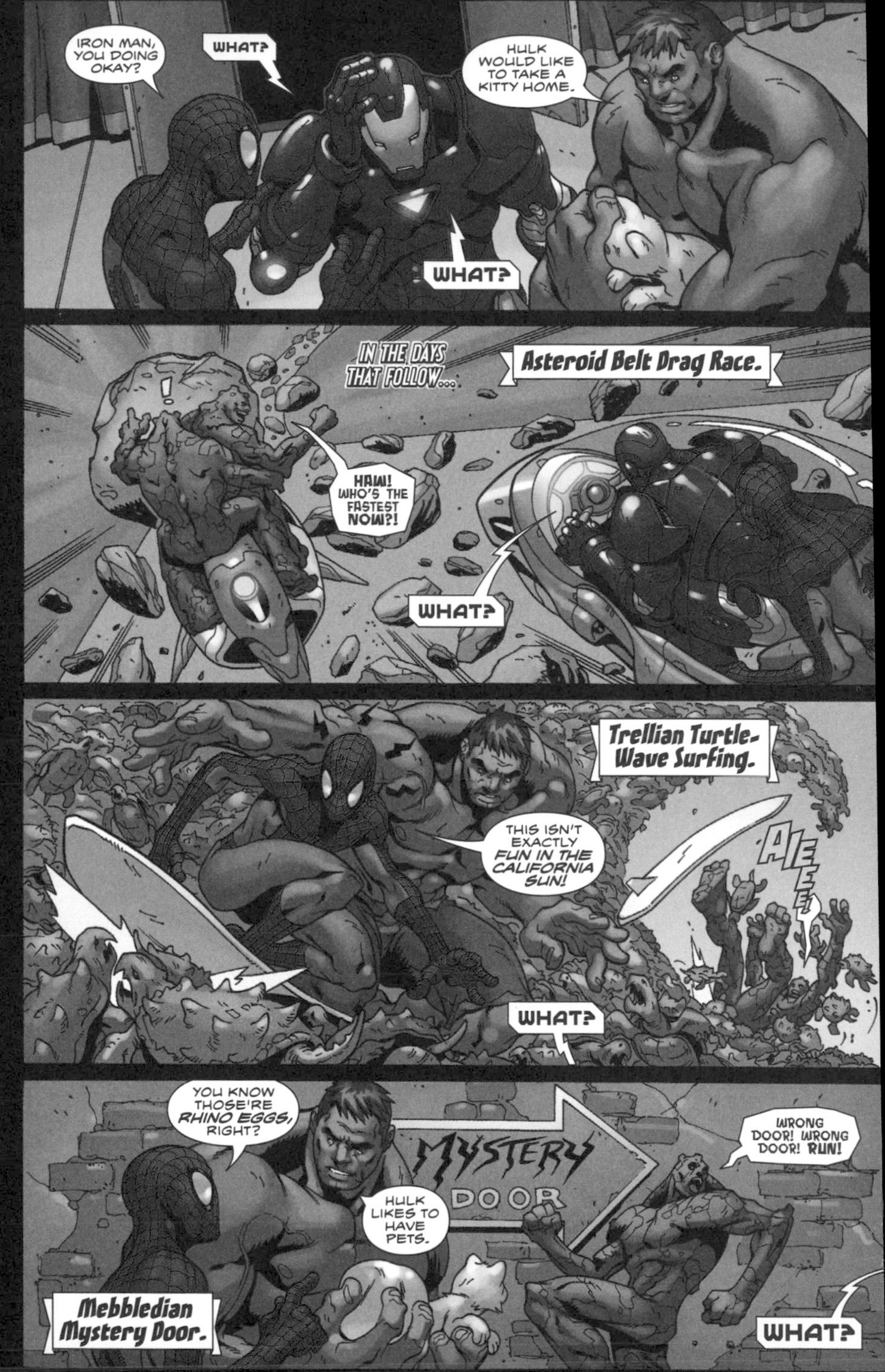
IRON MAN, YOU DOING OKAY?
WHAT?
HULK WOULD LIKE TO TAKE A KITTY HOME.
WHAT?
IN THE DAYS THAT FOLLOW...
Asteroid Belt Drag Race.
!
HAW! WHO'S THE FASTEST NOW?!
WHAT?
Trellian Turtle-Wave Surfing.
THIS ISN'T EXACTLY FUN IN THE CALIFORNIA SUN!
AIEEE!
WHAT?
Mebbledian Mystery Door.
YOU KNOW THOSE'RE RHINO EGGS, RIGHT?
HULK LIKES TO HAVE PETS.
MYSTERY DOOR
WRONG DOOR! WRONG DOOR! RUN!
WHAT?

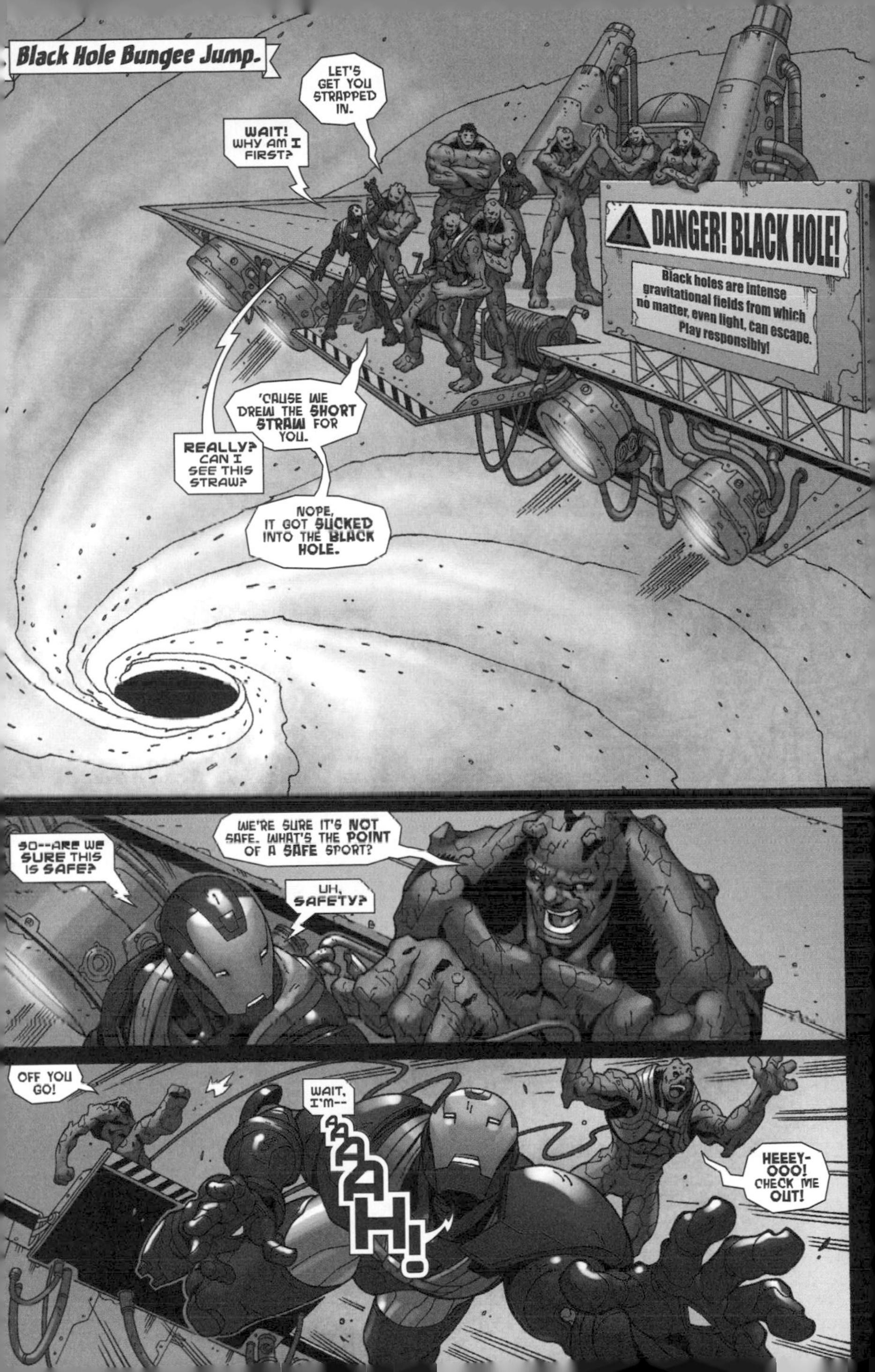
Black Hole Bungee Jump.
LET'S GET YOU STRAPPED IN.
WAIT! WHY AM I FIRST?
'CAUSE WE DREW THE SHORT STRAW FOR YOU.
REALLY? CAN I SEE THIS STRAW?
NOPE, IT GOT SUCKED INTO THE BLACK HOLE.
DANGER! BLACK HOLE!
Black holes are intense gravitational fields from which no matter, even light, can escape. Play responsibly!
SO--ARE WE SURE THIS IS SAFE?
WE'RE SURE IT'S NOT SAFE. WHAT'S THE POINT OF A SAFE SPORT?
UH, SAFETY?
OFF YOU GO!
WAIT, I'M--
AAAAH!
HEEEY-OOO! CHECK ME OUT!

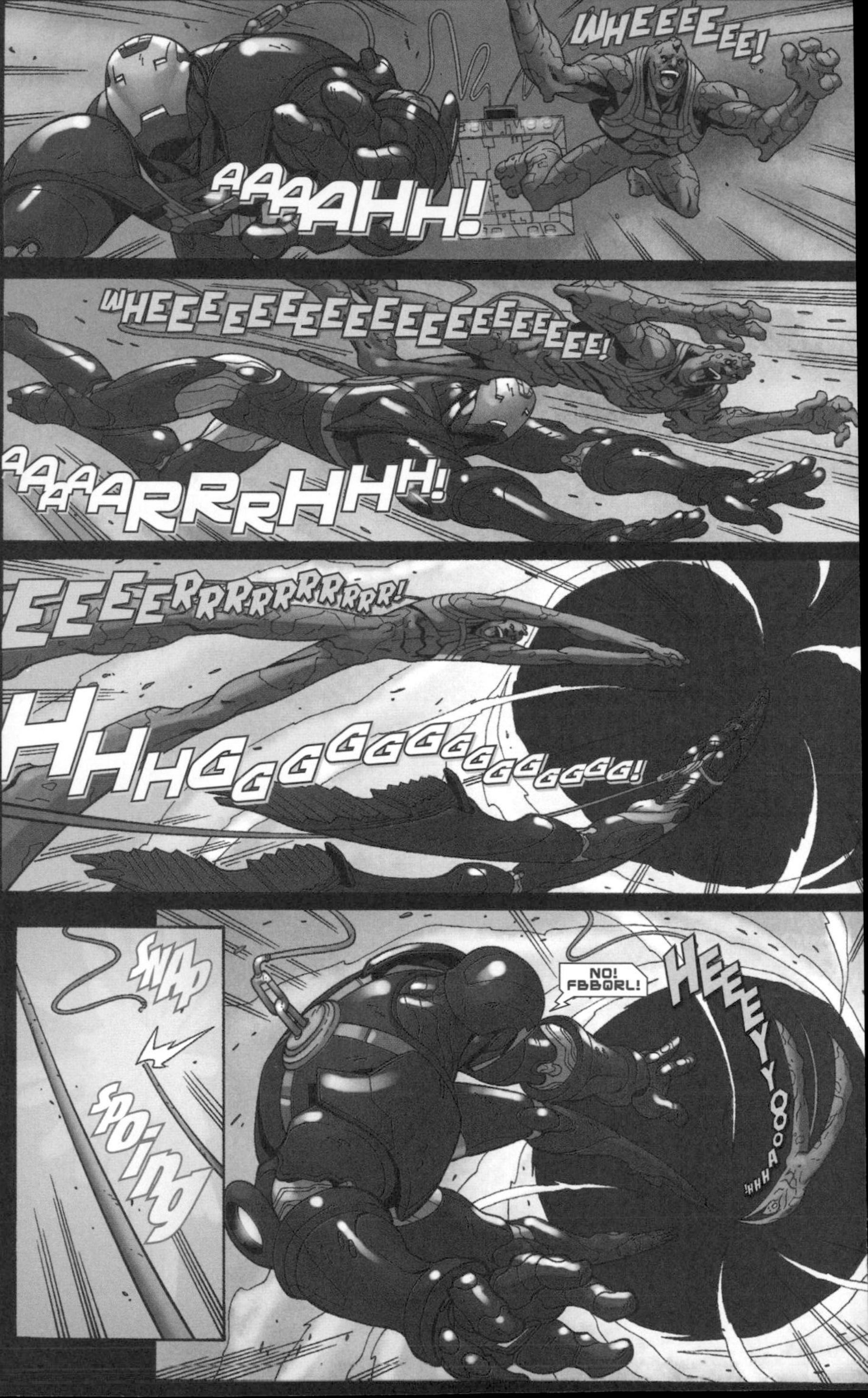
WHEEEEEE!
AAAAAHH!
WHEEEEEEEEEEEEEEEEEEEE!
AAAAARRRRHHH!
EEEEERRRRRRRRRR!
HHHGGGGGGGGGGGG!
SNAP
SPOING
NO! FBBORL!
HEEEYYOOOAHHH!

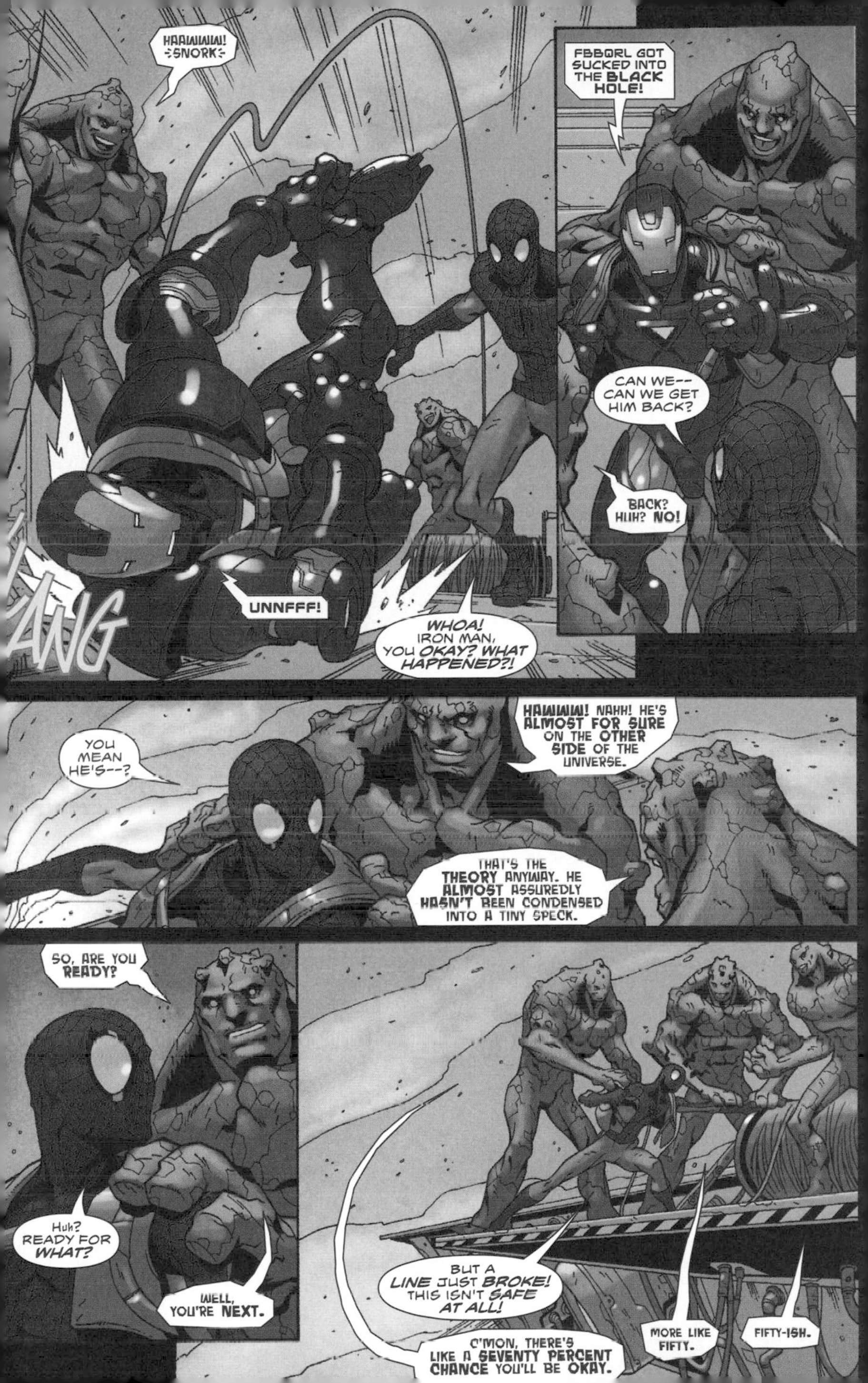
HAAWWW! -SNORK-
UNNFFF!
WHOA! IRON MAN, YOU OKAY? WHAT HAPPENED?!
FBBQRL GOT SUCKED INTO THE BLACK HOLE!
CAN WE-- CAN WE GET HIM BACK?
BACK? HUH? NO!
YOU MEAN HE'S--?
HAWWW! NAHH! HE'S ALMOST FOR SURE ON THE OTHER SIDE OF THE UNIVERSE.
THAT'S THE THEORY ANYWAY. HE ALMOST ASSUREDLY HASN'T BEEN CONDENSED INTO A TINY SPECK.
SO, ARE YOU READY?
Huh? READY FOR WHAT?
WELL, YOU'RE NEXT.
BUT A LINE JUST BROKE! THIS ISN'T SAFE AT ALL!
C'MON, THERE'S LIKE A SEVENTY PERCENT CHANCE YOU'LL BE OKAY.
MORE LIKE FIFTY.
FIFTY-ISH.

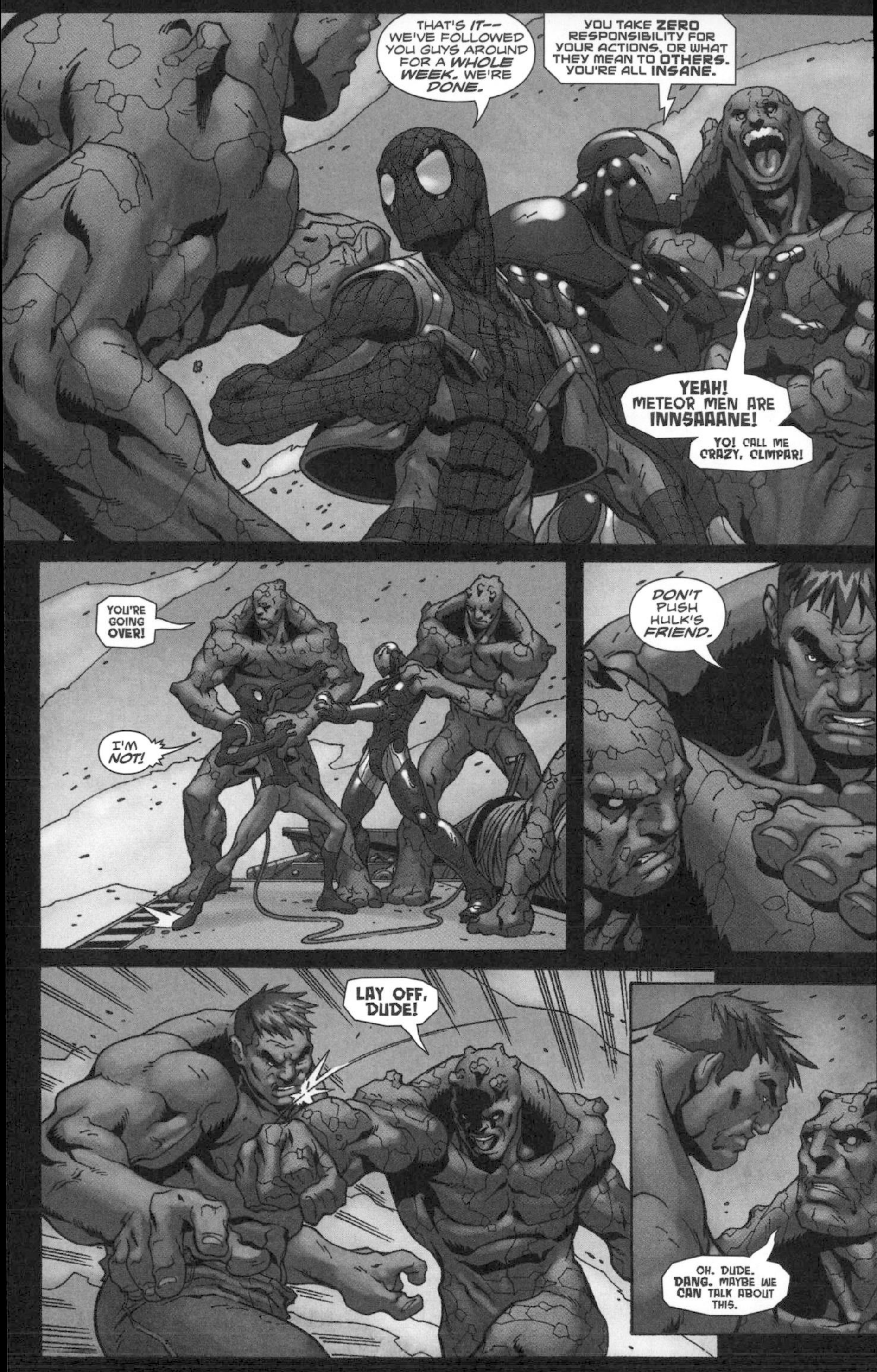
THAT'S IT-- WE'VE FOLLOWED YOU GUYS AROUND FOR A WHOLE WEEK. WE'RE DONE.
YOU TAKE ZERO RESPONSIBILITY FOR YOUR ACTIONS, OR WHAT THEY MEAN TO OTHERS. YOU'RE ALL INSANE.
YEAH! METEOR MEN ARE INNSAAANE!
YO! CALL ME CRAZY, CLMPAR!
YOU'RE GOING OVER!
I'M NOT!
DON'T PUSH HULK'S FRIEND.
LAY OFF, DUDE!
OH. DUDE. DANG. MAYBE WE CAN TALK ABOUT THIS.

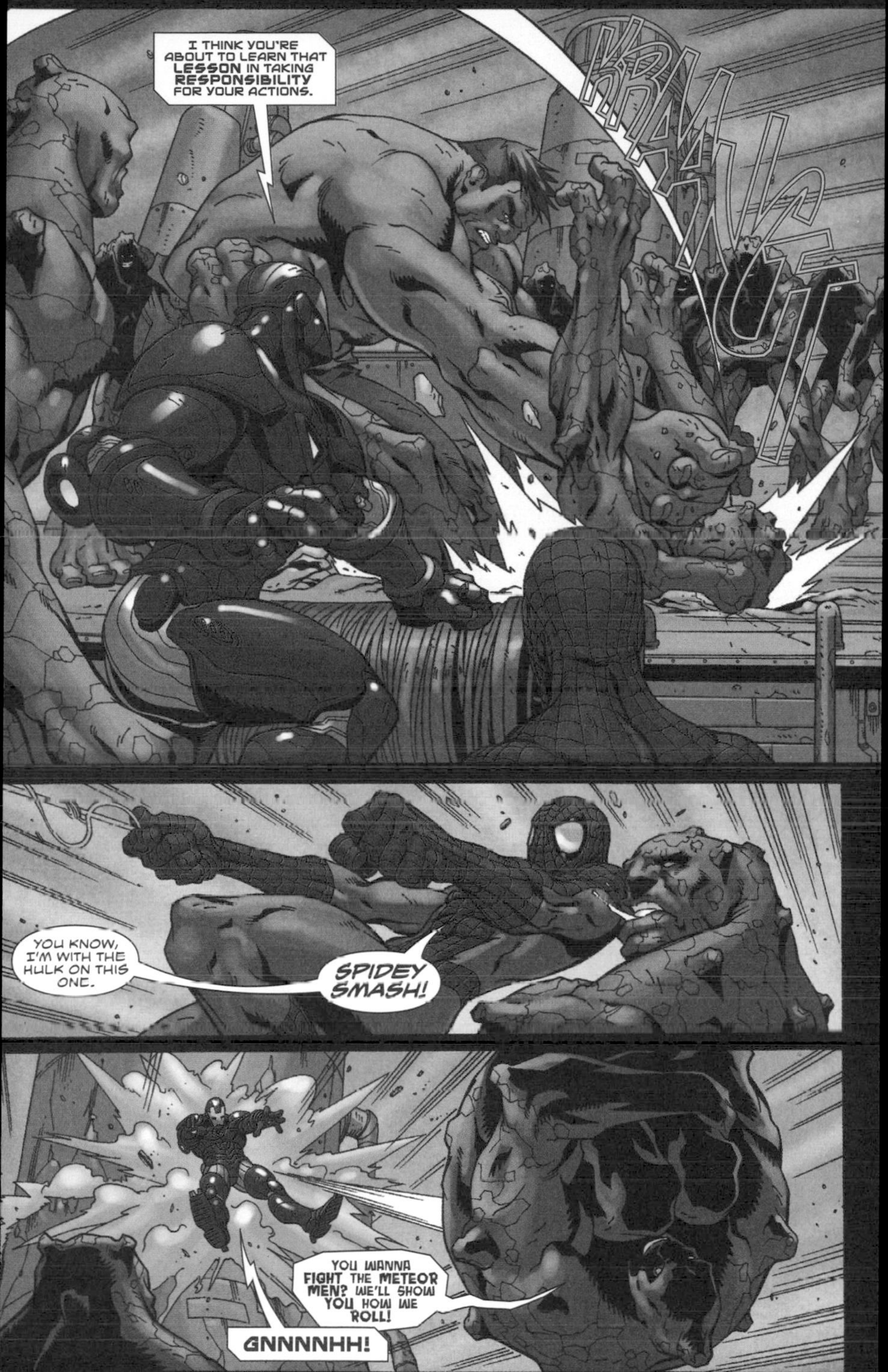
I THINK YOU'RE ABOUT TO LEARN THAT LESSON IN TAKING RESPONSIBILITY FOR YOUR ACTIONS.
KRAKOOM
YOU KNOW, I'M WITH THE HULK ON THIS ONE.
SPIDEY SMASH!
YOU WANNA FIGHT THE METEOR MEN? WE'LL SHOW YOU HOW WE ROLL!
GNNNNHH!

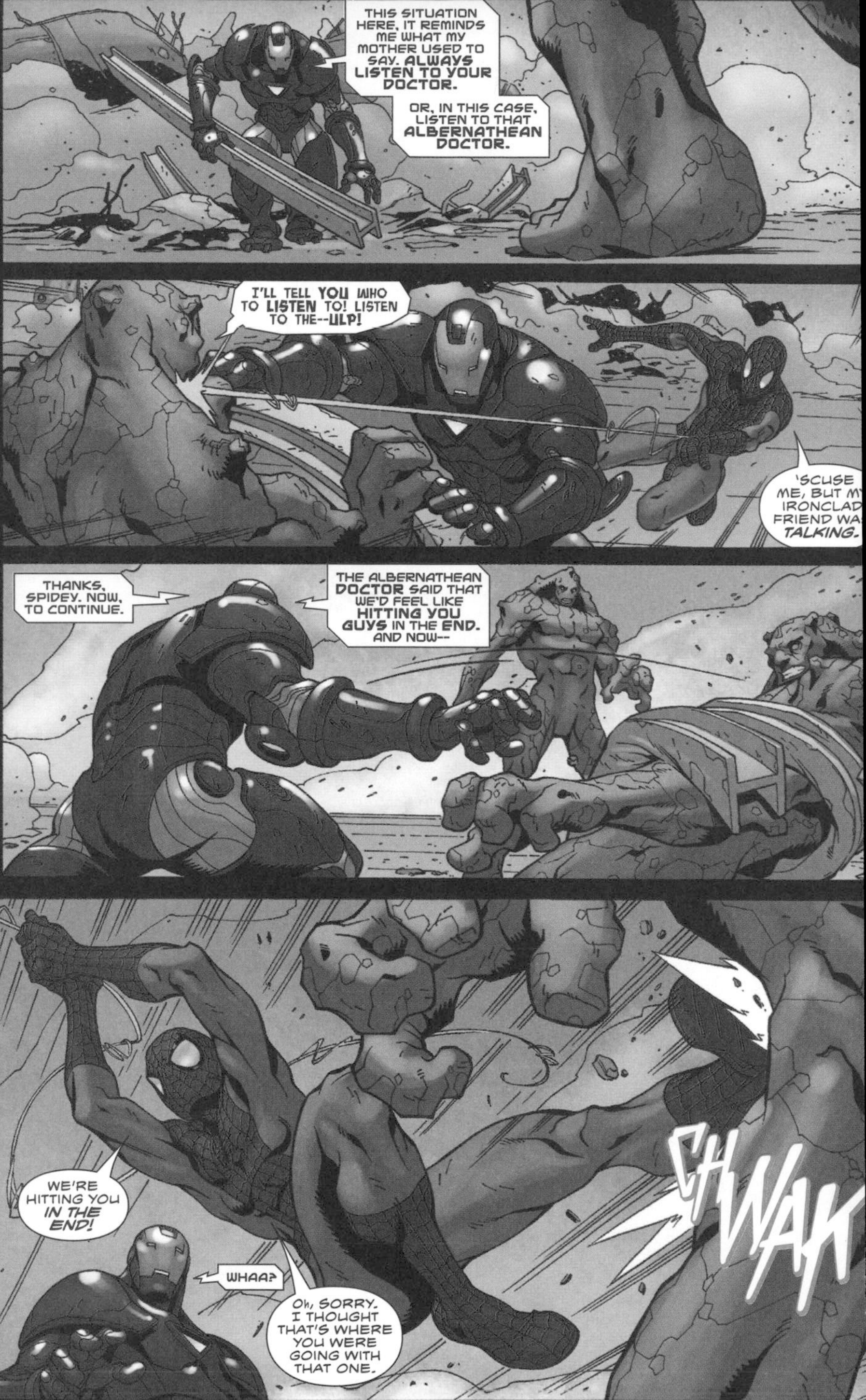
THIS SITUATION HERE, IT REMINDS ME WHAT MY MOTHER USED TO SAY. ALWAYS LISTEN TO YOUR DOCTOR.
OR, IN THIS CASE, LISTEN TO THAT ALBERNATHEAN DOCTOR.
I'LL TELL YOU WHO TO LISTEN TO! LISTEN TO THE--ULP!
'SCUSE ME, BUT MY IRONCLAD FRIEND WAS TALKING.
THANKS, SPIDEY. NOW, TO CONTINUE.
THE ALBERNATHEAN DOCTOR SAID THAT WE'D FEEL LIKE HITTING YOU GUYS IN THE END. AND NOW--
WE'RE HITTING YOU IN THE END!
CHWAK
WHAA?
OH, SORRY. I THOUGHT THAT'S WHERE YOU WERE GOING WITH THAT ONE.

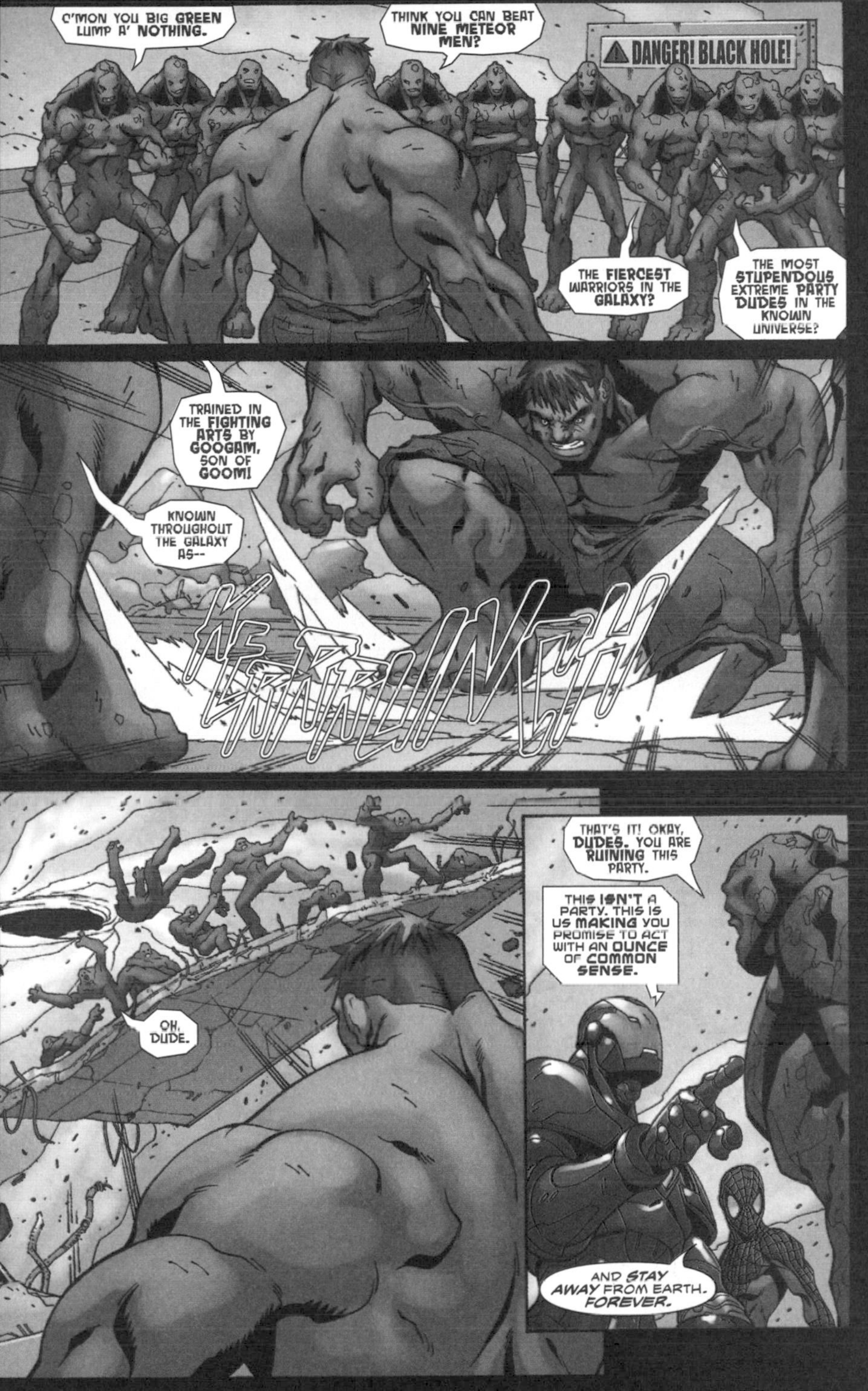

C'MON YOU BIG GREEN LUMP A' NOTHING.
THINK YOU CAN BEAT NINE METEOR MEN?
DANGER! BLACK HOLE!
THE FIERCEST WARRIORS IN THE GALAXY?
THE MOST STUPENDOUS EXTREME PARTY DUDES IN THE KNOWN UNIVERSE?
TRAINED IN THE FIGHTING ARTS BY GOOGAM, SON OF GOOM!
KNOWN THROUGHOUT THE GALAXY AS--
KERRRUNCH
OH, DUDE.
THAT'S IT! OKAY, DUDES. YOU ARE RUINING THIS PARTY.
THIS ISN'T A PARTY. THIS IS US MAKING YOU PROMISE TO ACT WITH AN OUNCE OF COMMON SENSE.
AND STAY AWAY FROM EARTH. FOREVER.

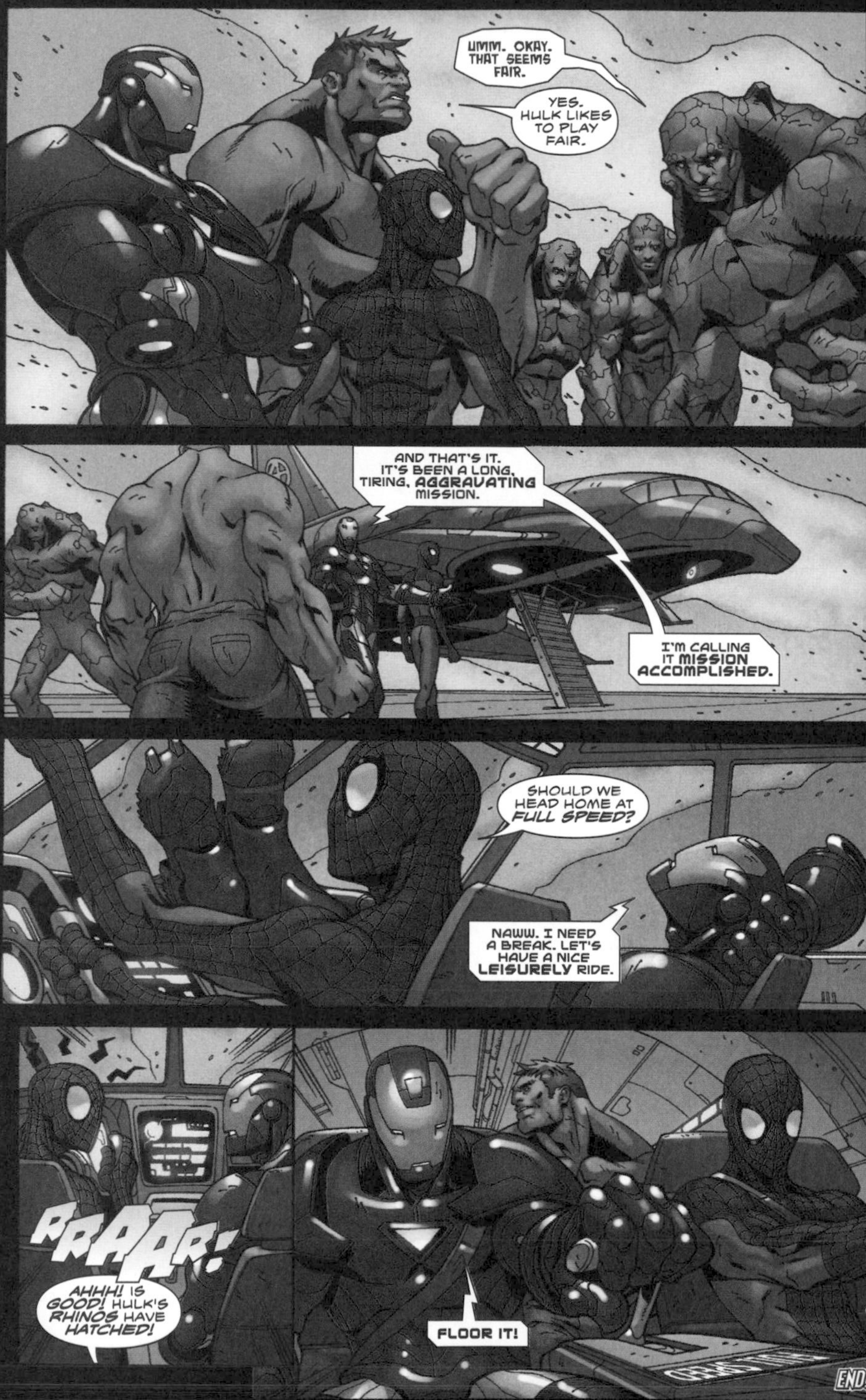
UMM. OKAY. THAT SEEMS FAIR.
YES. HULK LIKES TO PLAY FAIR.
AND THAT'S IT. IT'S BEEN A LONG, TIRING, AGGRAVATING MISSION.
I'M CALLING IT MISSION ACCOMPLISHED.
SHOULD WE HEAD HOME AT FULL SPEED?
NAWW. I NEED A BREAK. LET'S HAVE A NICE LEISURELY RIDE.
RRAAAR!
AHHH! IS GOOD! HULK'S RHINOS HAVE HATCHED!
FLOOR IT!
END

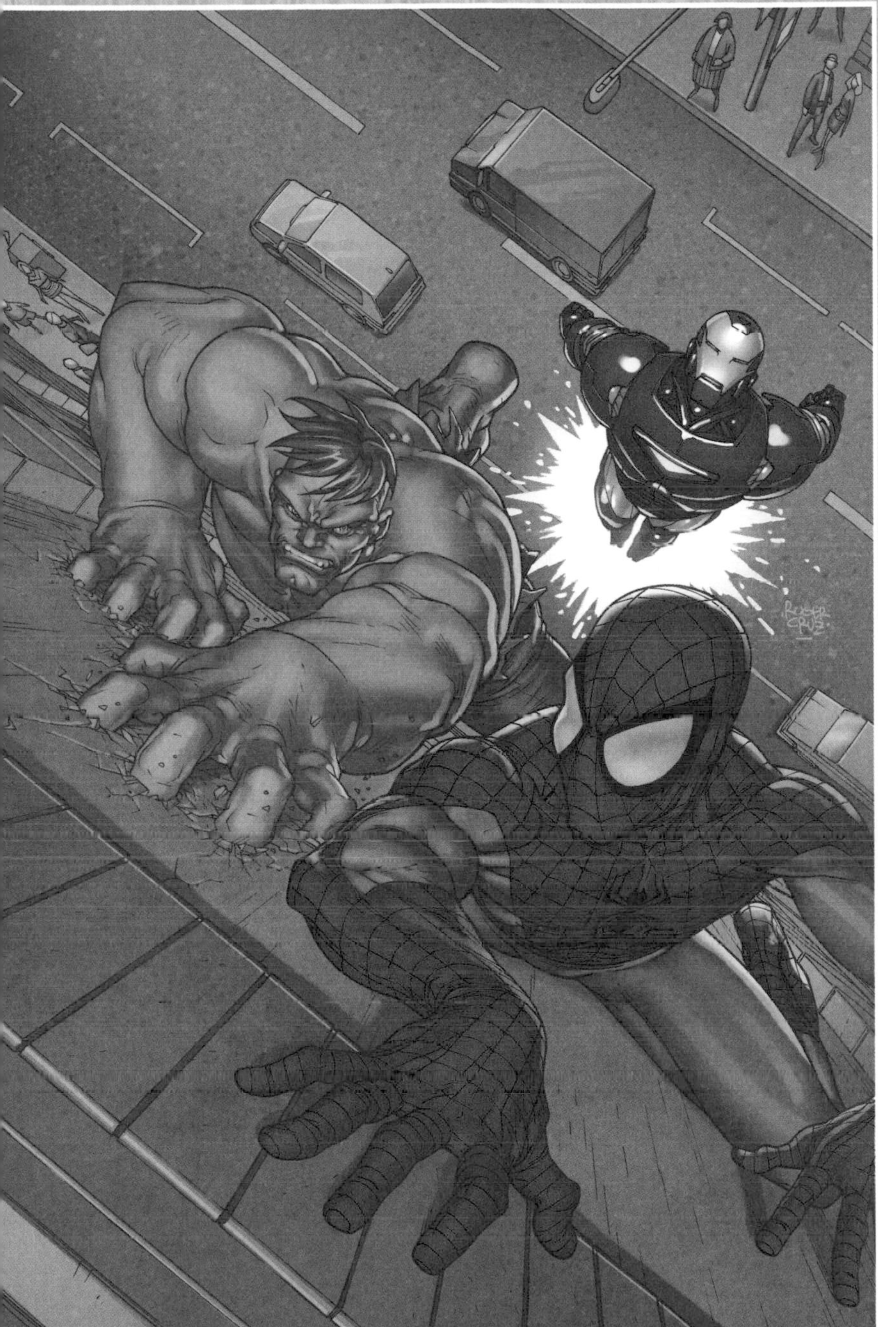

#3

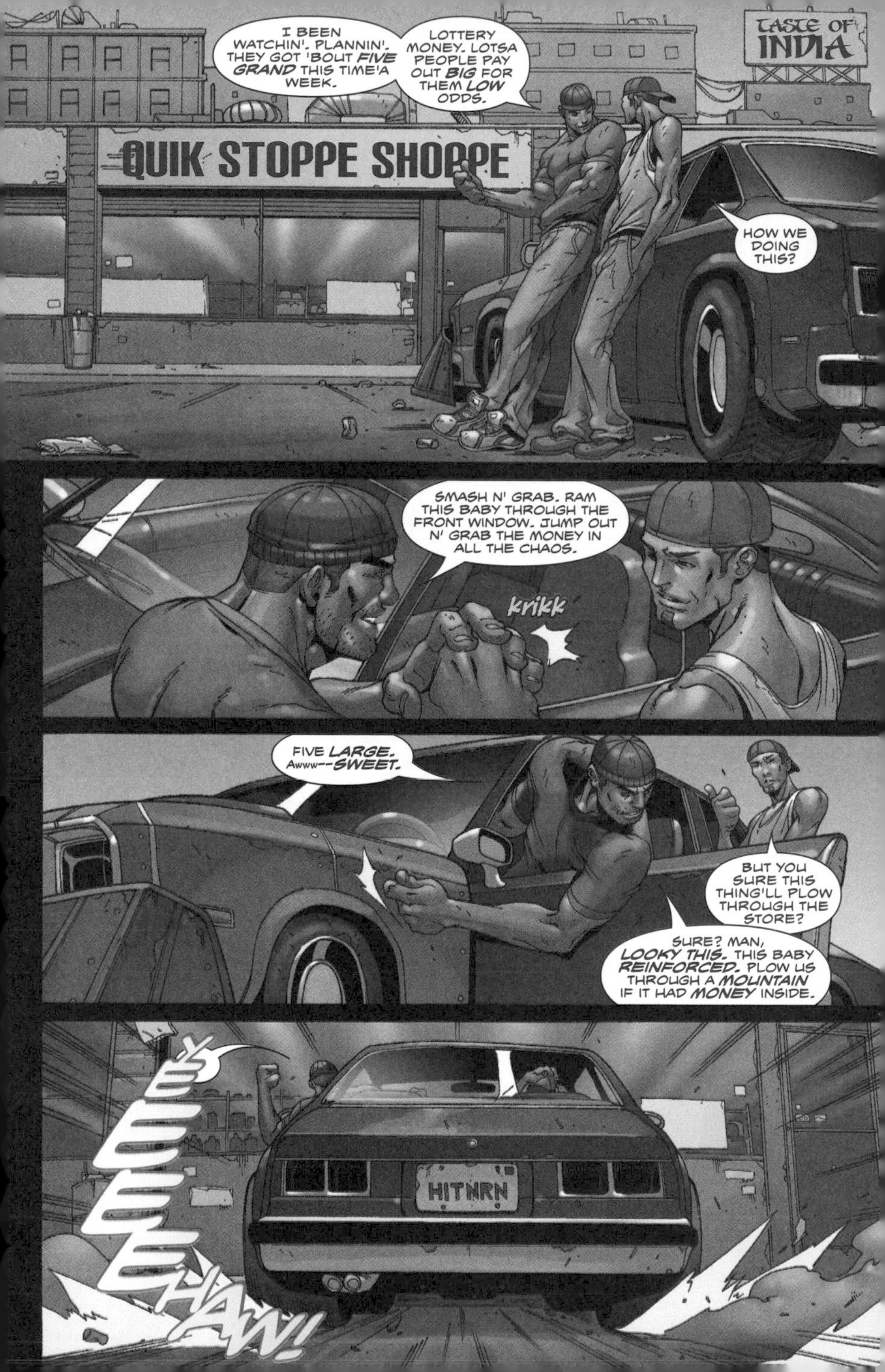
TASTE OF INDIA
QUIK STOPPE SHOPPE
I BEEN WATCHIN'. PLANNIN'. THEY GOT 'BOUT FIVE GRAND THIS TIME'A WEEK.
LOTTERY MONEY. LOTSA PEOPLE PAY OUT BIG FOR THEM LOW ODDS.
HOW WE DOING THIS?
SMASH N' GRAB. RAM THIS BABY THROUGH THE FRONT WINDOW. JUMP OUT N' GRAB THE MONEY IN ALL THE CHAOS.
krikk
FIVE LARGE. Awww--SWEET.
BUT YOU SURE THIS THING'LL PLOW THROUGH THE STORE?
SURE? MAN, LOOKY THIS. THIS BABY REINFORCED. PLOW US THROUGH A MOUNTAIN IF IT HAD MONEY INSIDE.
HITNRN
YEEEEEEHAW!

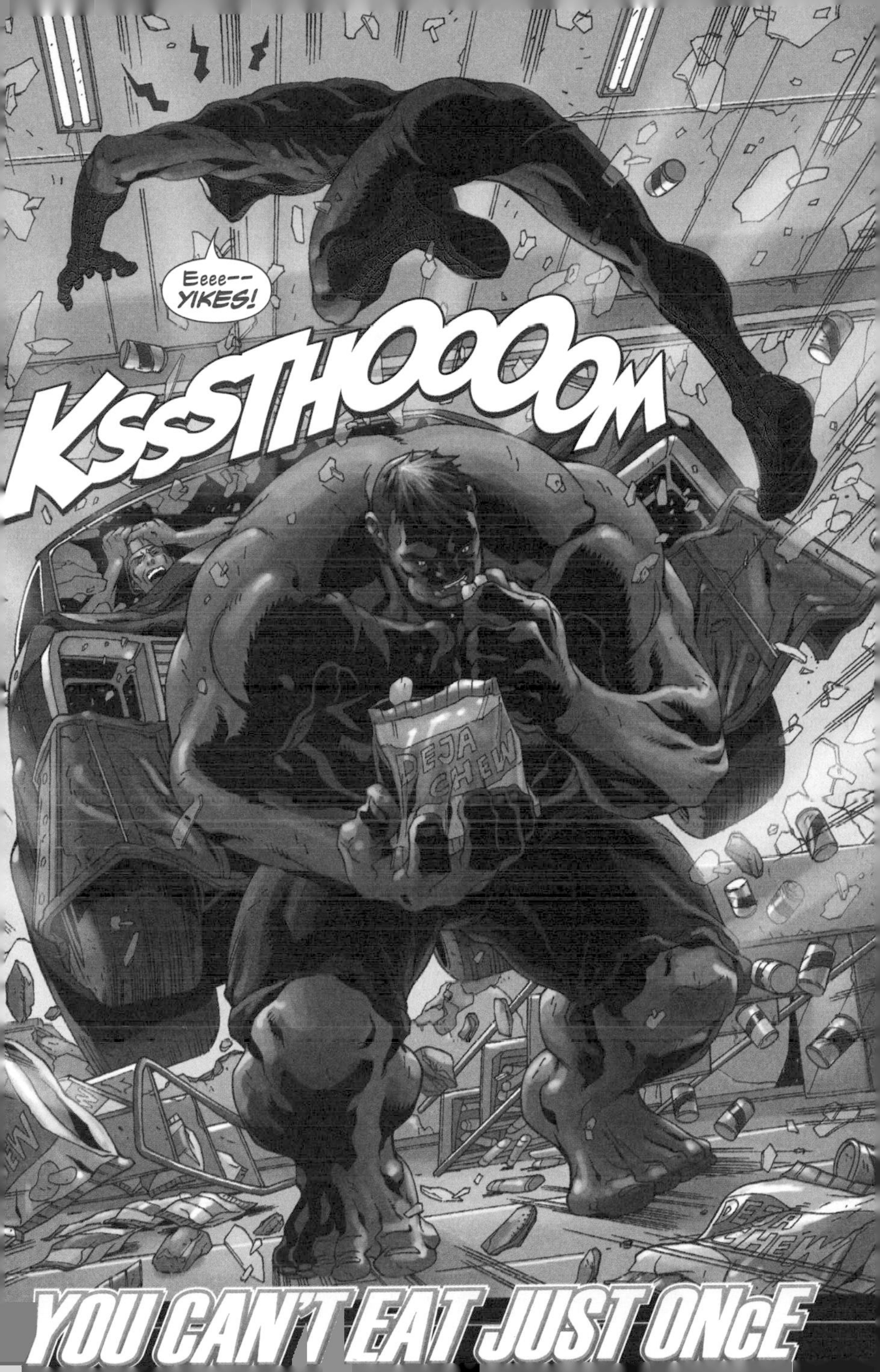
Eeee--
YIKES!
KSSTHOOOOM
DEJA CHEW
YOU CAN'T EAT JUST ONcE

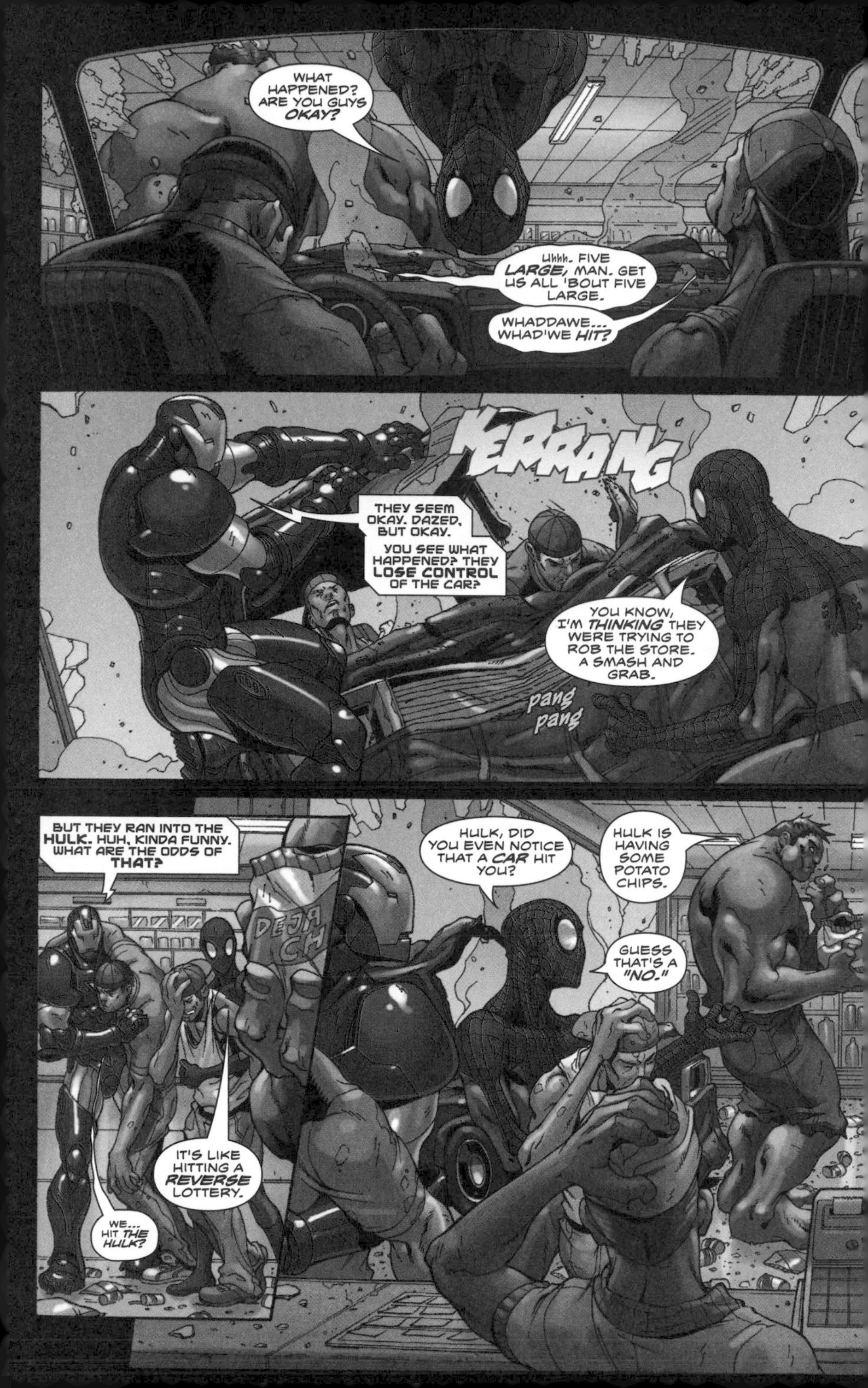
WHAT HAPPENED? ARE YOU GUYS OKAY?
Uhhh. FIVE LARGE, MAN. GET US ALL 'BOUT FIVE LARGE.
WHADDAWE... WHAD'WE HIT?
KERRANG
THEY SEEM OKAY. DAZED, BUT OKAY.
YOU SEE WHAT HAPPENED? THEY LOSE CONTROL OF THE CAR?
YOU KNOW, I'M THINKING THEY WERE TRYING TO ROB THE STORE. A SMASH AND GRAB.
pang pang
BUT THEY RAN INTO THE HULK. HUH, KINDA FUNNY. WHAT ARE THE ODDS OF THAT?
HULK, DID YOU EVEN NOTICE THAT A CAR HIT YOU?
HULK IS HAVING SOME POTATO CHIPS.
GUESS THAT'S A "NO."
IT'S LIKE HITTING A REVERSE LOTTERY.
WE... HIT THE HULK?

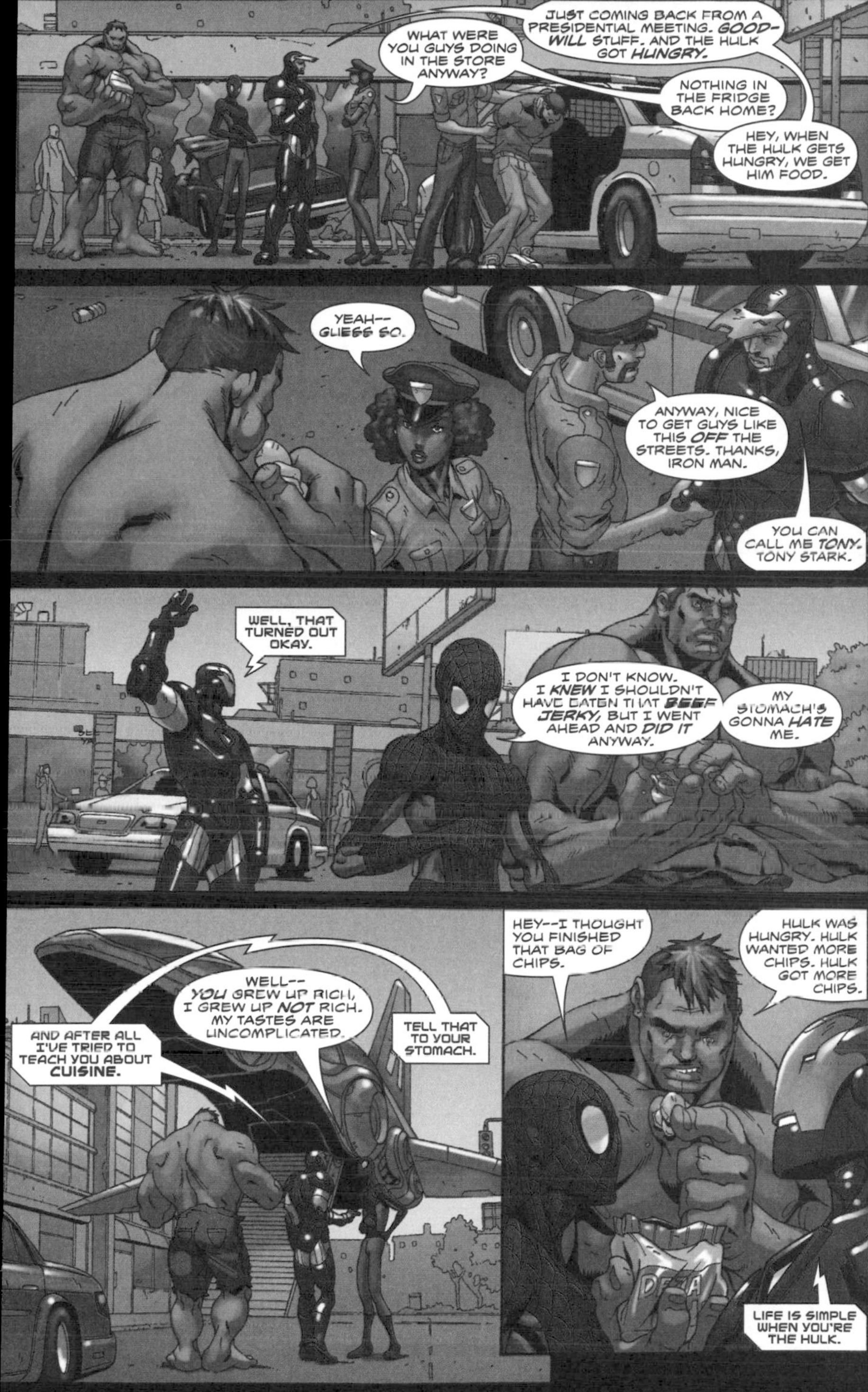
WHAT WERE YOU GUYS DOING IN THE STORE ANYWAY?
JUST COMING BACK FROM A PRESIDENTIAL MEETING. GOOD-WILL STUFF. AND THE HULK GOT HUNGRY.
NOTHING IN THE FRIDGE BACK HOME?
HEY, WHEN THE HULK GETS HUNGRY, WE GET HIM FOOD.
YEAH-- GUESS SO.
ANYWAY, NICE TO GET GUYS LIKE THIS OFF THE STREETS. THANKS, IRON MAN.
YOU CAN CALL ME TONY. TONY STARK.
WELL, THAT TURNED OUT OKAY.
I DON'T KNOW. I KNEW I SHOULDN'T HAVE EATEN THAT BEEF JERKY, BUT I WENT AHEAD AND DID IT ANYWAY.
MY STOMACH'S GONNA HATE ME.
AND AFTER ALL I'VE TRIED TO TEACH YOU ABOUT CUISINE.
WELL-- YOU GREW UP RICH, I GREW UP NOT RICH. MY TASTES ARE UNCOMPLICATED.
TELL THAT TO YOUR STOMACH.
HEY--I THOUGHT YOU FINISHED THAT BAG OF CHIPS.
HULK WAS HUNGRY. HULK WANTED MORE CHIPS. HULK GOT MORE CHIPS.
LIFE IS SIMPLE WHEN YOU'RE THE HULK.

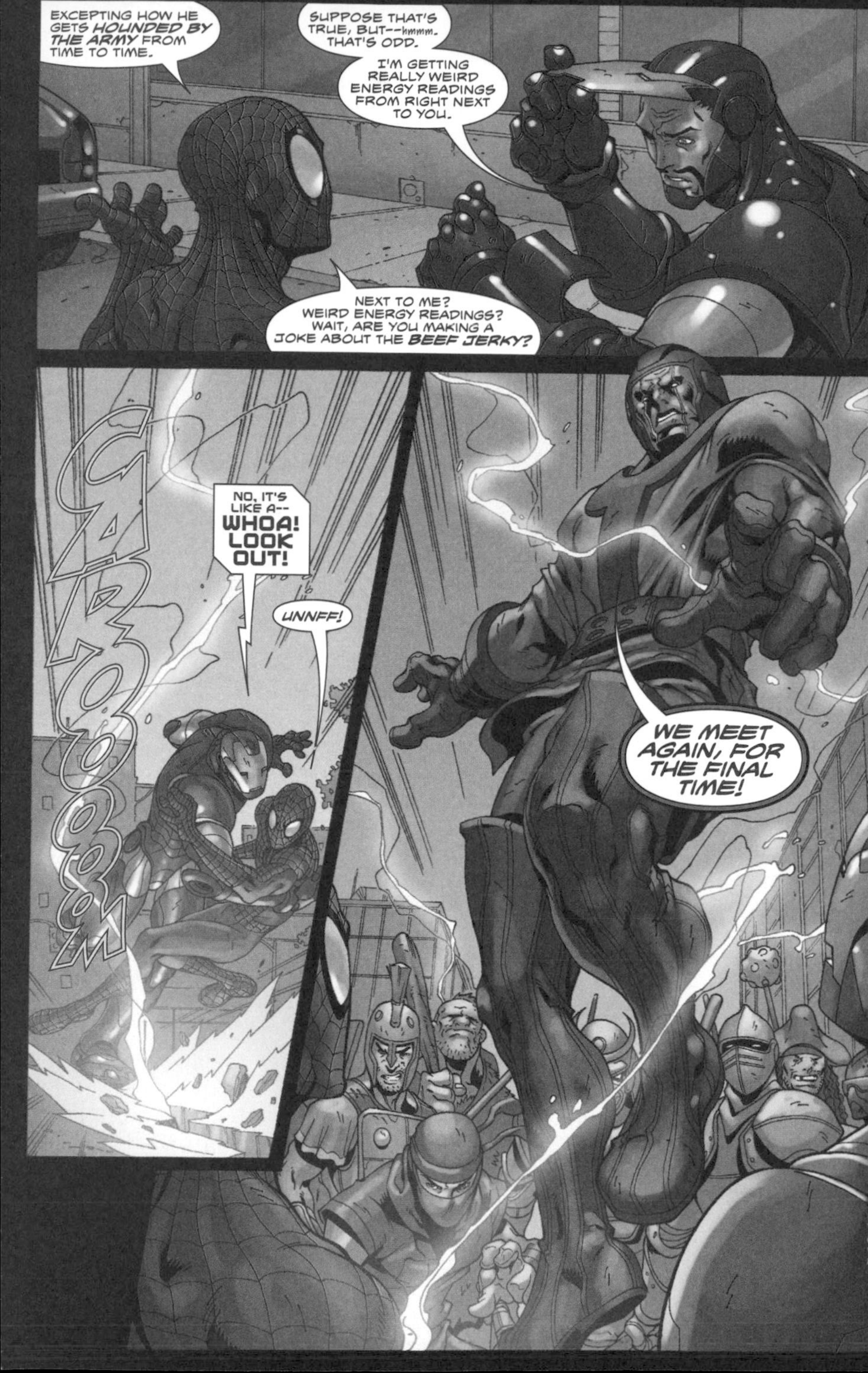
EXCEPTING HOW HE GETS HOUNDED BY THE ARMY FROM TIME TO TIME.
SUPPOSE THAT'S TRUE, BUT--hmmm. THAT'S ODD.
I'M GETTING REALLY WEIRD ENERGY READINGS FROM RIGHT NEXT TO YOU.
NEXT TO ME? WEIRD ENERGY READINGS? WAIT, ARE YOU MAKING A JOKE ABOUT THE BEEF JERKY?
NO, IT'S LIKE A-- WHOA! LOOK OUT!
UNNFF!
WE MEET AGAIN, FOR THE FINAL TIME!

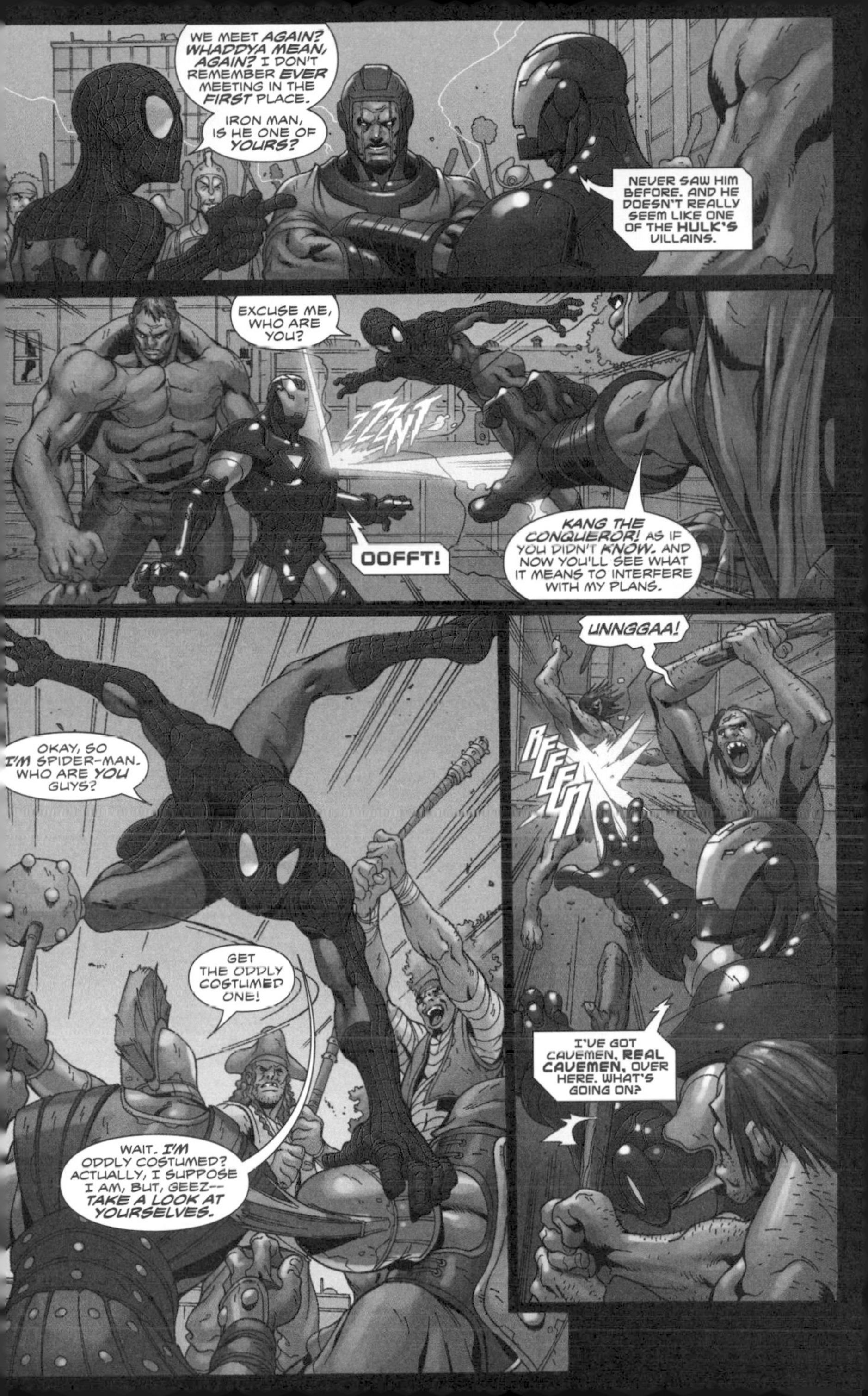

WE MEET AGAIN? WHADDYA MEAN, AGAIN? I DON'T REMEMBER EVER MEETING IN THE FIRST PLACE.
IRON MAN, IS HE ONE OF YOURS?
NEVER SAW HIM BEFORE. AND HE DOESN'T REALLY SEEM LIKE ONE OF THE HULK'S VILLAINS.
EXCUSE ME, WHO ARE YOU?
ZZZZNT
OOFFT!
KANG THE CONQUEROR! AS IF YOU DIDN'T KNOW. AND NOW YOU'LL SEE WHAT IT MEANS TO INTERFERE WITH MY PLANS.
OKAY, SO I'M SPIDER-MAN. WHO ARE YOU GUYS?
GET THE ODDLY COSTUMED ONE!
WAIT. I'M ODDLY COSTUMED? ACTUALLY, I SUPPOSE I AM, BUT, GEEZ-- TAKE A LOOK AT YOURSELVES.
UNNGGAA!
I'VE GOT CAVEMEN, REAL CAVEMEN, OVER HERE. WHAT'S GOING ON?

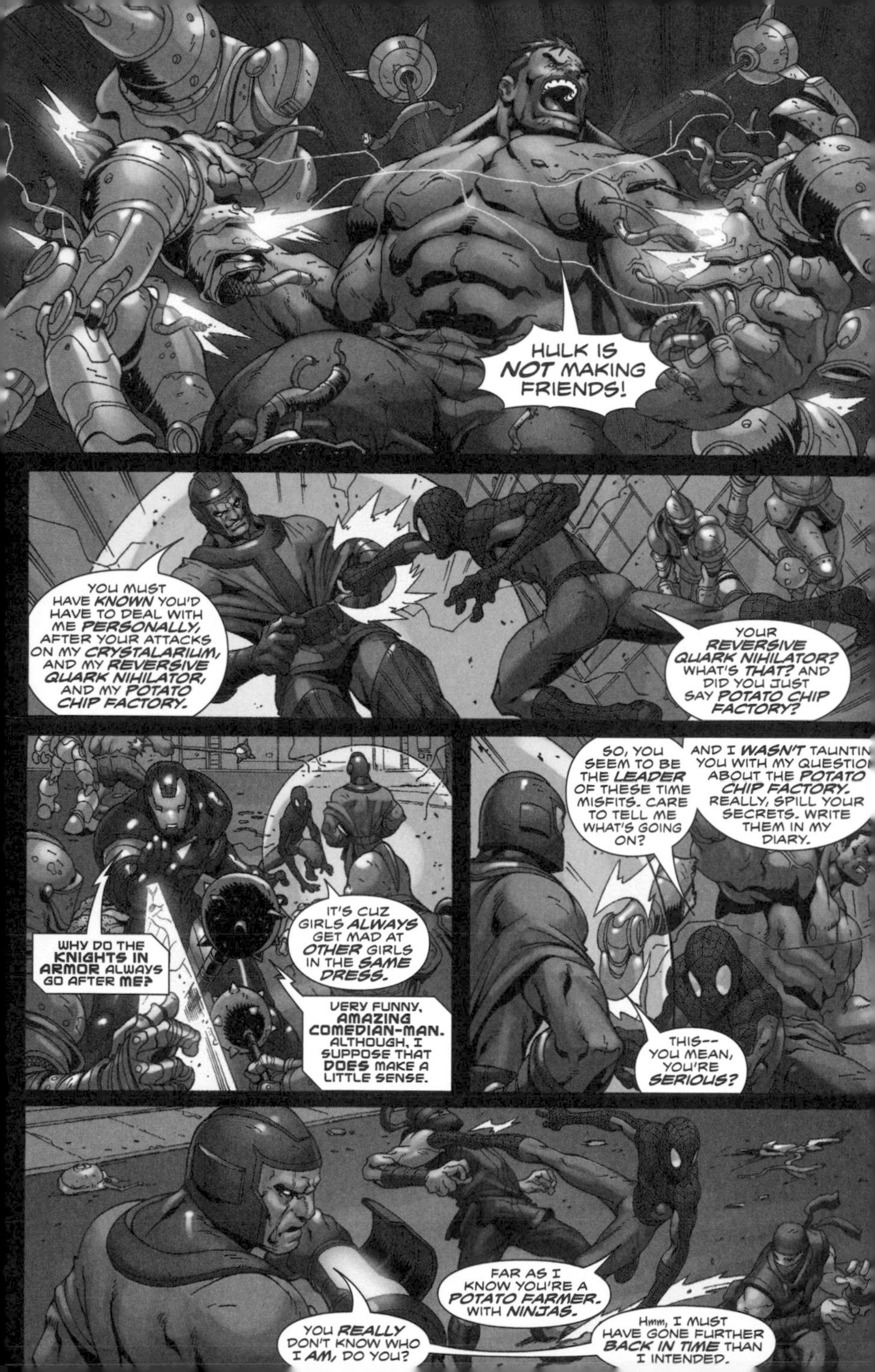
HULK IS NOT MAKING FRIENDS!
YOU MUST HAVE KNOWN YOU'D HAVE TO DEAL WITH ME PERSONALLY, AFTER YOUR ATTACKS ON MY CRYSTALARIUM, AND MY REVERSIVE QUARK NIHILATOR, AND MY POTATO CHIP FACTORY.
YOUR REVERSIVE QUARK NIHILATOR? WHAT'S THAT? AND DID YOU JUST SAY POTATO CHIP FACTORY?
WHY DO THE KNIGHTS IN ARMOR ALWAYS GO AFTER ME?
IT'S CUZ GIRLS ALWAYS GET MAD AT OTHER GIRLS IN THE SAME DRESS.
VERY FUNNY, AMAZING COMEDIAN-MAN. ALTHOUGH, I SUPPOSE THAT DOES MAKE A LITTLE SENSE.
SO, YOU SEEM TO BE THE LEADER OF THESE TIME MISFITS. CARE TO TELL ME WHAT'S GOING ON?
AND I WASN'T TAUNTIN YOU WITH MY QUESTIO ABOUT THE POTATO CHIP FACTORY. REALLY, SPILL YOUR SECRETS. WRITE THEM IN MY DIARY.
THIS-- YOU MEAN, YOU'RE SERIOUS?
YOU REALLY DON'T KNOW WHO I AM, DO YOU?
FAR AS I KNOW YOU'RE A POTATO FARMER. WITH NINJAS.
Hmm, I MUST HAVE GONE FURTHER BACK IN TIME THAN I INTENDED.

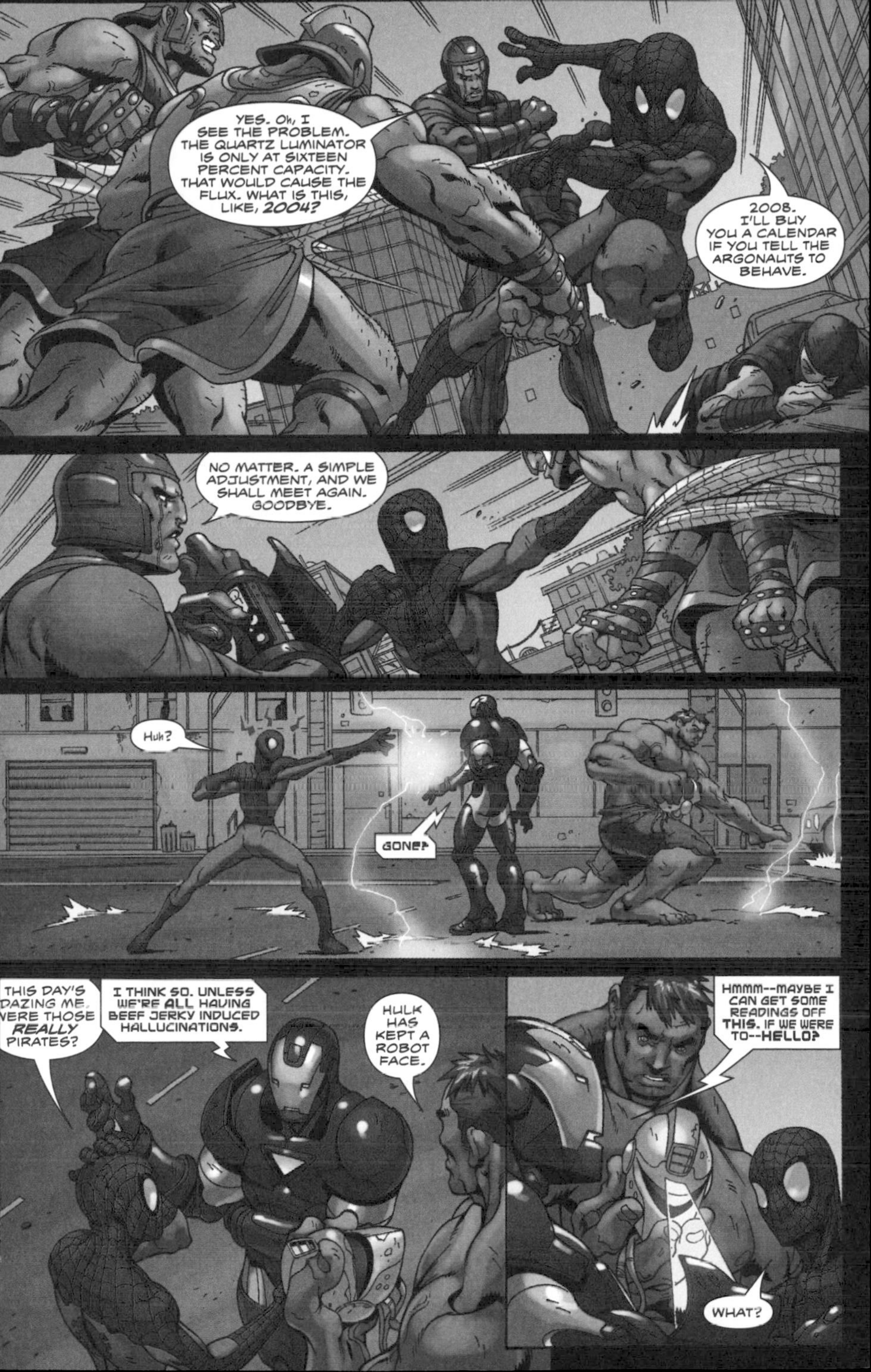
YES. Oh, I SEE THE PROBLEM. THE QUARTZ LUMINATOR IS ONLY AT SIXTEEN PERCENT CAPACITY. THAT WOULD CAUSE THE FLUX. WHAT IS THIS, LIKE, 2004?
2008. I'LL BUY YOU A CALENDAR IF YOU TELL THE ARGONAUTS TO BEHAVE.
NO MATTER. A SIMPLE ADJUSTMENT, AND WE SHALL MEET AGAIN. GOODBYE.
Huh?
GONE?
THIS DAY'S DAZING ME. WERE THOSE REALLY PIRATES?
I THINK SO. UNLESS WE'RE ALL HAVING BEEF JERKY INDUCED HALLUCINATIONS.
HULK HAS KEPT A ROBOT FACE.
HMMM--MAYBE I CAN GET SOME READINGS OFF THIS. IF WE WERE TO--HELLO?
WHAT?

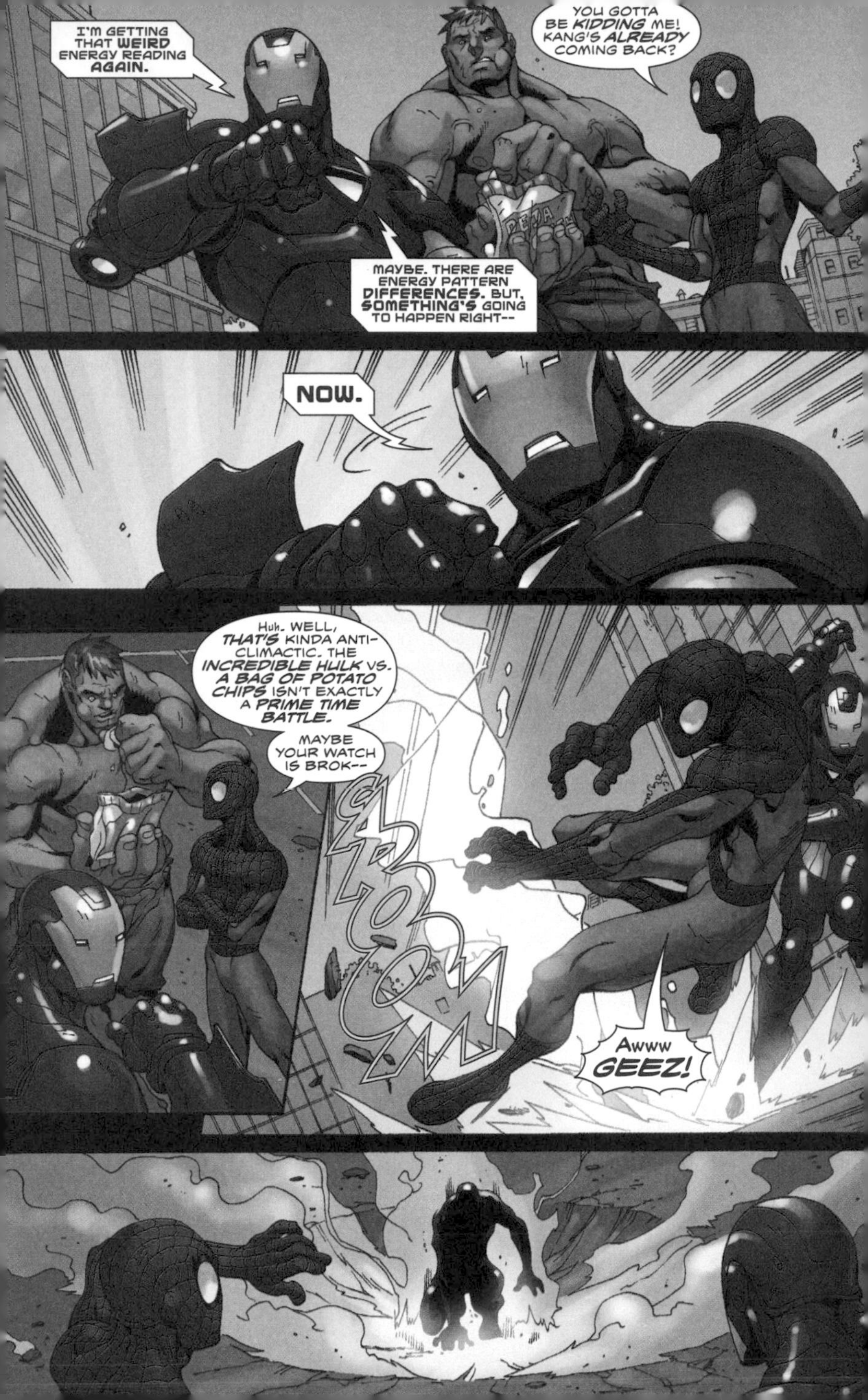
I'M GETTING THAT WEIRD ENERGY READING AGAIN.
YOU GOTTA BE KIDDING ME! KANG'S ALREADY COMING BACK?
MAYBE. THERE ARE ENERGY PATTERN DIFFERENCES. BUT, SOMETHING'S GOING TO HAPPEN RIGHT--
NOW.
Huh. WELL, THAT'S KINDA ANTI-CLIMACTIC. THE INCREDIBLE HULK VS. A BAG OF POTATO CHIPS ISN'T EXACTLY A PRIME TIME BATTLE.
MAYBE YOUR WATCH IS BROK--
Awww GEEZ!

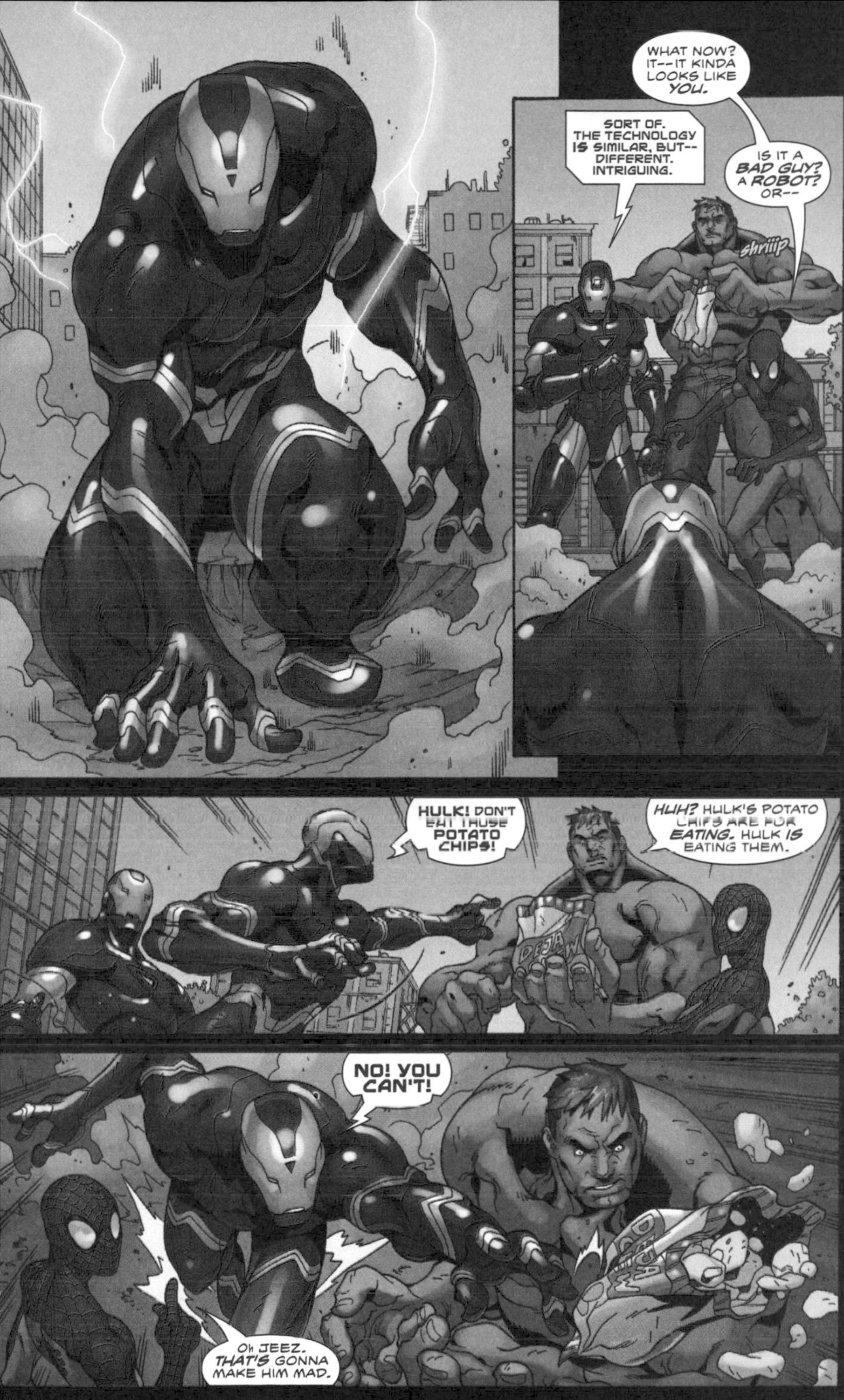

WHAT NOW? IT--IT KINDA LOOKS LIKE *YOU.*
SORT OF. THE TECHNOLOGY **IS** SIMILAR, BUT-- DIFFERENT. INTRIGUING.
IS IT A *BAD GUY?* A *ROBOT?* OR--
shriiip
HULK! DON'T **EAT THOSE POTATO CHIPS!**
HUH? HULK'S POTATO CHIPS ARE FOR *EATING.* HULK *IS* EATING THEM.
NO! YOU CAN'T!
Oh JEEZ. *THAT'S* GONNA MAKE HIM MAD.

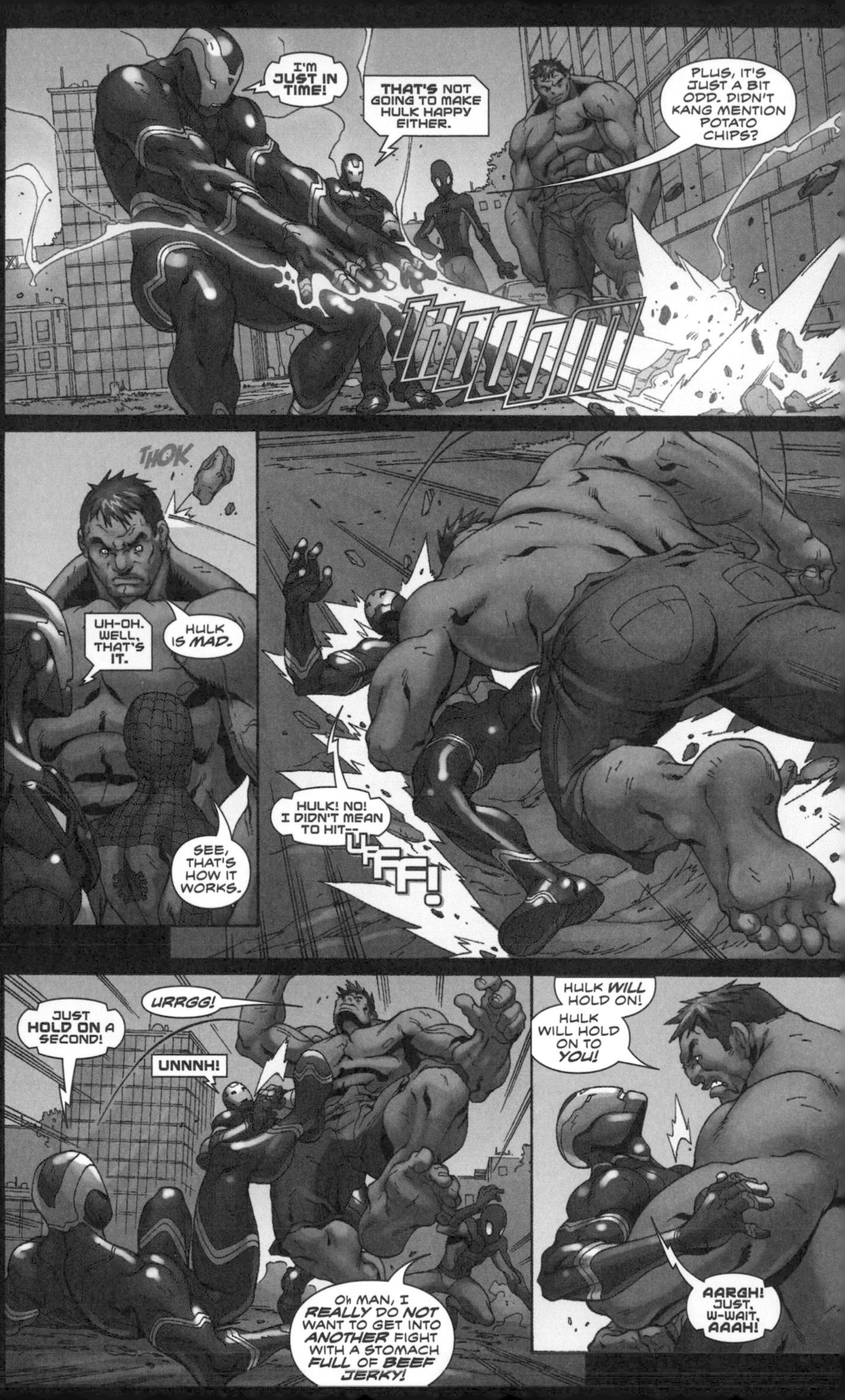
I'M JUST IN TIME!
THAT'S NOT GOING TO MAKE HULK HAPPY EITHER.
PLUS, IT'S JUST A BIT ODD. DIDN'T KANG MENTION POTATO CHIPS?
THOOOM
THOK
UH-OH. WELL, THAT'S IT.
HULK IS MAD.
SEE, THAT'S HOW IT WORKS.
HULK! NO! I DIDN'T MEAN TO HIT--
UFFF!
JUST HOLD ON A SECOND!
URRGG!
UNNNH!
OH MAN, I REALLY DO NOT WANT TO GET INTO ANOTHER FIGHT WITH A STOMACH FULL OF BEEF JERKY!
HULK WILL HOLD ON!
HULK WILL HOLD ON TO YOU!
AARGH! JUST, W-WAIT, AAAH!

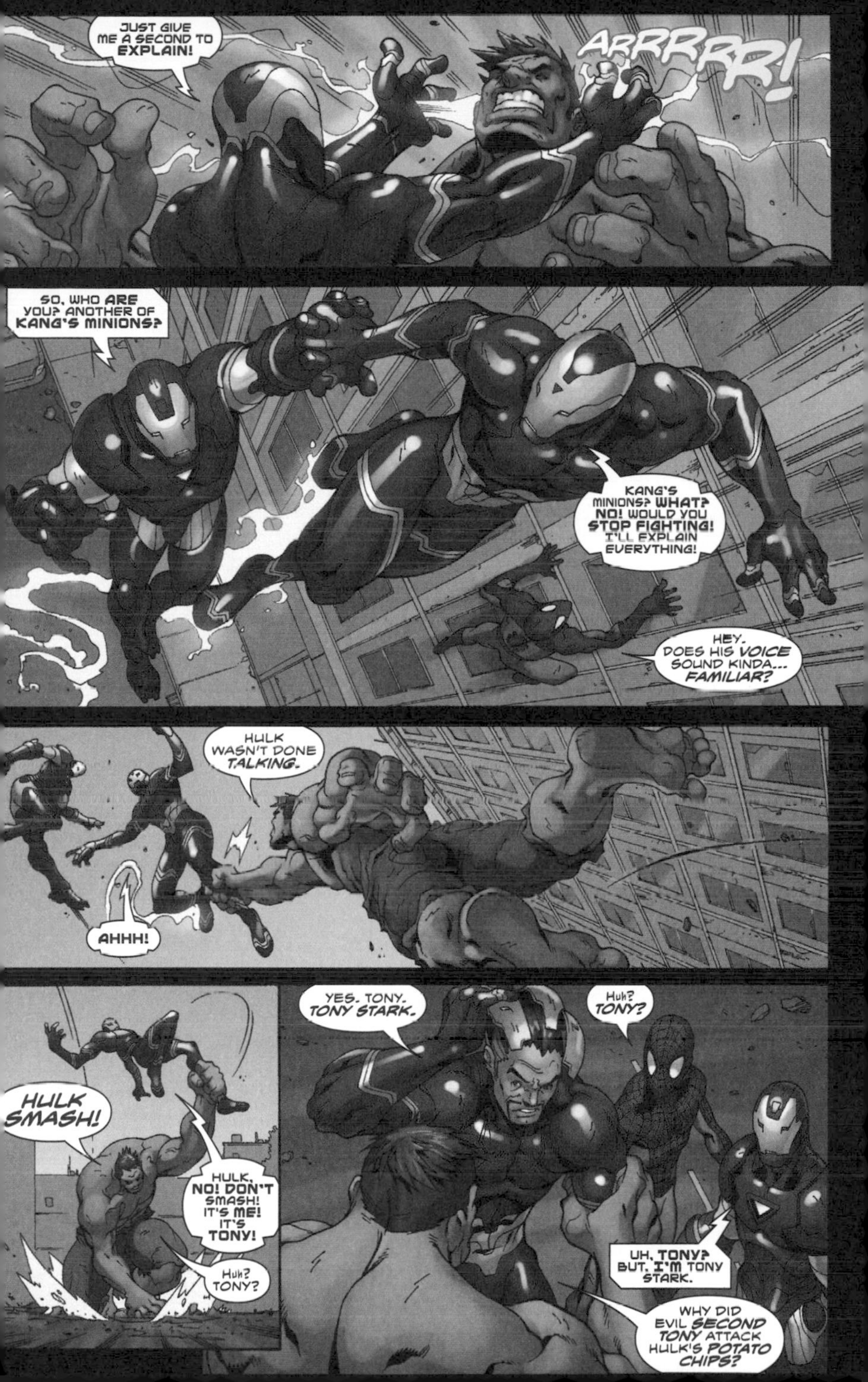
JUST GIVE ME A SECOND TO EXPLAIN!
ARRRRR!
SO, WHO ARE YOU? ANOTHER OF KANG'S MINIONS?
KANG'S MINIONS? WHAT? NO! WOULD YOU STOP FIGHTING! I'LL EXPLAIN EVERYTHING!
HEY. DOES HIS VOICE SOUND KINDA... FAMILIAR?
HULK WASN'T DONE TALKING.
AHHH!
HULK SMASH!
HULK, NO! DON'T SMASH! IT'S ME! IT'S TONY!
Huh? TONY?
YES. TONY. TONY STARK.
Huh? TONY?
UH, TONY? BUT, I'M TONY STARK.
WHY DID EVIL SECOND TONY ATTACK HULK'S POTATO CHIPS?

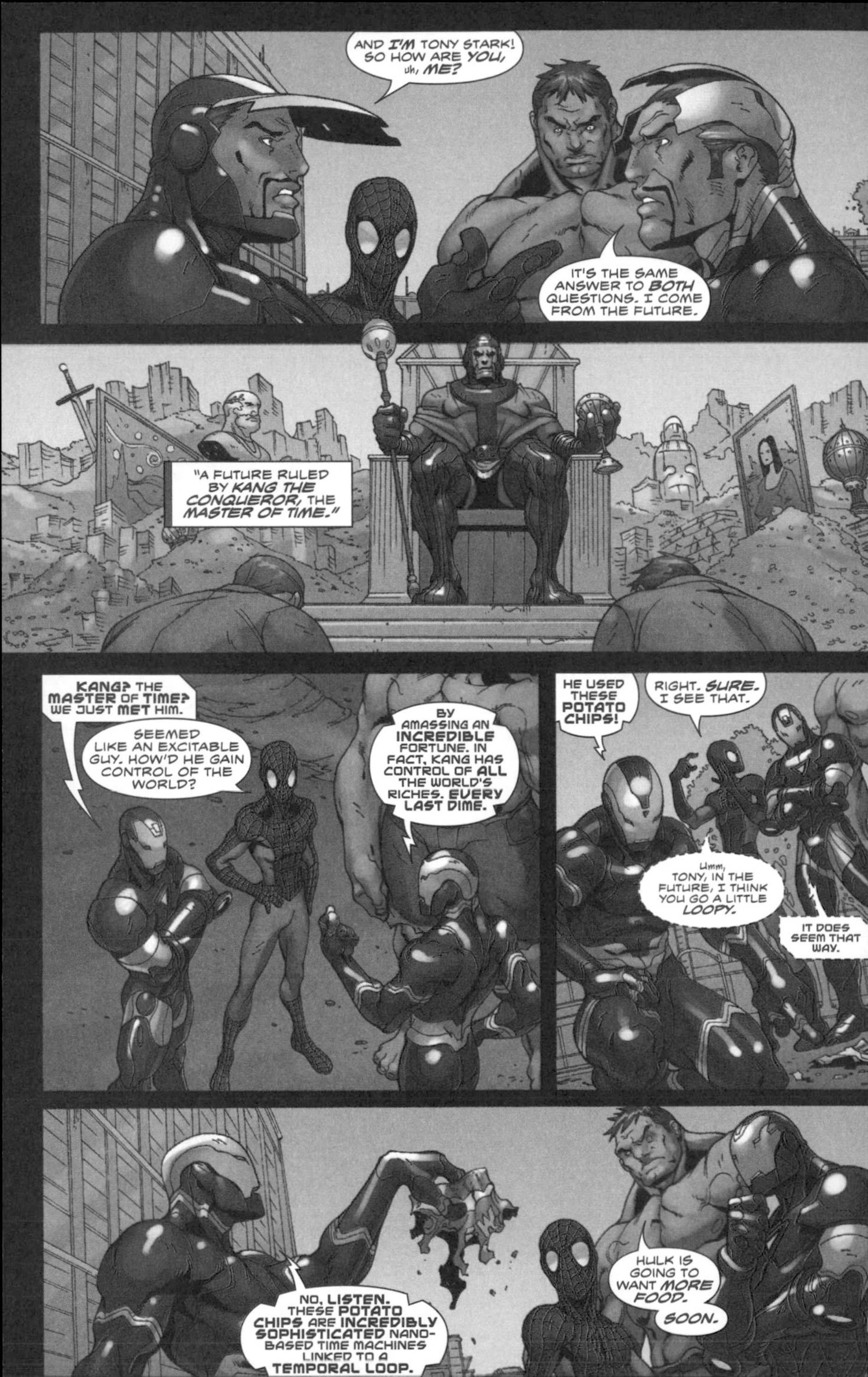
AND I'M TONY STARK! SO HOW ARE YOU, uh, ME?
IT'S THE SAME ANSWER TO BOTH QUESTIONS. I COME FROM THE FUTURE.
"A FUTURE RULED BY KANG THE CONQUEROR, THE MASTER OF TIME."
KANG? THE MASTER OF TIME? WE JUST MET HIM.
SEEMED LIKE AN EXCITABLE GUY. HOW'D HE GAIN CONTROL OF THE WORLD?
BY AMASSING AN INCREDIBLE FORTUNE. IN FACT, KANG HAS CONTROL OF ALL THE WORLD'S RICHES. EVERY LAST DIME.
HE USED THESE POTATO CHIPS!
RIGHT. SURE. I SEE THAT.
Umm, TONY, IN THE FUTURE, I THINK YOU GO A LITTLE LOOPY.
IT DOES SEEM THAT WAY.
NO, LISTEN. THESE POTATO CHIPS ARE INCREDIBLY SOPHISTICATED NANO-BASED TIME MACHINES LINKED TO A TEMPORAL LOOP.
HULK IS GOING TO WANT MORE FOOD.
SOON.

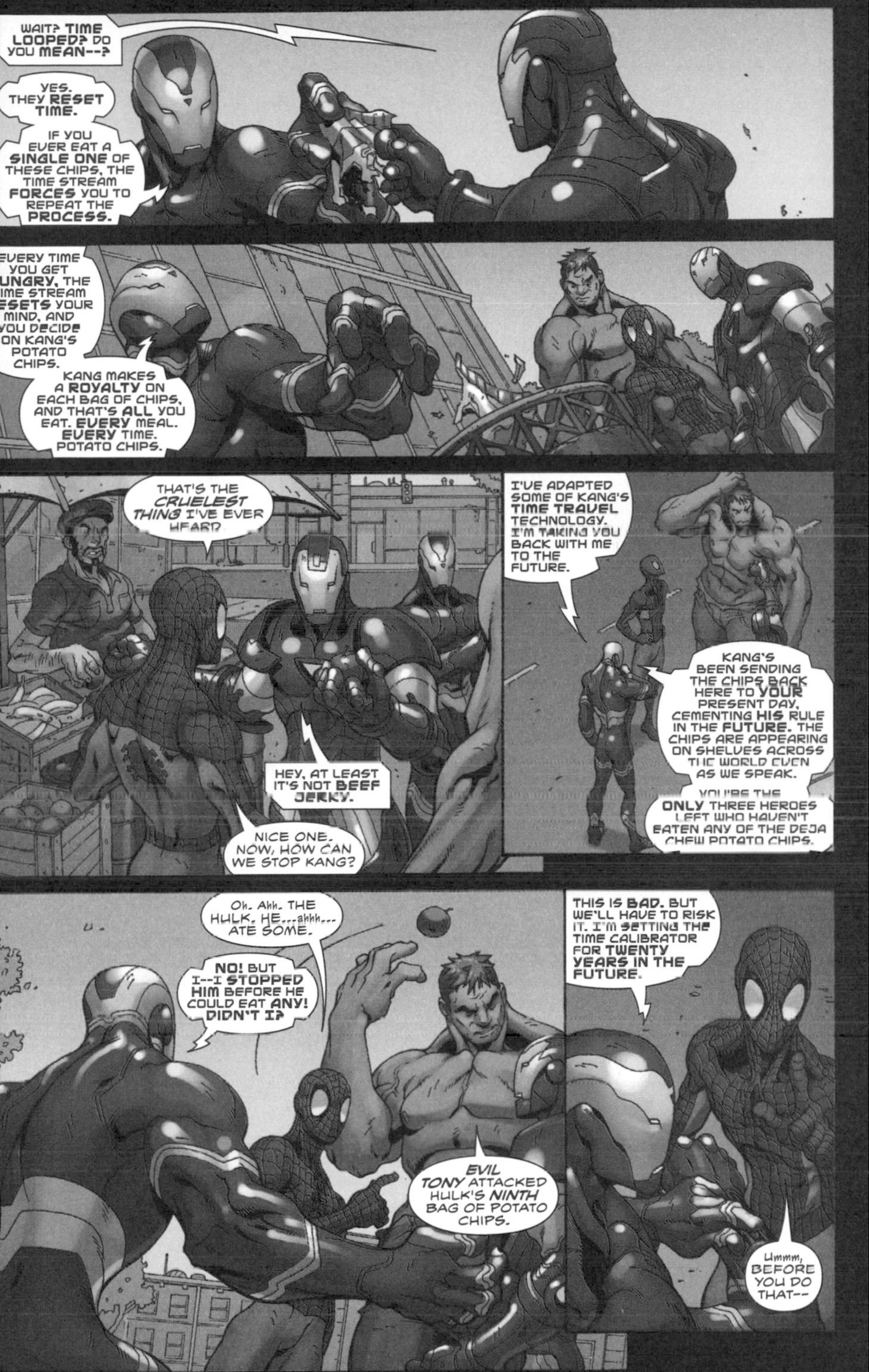
WAIT? TIME LOOPED? DO YOU MEAN--?
YES. THEY RESET TIME.
IF YOU EVER EAT A SINGLE ONE OF THESE CHIPS, THE TIME STREAM FORCES YOU TO REPEAT THE PROCESS.
EVERY TIME YOU GET HUNGRY, THE TIME STREAM RESETS YOUR MIND, AND YOU DECIDE ON KANG'S POTATO CHIPS.
KANG MAKES A ROYALTY ON EACH BAG OF CHIPS, AND THAT'S ALL YOU EAT. EVERY MEAL. EVERY TIME. POTATO CHIPS.
THAT'S THE CRUELEST THING I'VE EVER HEARD.
HEY, AT LEAST IT'S NOT BEEF JERKY.
NICE ONE. NOW, HOW CAN WE STOP KANG?
I'VE ADAPTED SOME OF KANG'S TIME TRAVEL TECHNOLOGY. I'M TAKING YOU BACK WITH ME TO THE FUTURE.
KANG'S BEEN SENDING THE CHIPS BACK HERE TO YOUR PRESENT DAY, CEMENTING HIS RULE IN THE FUTURE. THE CHIPS ARE APPEARING ON SHELVES ACROSS THE WORLD EVEN AS WE SPEAK.
YOU'RE THE ONLY THREE HEROES LEFT WHO HAVEN'T EATEN ANY OF THE DEJA CHEW POTATO CHIPS.
Oh. Ahh. THE HULK. HE...ahhh... ATE SOME.
NO! BUT I--I STOPPED HIM BEFORE HE COULD EAT ANY! DIDN'T I?
EVIL TONY ATTACKED HULK'S NINTH BAG OF POTATO CHIPS.
THIS IS BAD. BUT WE'LL HAVE TO RISK IT. I'M SETTING THE TIME CALIBRATOR FOR TWENTY YEARS IN THE FUTURE.
Ummm, BEFORE YOU DO THAT--

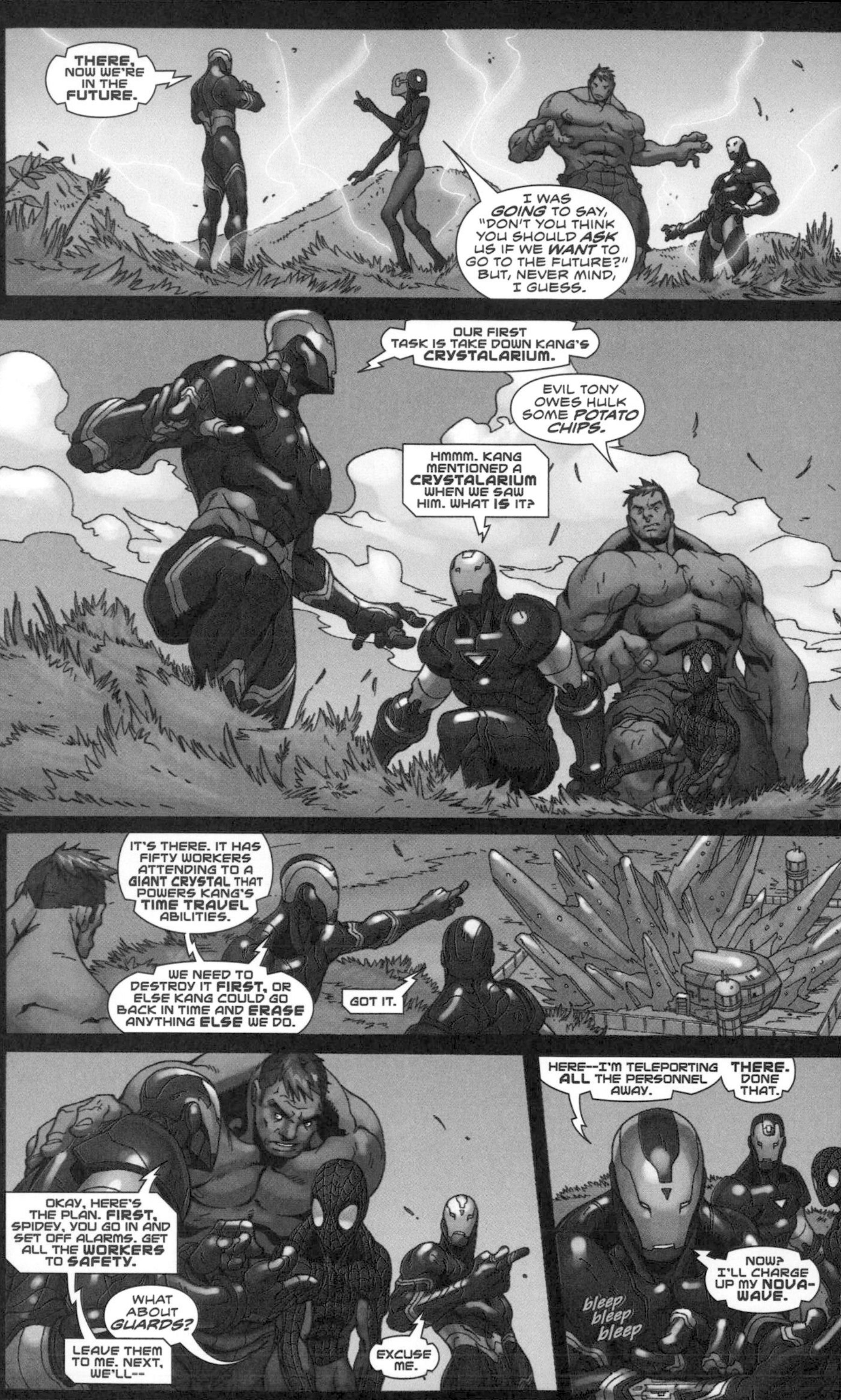
THERE, NOW WE'RE IN THE FUTURE.
I WAS GOING TO SAY, "DON'T YOU THINK YOU SHOULD ASK US IF WE WANT TO GO TO THE FUTURE?" BUT, NEVER MIND, I GUESS.
OUR FIRST TASK IS TAKE DOWN KANG'S CRYSTALARIUM.
EVIL TONY OWES HULK SOME POTATO CHIPS.
HMMM. KANG MENTIONED A CRYSTALARIUM WHEN WE SAW HIM. WHAT IS IT?
IT'S THERE. IT HAS FIFTY WORKERS ATTENDING TO A GIANT CRYSTAL THAT POWERS KANG'S TIME TRAVEL ABILITIES.
WE NEED TO DESTROY IT FIRST, OR ELSE KANG COULD GO BACK IN TIME AND ERASE ANYTHING ELSE WE DO.
GOT IT.
OKAY, HERE'S THE PLAN. FIRST, SPIDEY, YOU GO IN AND SET OFF ALARMS. GET ALL THE WORKERS TO SAFETY.
WHAT ABOUT GUARDS?
LEAVE THEM TO ME. NEXT, WE'LL--
EXCUSE ME.
HERE--I'M TELEPORTING ALL THE PERSONNEL AWAY.
THERE. DONE THAT.
bleep bleep bleep
NOW? I'LL CHARGE UP MY NOVA-WAVE.

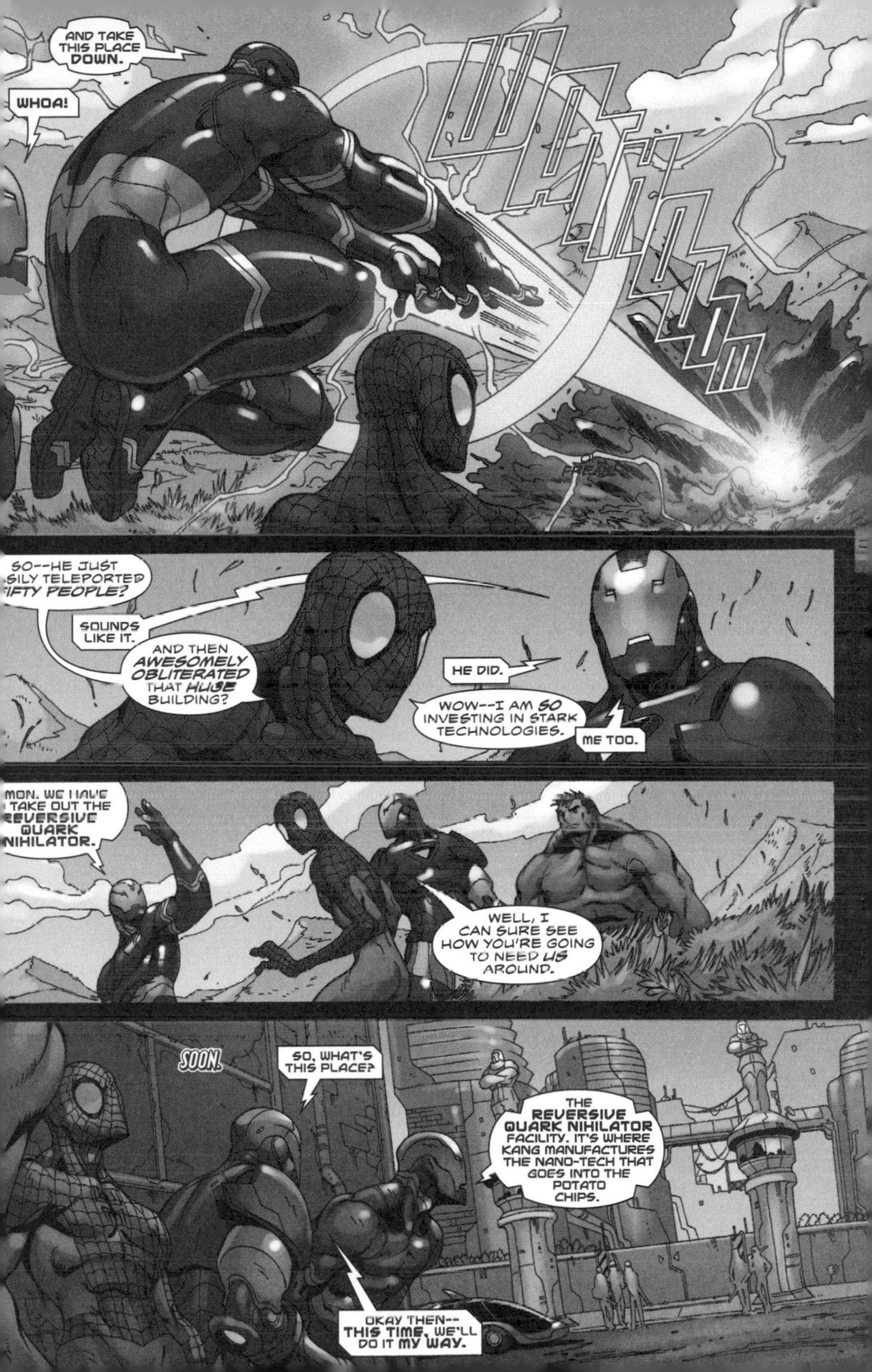
AND TAKE THIS PLACE DOWN.
WHOA!
SO--HE JUST SILY TELEPORTED FIFTY PEOPLE?
SOUNDS LIKE IT.
AND THEN AWESOMELY OBLITERATED THAT HUGE BUILDING?
HE DID.
WOW--I AM SO INVESTING IN STARK TECHNOLOGIES.
ME TOO.
MON. WE HAVE TAKE OUT THE REVERSIVE QUARK NIHILATOR.
WELL, I CAN SURE SEE HOW YOU'RE GOING TO NEED US AROUND.
SOON.
SO, WHAT'S THIS PLACE?
THE REVERSIVE QUARK NIHILATOR FACILITY. IT'S WHERE KANG MANUFACTURES THE NANO-TECH THAT GOES INTO THE POTATO CHIPS.
OKAY THEN-- THIS TIME, WE'LL DO IT MY WAY.

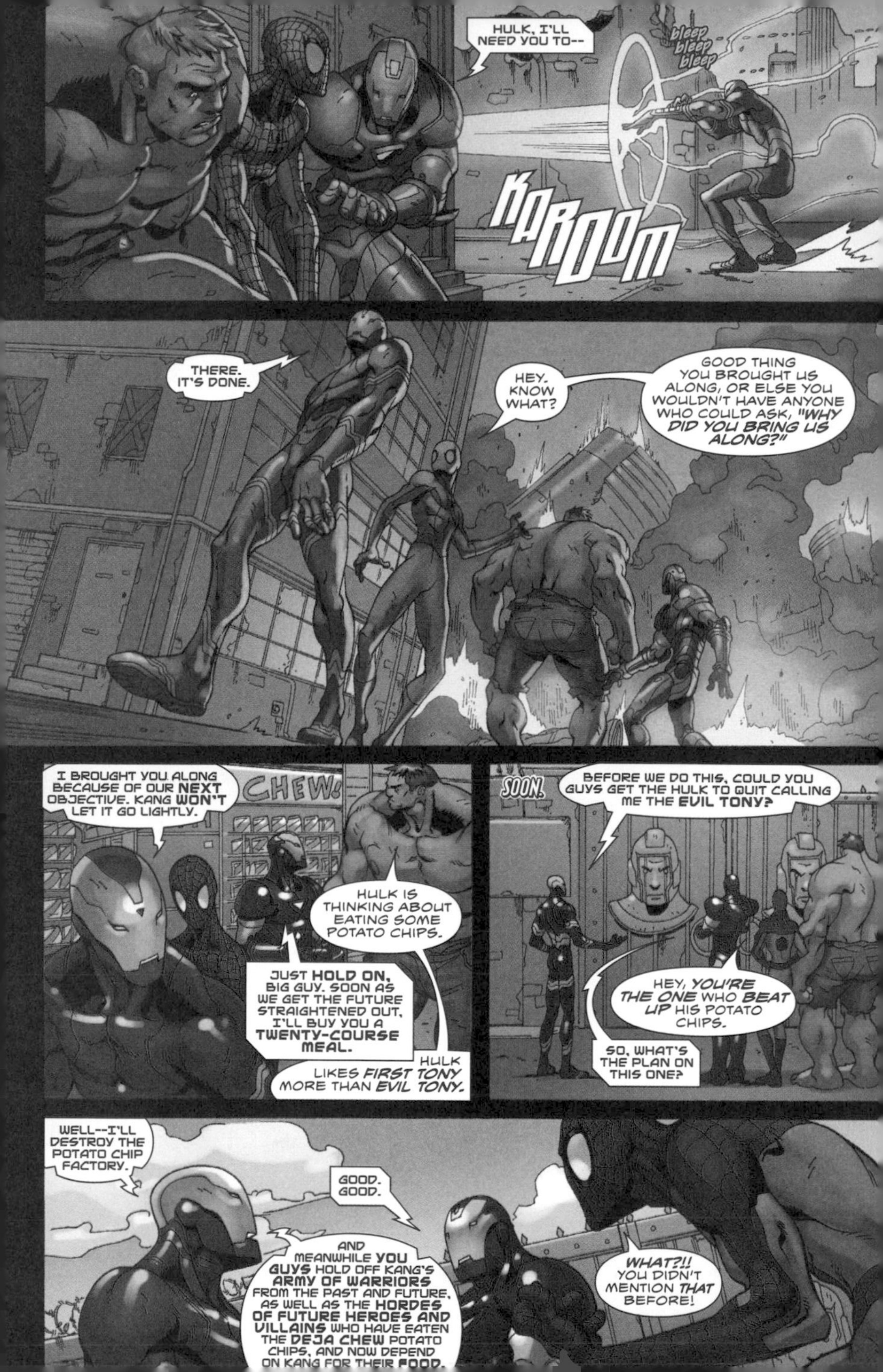

HULK, I'LL NEED YOU TO--
bleep bleep bleep
KAROOM
THERE. IT'S DONE.
HEY. KNOW WHAT?
GOOD THING YOU BROUGHT US ALONG, OR ELSE YOU WOULDN'T HAVE ANYONE WHO COULD ASK, "WHY DID YOU BRING US ALONG?"
I BROUGHT YOU ALONG BECAUSE OF OUR NEXT OBJECTIVE. KANG WON'T LET IT GO LIGHTLY.
CHEW!
HULK IS THINKING ABOUT EATING SOME POTATO CHIPS.
JUST HOLD ON, BIG GUY. SOON AS WE GET THE FUTURE STRAIGHTENED OUT, I'LL BUY YOU A TWENTY-COURSE MEAL.
HULK LIKES FIRST TONY MORE THAN EVIL TONY.
SOON.
BEFORE WE DO THIS, COULD YOU GUYS GET THE HULK TO QUIT CALLING ME THE EVIL TONY?
HEY, YOU'RE THE ONE WHO BEAT UP HIS POTATO CHIPS.
SO, WHAT'S THE PLAN ON THIS ONE?
WELL--I'LL DESTROY THE POTATO CHIP FACTORY.
GOOD. GOOD.
AND MEANWHILE YOU GUYS HOLD OFF KANG'S ARMY OF WARRIORS FROM THE PAST AND FUTURE, AS WELL AS THE HORDES OF FUTURE HEROES AND VILLAINS WHO HAVE EATEN THE DEJA CHEW POTATO CHIPS, AND NOW DEPEND ON KANG FOR THEIR FOOD.
WHAT?!! YOU DIDN'T MENTION THAT BEFORE!

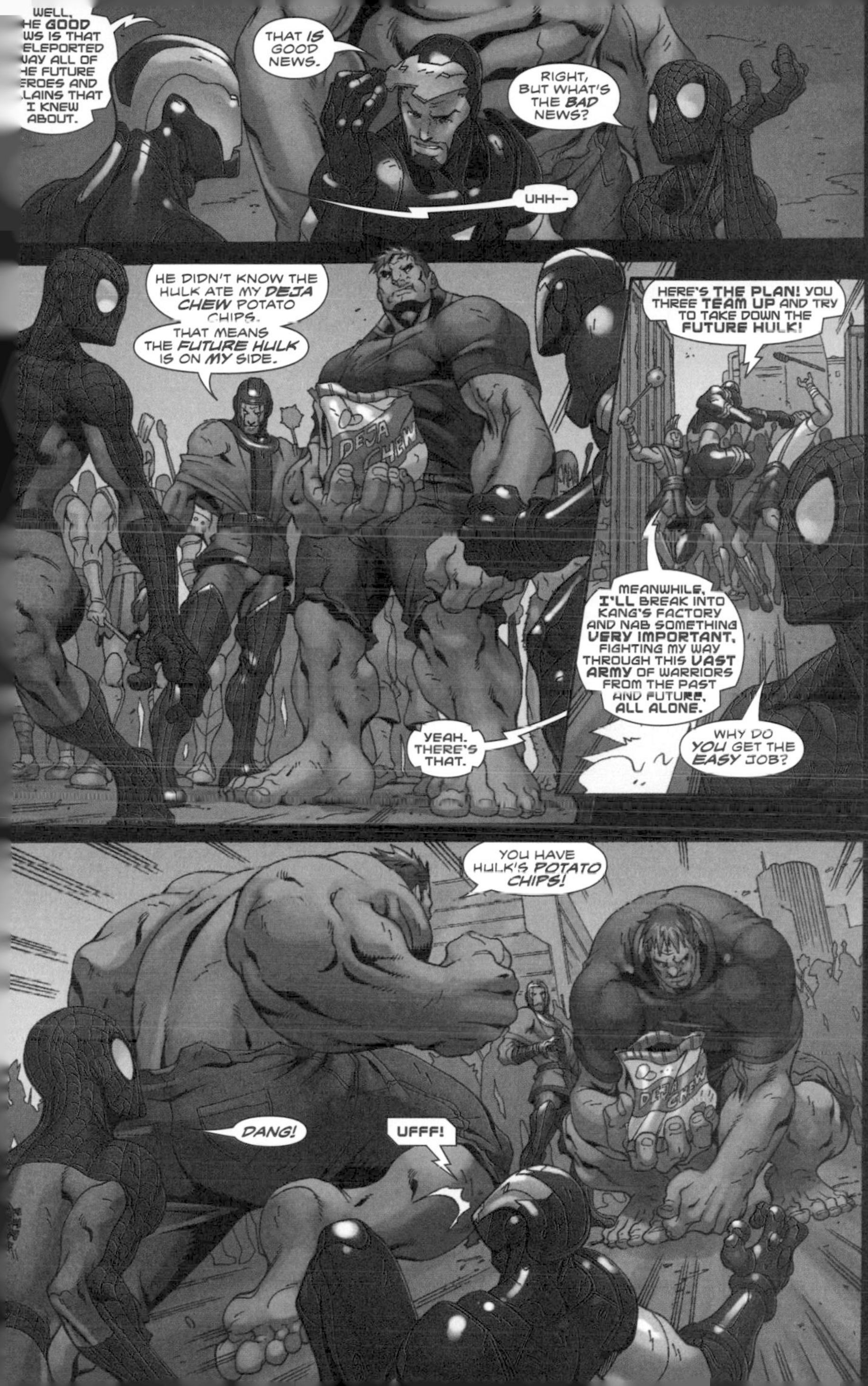
WELL, HE GOOD WS IS THAT ELEPORTED WAY ALL OF HE FUTURE EROES AND LAINS THAT I KNEW ABOUT.
THAT IS GOOD NEWS.
RIGHT, BUT WHAT'S THE BAD NEWS?
UHH--
HE DIDN'T KNOW THE HULK ATE MY DEJA CHEW POTATO CHIPS.
THAT MEANS THE FUTURE HULK IS ON MY SIDE.
DEJA CHEW
HERE'S THE PLAN! YOU THREE TEAM UP AND TRY TO TAKE DOWN THE FUTURE HULK!
MEANWHILE, I'LL BREAK INTO KANG'S FACTORY AND NAB SOMETHING VERY IMPORTANT, FIGHTING MY WAY THROUGH THIS VAST ARMY OF WARRIORS FROM THE PAST AND FUTURE, ALL ALONE.
YEAH. THERE'S THAT.
WHY DO YOU GET THE EASY JOB?
YOU HAVE HULK'S POTATO CHIPS!
DEJA CHEW
DANG!
UFFF!

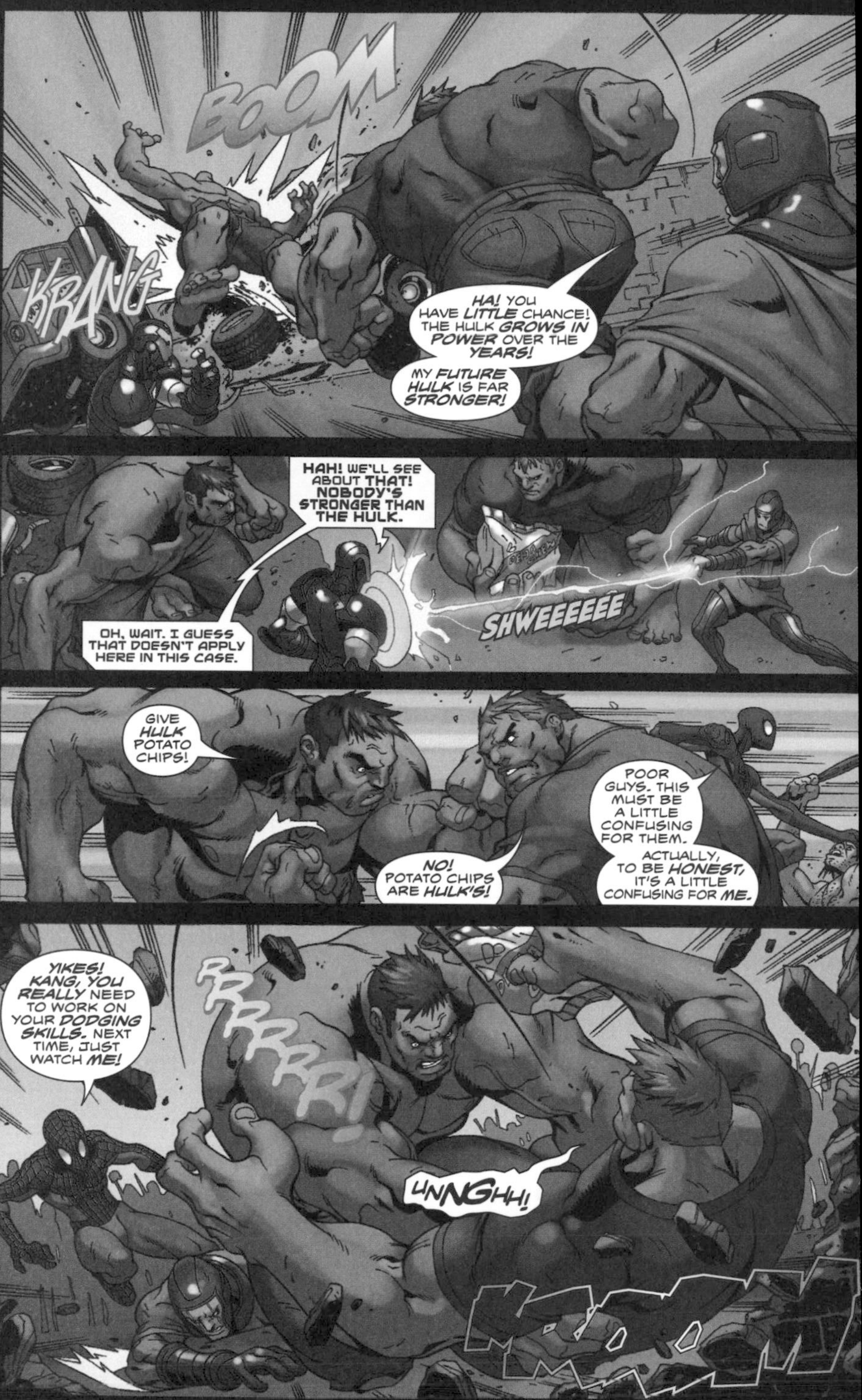
BOOM
KRANG
HA! YOU HAVE LITTLE CHANCE! THE HULK GROWS IN POWER OVER THE YEARS!
MY FUTURE HULK IS FAR STRONGER!
HAH! WE'LL SEE ABOUT THAT! NOBODY'S STRONGER THAN THE HULK.
OH, WAIT. I GUESS THAT DOESN'T APPLY HERE IN THIS CASE.
SHWEEEEEE
GIVE HULK POTATO CHIPS!
NO! POTATO CHIPS ARE HULK'S!
POOR GUYS. THIS MUST BE A LITTLE CONFUSING FOR THEM.
ACTUALLY, TO BE HONEST, IT'S A LITTLE CONFUSING FOR ME.
YIKES! KANG, YOU REALLY NEED TO WORK ON YOUR DODGING SKILLS. NEXT TIME, JUST WATCH ME!
RRRRRR!
UNNGHH!
KA-BOOM

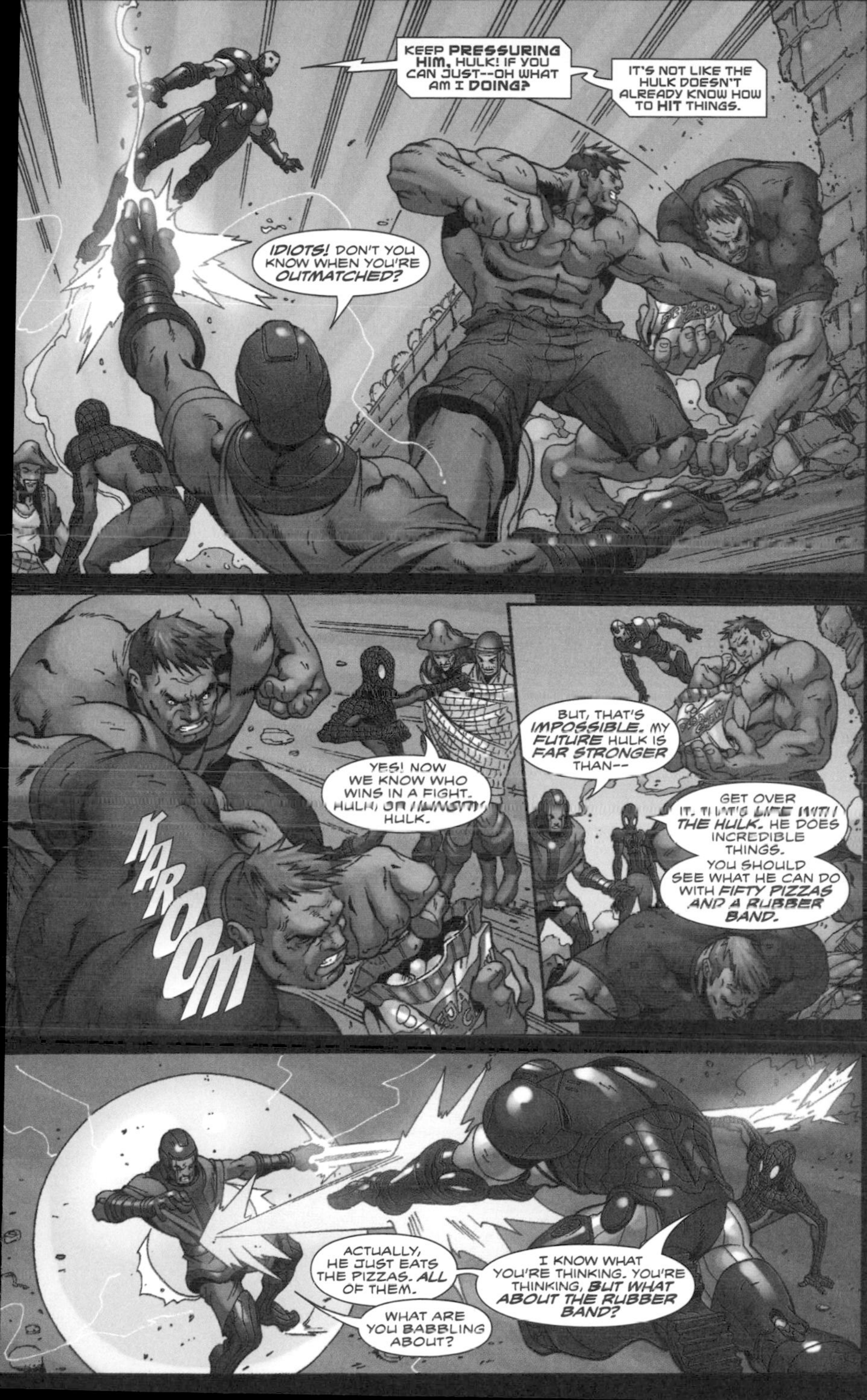
KEEP PRESSURING HIM, HULK! IF YOU CAN JUST--OH WHAT AM I DOING?
IT'S NOT LIKE THE HULK DOESN'T ALREADY KNOW HOW TO HIT THINGS.
IDIOTS! DON'T YOU KNOW WHEN YOU'RE OUTMATCHED?
KAROOOM
YES! NOW WE KNOW WHO WINS IN A FIGHT. HULK, OR HULK.
BUT, THAT'S IMPOSSIBLE. MY FUTURE HULK IS FAR STRONGER THAN--
GET OVER IT. THE HULK. HE DOES INCREDIBLE THINGS.
YOU SHOULD SEE WHAT HE CAN DO WITH FIFTY PIZZAS AND A RUBBER BAND.
ACTUALLY, HE JUST EATS THE PIZZAS. ALL OF THEM.
I KNOW WHAT YOU'RE THINKING. YOU'RE THINKING, BUT WHAT ABOUT THE RUBBER BAND?
WHAT ARE YOU BABBLING ABOUT?

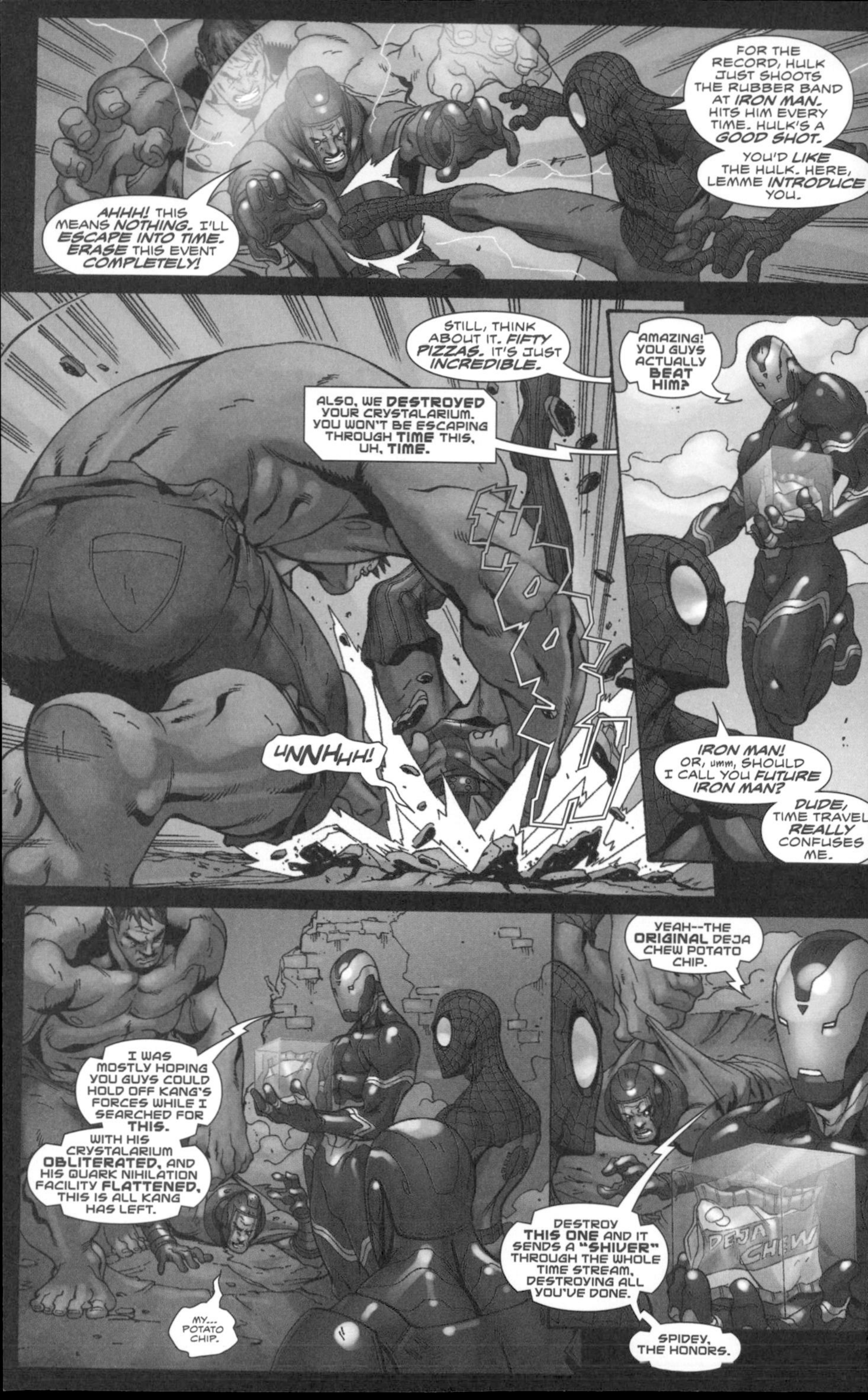
FOR THE RECORD, HULK JUST SHOOTS THE RUBBER BAND AT IRON MAN. HITS HIM EVERY TIME. HULK'S A GOOD SHOT.
YOU'D LIKE THE HULK. HERE, LEMME INTRODUCE YOU.
AHHH! THIS MEANS NOTHING. I'LL ESCAPE INTO TIME. ERASE THIS EVENT COMPLETELY!
STILL, THINK ABOUT IT. FIFTY PIZZAS. IT'S JUST INCREDIBLE.
ALSO, WE DESTROYED YOUR CRYSTALARIUM. YOU WON'T BE ESCAPING THROUGH TIME THIS, UH, TIME.
UNNHHH!
AMAZING! YOU GUYS ACTUALLY BEAT HIM?
IRON MAN! OR, umm, SHOULD I CALL YOU FUTURE IRON MAN?
DUDE, TIME TRAVEL REALLY CONFUSES ME.
I WAS MOSTLY HOPING YOU GUYS COULD HOLD OFF KANG'S FORCES WHILE I SEARCHED FOR THIS.
WITH HIS CRYSTALARIUM OBLITERATED, AND HIS QUARK NIHILATION FACILITY FLATTENED, THIS IS ALL KANG HAS LEFT.
MY... POTATO CHIP.
YEAH--THE ORIGINAL DEJA CHEW POTATO CHIP.
DESTROY THIS ONE AND IT SENDS A "SHIVER" THROUGH THE WHOLE TIME STREAM, DESTROYING ALL YOU'VE DONE.
SPIDEY, THE HONORS.
DEJA CHEW

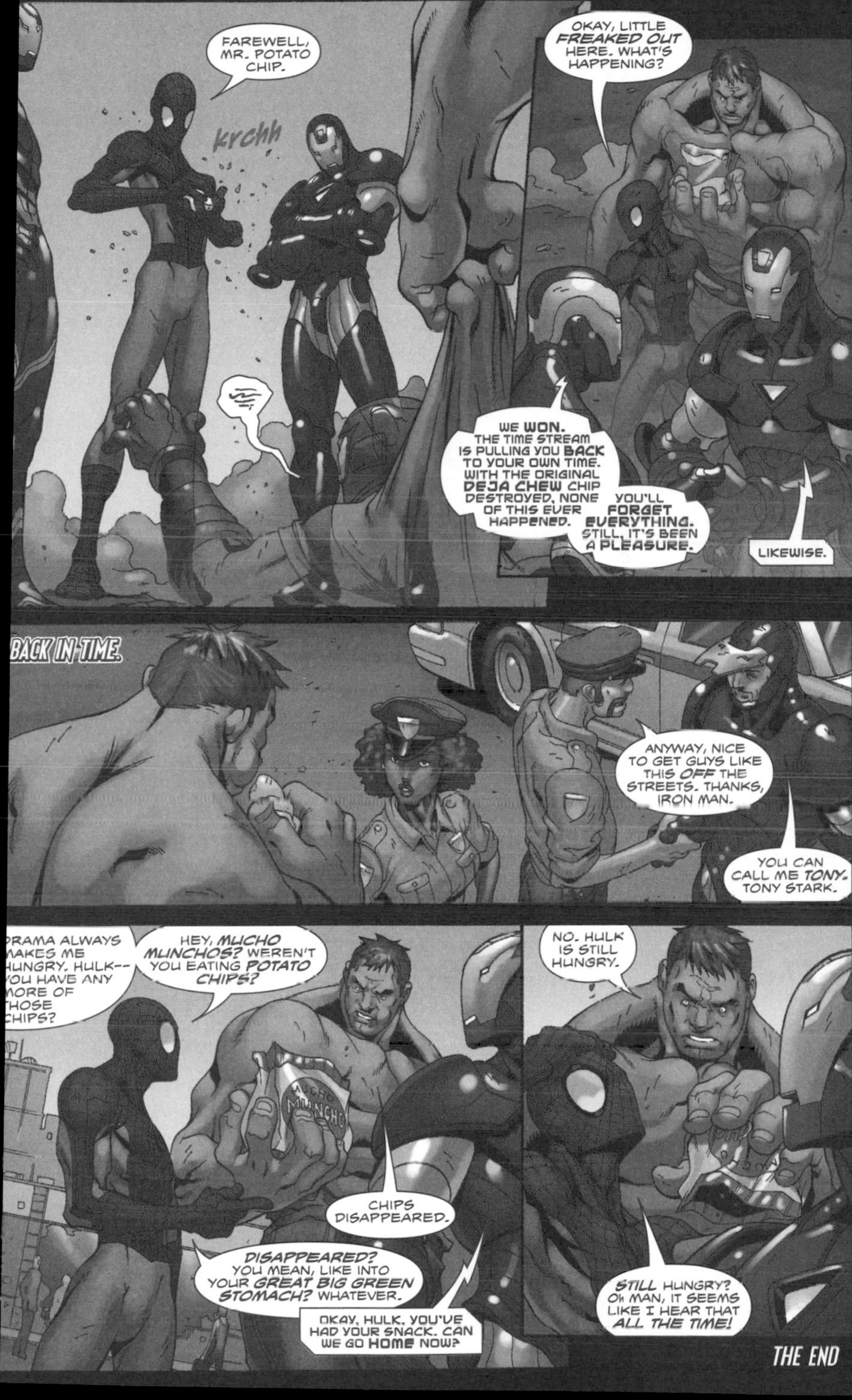
FAREWELL, MR. POTATO CHIP.
krchh
OKAY, LITTLE FREAKED OUT HERE. WHAT'S HAPPENING?
WE WON. THE TIME STREAM IS PULLING YOU BACK TO YOUR OWN TIME. WITH THE ORIGINAL DEJA CHEW CHIP DESTROYED, NONE OF THIS EVER HAPPENED.
YOU'LL FORGET EVERYTHING. STILL, IT'S BEEN A PLEASURE.
LIKEWISE.
BACK IN TIME.
ANYWAY, NICE TO GET GUYS LIKE THIS OFF THE STREETS. THANKS, IRON MAN.
YOU CAN CALL ME TONY. TONY STARK.
DRAMA ALWAYS MAKES ME HUNGRY. HULK-- YOU HAVE ANY MORE OF THOSE CHIPS?
HEY, MUCHO MUNCHOS? WEREN'T YOU EATING POTATO CHIPS?
MUCHO MUNCHO
CHIPS DISAPPEARED.
DISAPPEARED? YOU MEAN, LIKE INTO YOUR GREAT BIG GREEN STOMACH? WHATEVER.
OKAY, HULK. YOU'VE HAD YOUR SNACK. CAN WE GO HOME NOW?
NO. HULK IS STILL HUNGRY.
STILL HUNGRY? OH MAN, IT SEEMS LIKE I HEAR THAT ALL THE TIME!
THE END

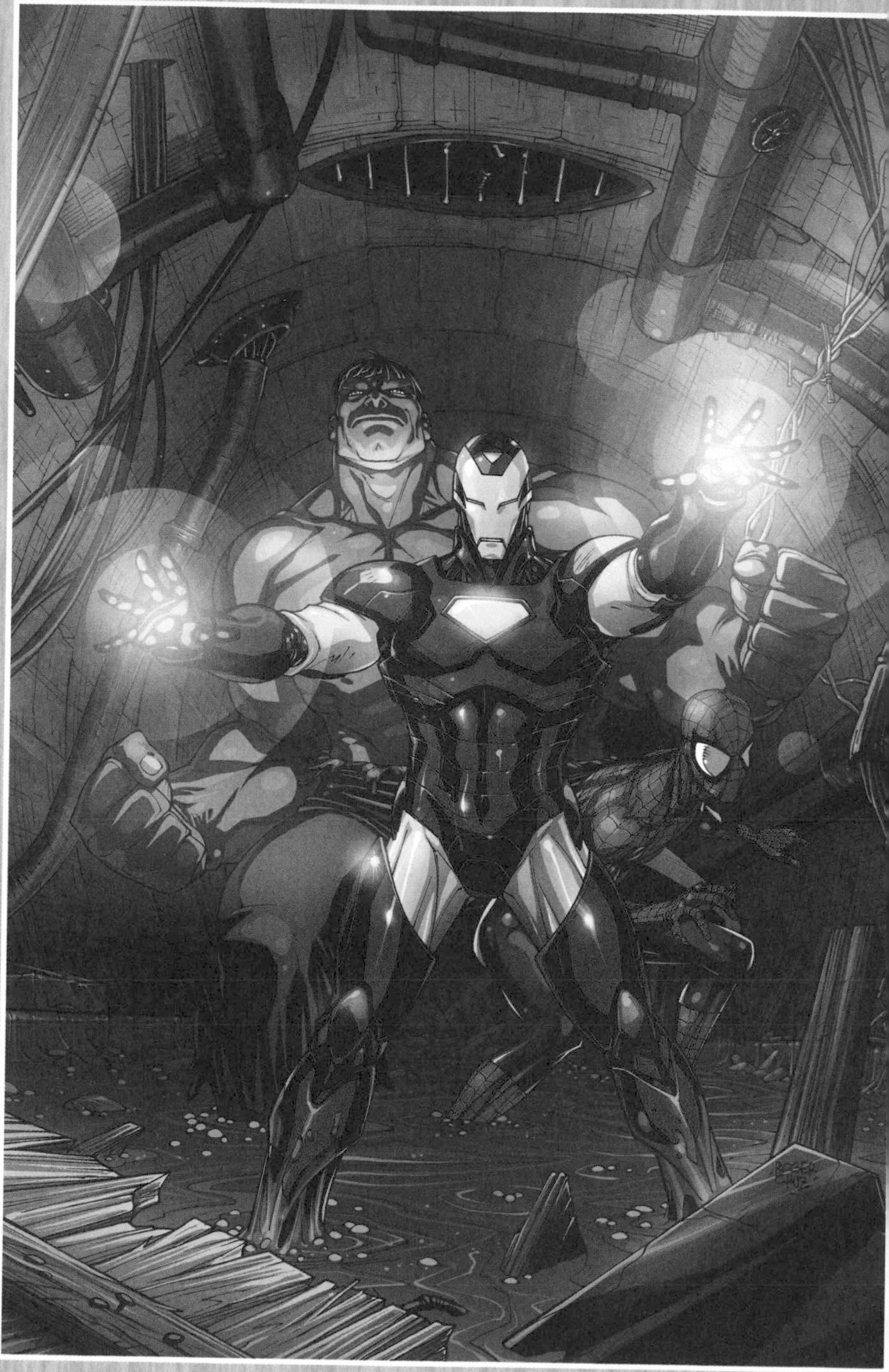

#4

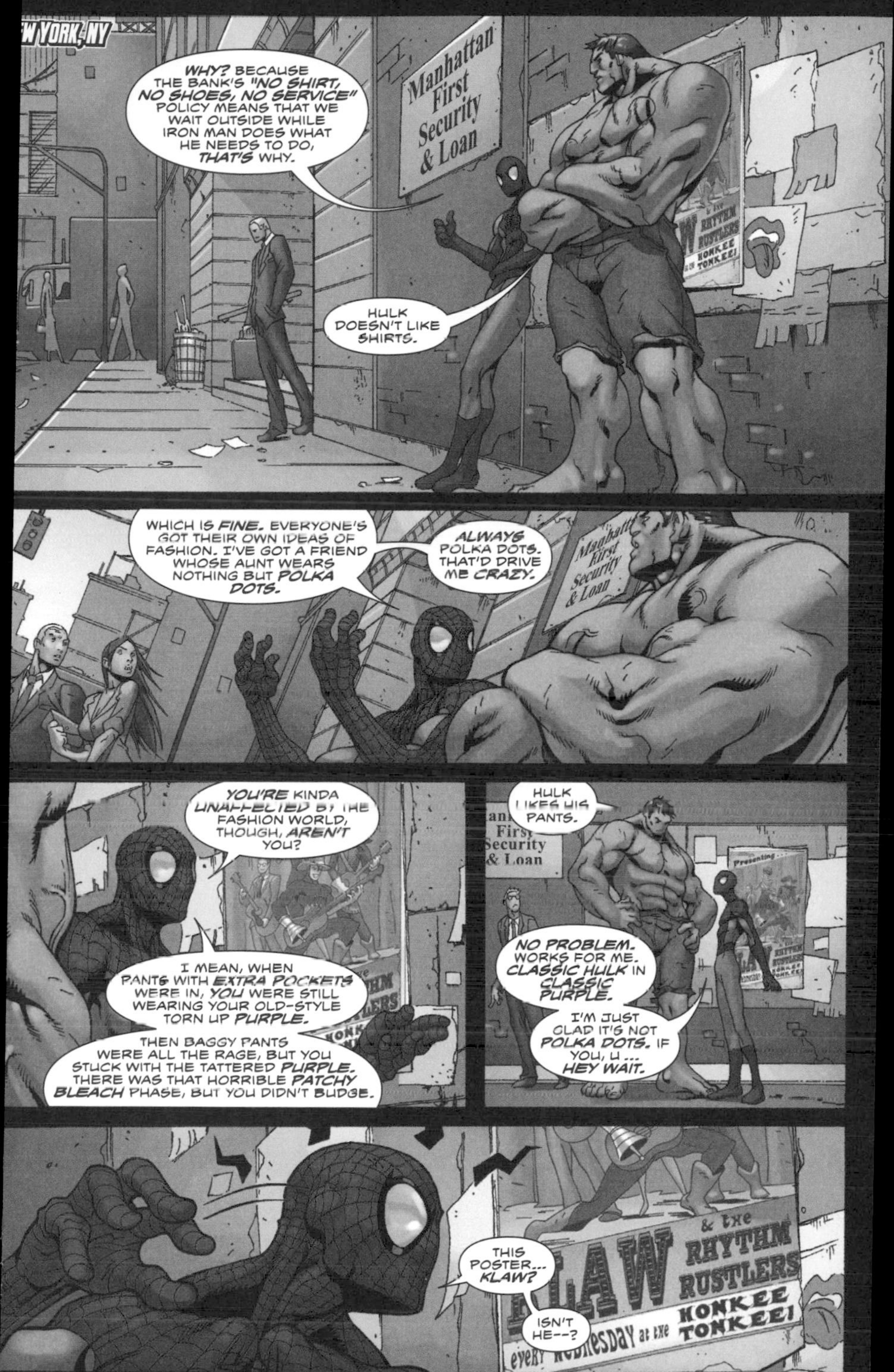
EW YORK, NY
Manhattan First Security & Loan
WHY? BECAUSE THE BANK'S "NO SHIRT, NO SHOES, NO SERVICE" POLICY MEANS THAT WE WAIT OUTSIDE WHILE IRON MAN DOES WHAT HE NEEDS TO DO, THAT'S WHY.
HULK DOESN'T LIKE SHIRTS.
WHICH IS FINE. EVERYONE'S GOT THEIR OWN IDEAS OF FASHION. I'VE GOT A FRIEND WHOSE AUNT WEARS NOTHING BUT POLKA DOTS.
ALWAYS POLKA DOTS. THAT'D DRIVE ME CRAZY.
YOU'RE KINDA UNAFFECTED BY THE FASHION WORLD, THOUGH, AREN'T YOU?
I MEAN, WHEN PANTS WITH EXTRA POCKETS WERE IN, YOU WERE STILL WEARING YOUR OLD-STYLE TORN UP PURPLE.
THEN BAGGY PANTS WERE ALL THE RAGE, BUT YOU STUCK WITH THE TATTERED PURPLE. THERE WAS THAT HORRIBLE PATCHY BLEACH PHASE, BUT YOU DIDN'T BUDGE.
HULK LIKES HIS PANTS.
NO PROBLEM. WORKS FOR ME. CLASSIC HULK IN CLASSIC PURPLE.
I'M JUST GLAD IT'S NOT POLKA DOTS. IF YOU, U ... HEY WAIT.
& the RHYTHM RUSTLERS
HONKEE TONKEE!
THIS POSTER... KLAW?
ISN'T HE--?

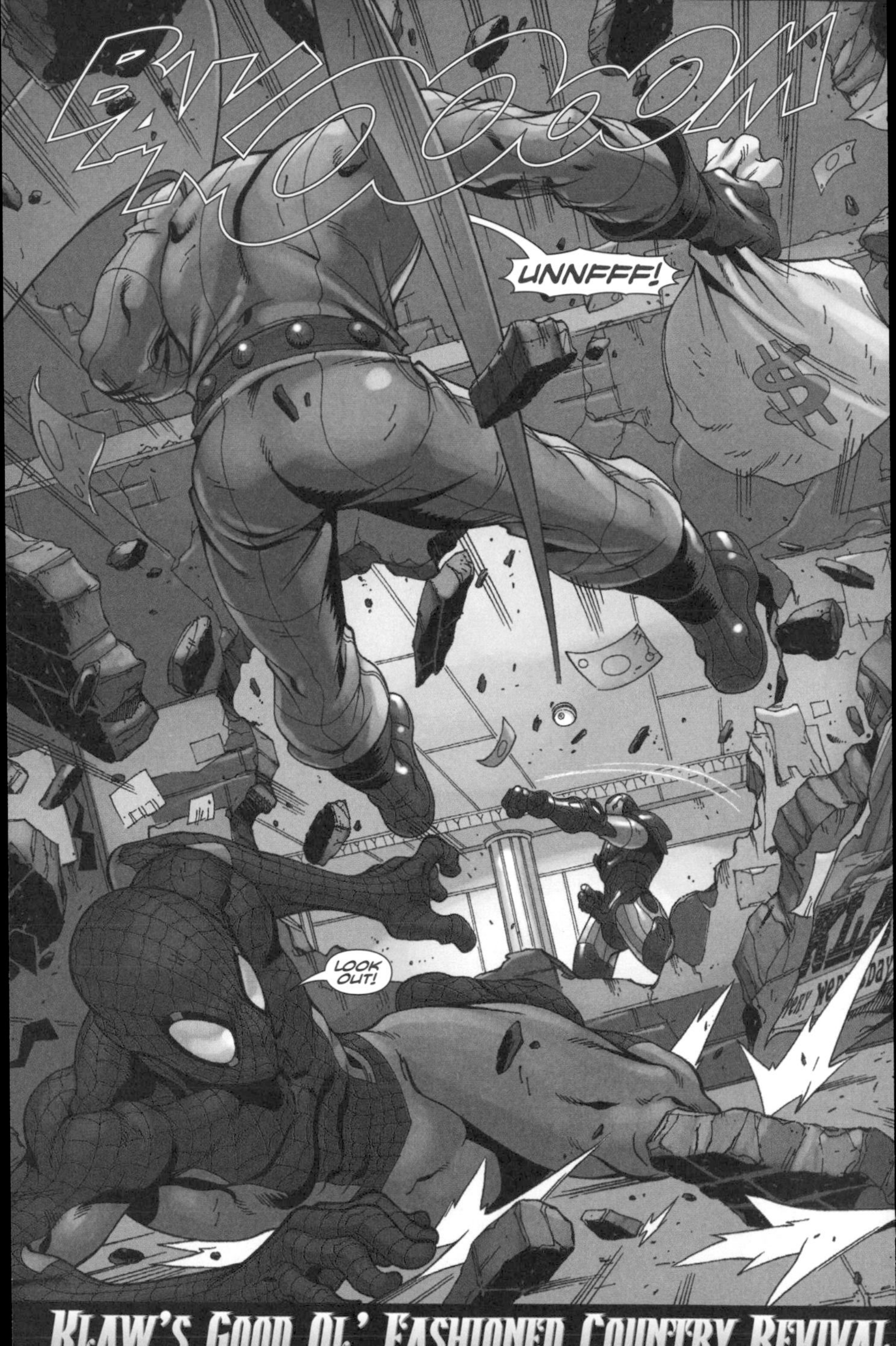
UNNFFF!
LOOK OUT!

KLAW'S GOOD OL' FASHIONED COUNTRY REVIVAL

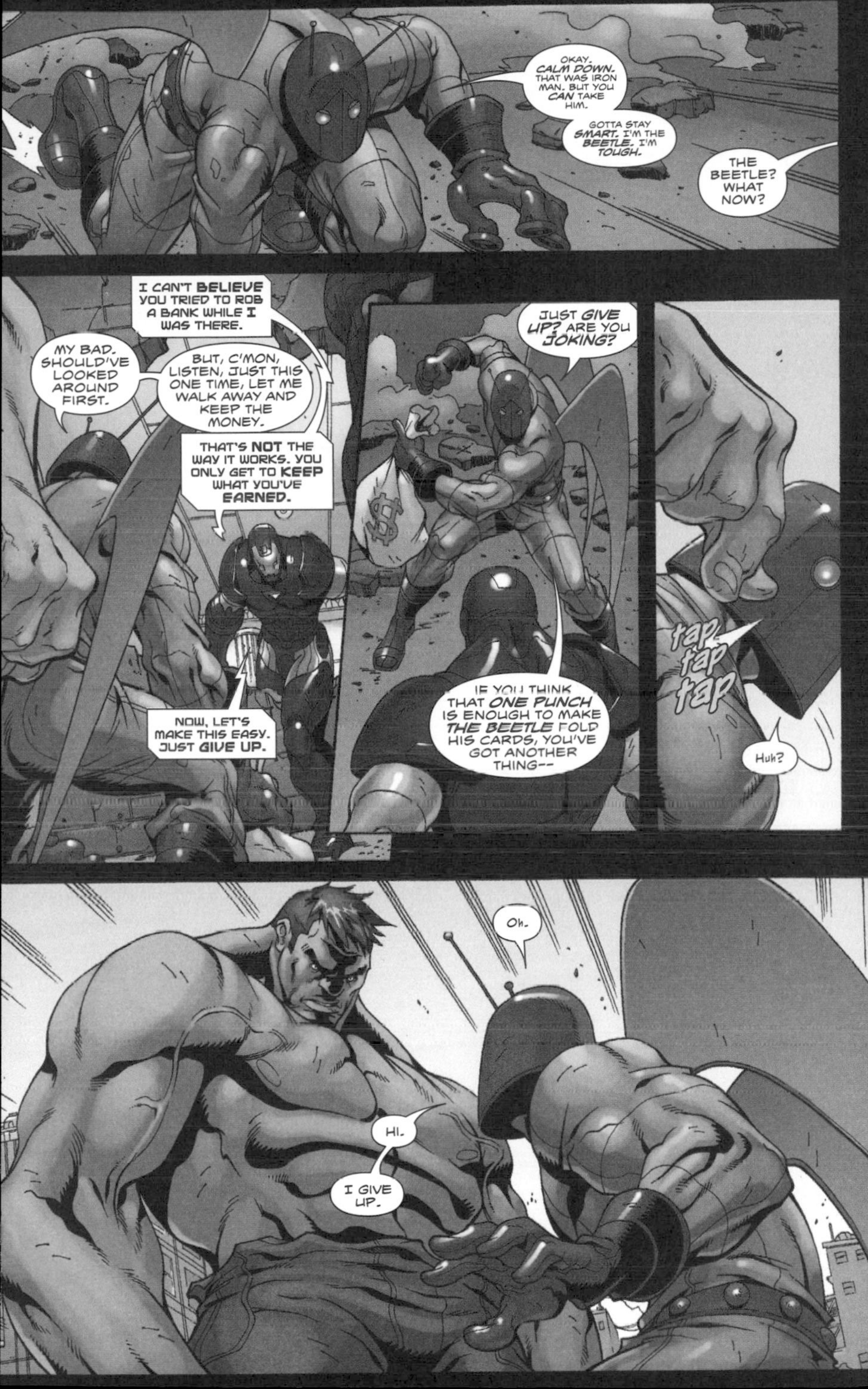

OKAY. CALM DOWN. THAT WAS IRON MAN. BUT YOU CAN TAKE HIM.
GOTTA STAY SMART. I'M THE BEETLE. I'M TOUGH.
THE BEETLE? WHAT NOW?
I CAN'T BELIEVE YOU TRIED TO ROB A BANK WHILE I WAS THERE.
MY BAD. SHOULD'VE LOOKED AROUND FIRST.
BUT, C'MON, LISTEN, JUST THIS ONE TIME, LET ME WALK AWAY AND KEEP THE MONEY.
THAT'S NOT THE WAY IT WORKS. YOU ONLY GET TO KEEP WHAT YOU'VE EARNED.
NOW, LET'S MAKE THIS EASY. JUST GIVE UP.
JUST GIVE UP? ARE YOU JOKING?
IF YOU THINK THAT ONE PUNCH IS ENOUGH TO MAKE THE BEETLE FOLD HIS CARDS, YOU'VE GOT ANOTHER THING--
tap tap tap
Huh?
Oh.
HI.
I GIVE UP.

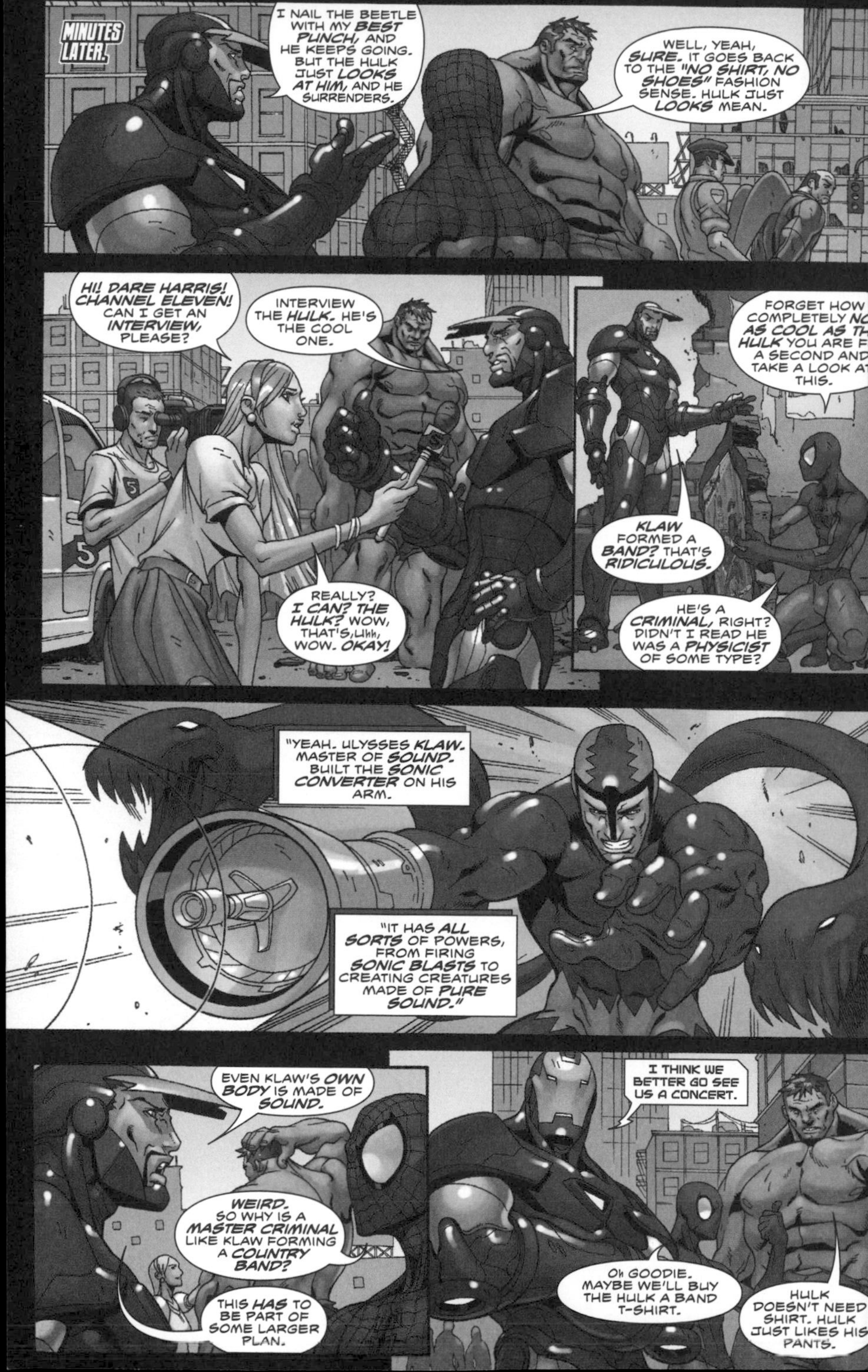
MINUTES LATER.
I NAIL THE BEETLE WITH MY BEST PUNCH, AND HE KEEPS GOING. BUT THE HULK JUST LOOKS AT HIM, AND HE SURRENDERS.
WELL, YEAH, SURE. IT GOES BACK TO THE "NO SHIRT, NO SHOES" FASHION SENSE. HULK JUST LOOKS MEAN.
HI! DARE HARRIS! CHANNEL ELEVEN! CAN I GET AN INTERVIEW, PLEASE?
INTERVIEW THE HULK. HE'S THE COOL ONE.
REALLY? I CAN? THE HULK? WOW, THAT'S, UHH, WOW. OKAY!
FORGET HOW COMPLETELY NO AS COOL AS TH HULK YOU ARE F A SECOND AND TAKE A LOOK AT THIS.
KLAW FORMED A BAND? THAT'S RIDICULOUS.
HE'S A CRIMINAL, RIGHT? DIDN'T I READ HE WAS A PHYSICIST OF SOME TYPE?
"YEAH. ULYSSES KLAW. MASTER OF SOUND. BUILT THE SONIC CONVERTER ON HIS ARM.
"IT HAS ALL SORTS OF POWERS, FROM FIRING SONIC BLASTS TO CREATING CREATURES MADE OF PURE SOUND."
EVEN KLAW'S OWN BODY IS MADE OF SOUND.
WEIRD. SO WHY IS A MASTER CRIMINAL LIKE KLAW FORMING A COUNTRY BAND?
THIS HAS TO BE PART OF SOME LARGER PLAN.
I THINK WE BETTER GO SEE US A CONCERT.
OH GOODIE. MAYBE WE'LL BUY THE HULK A BAND T-SHIRT.
HULK DOESN'T NEED SHIRT. HULK JUST LIKES HIS PANTS.

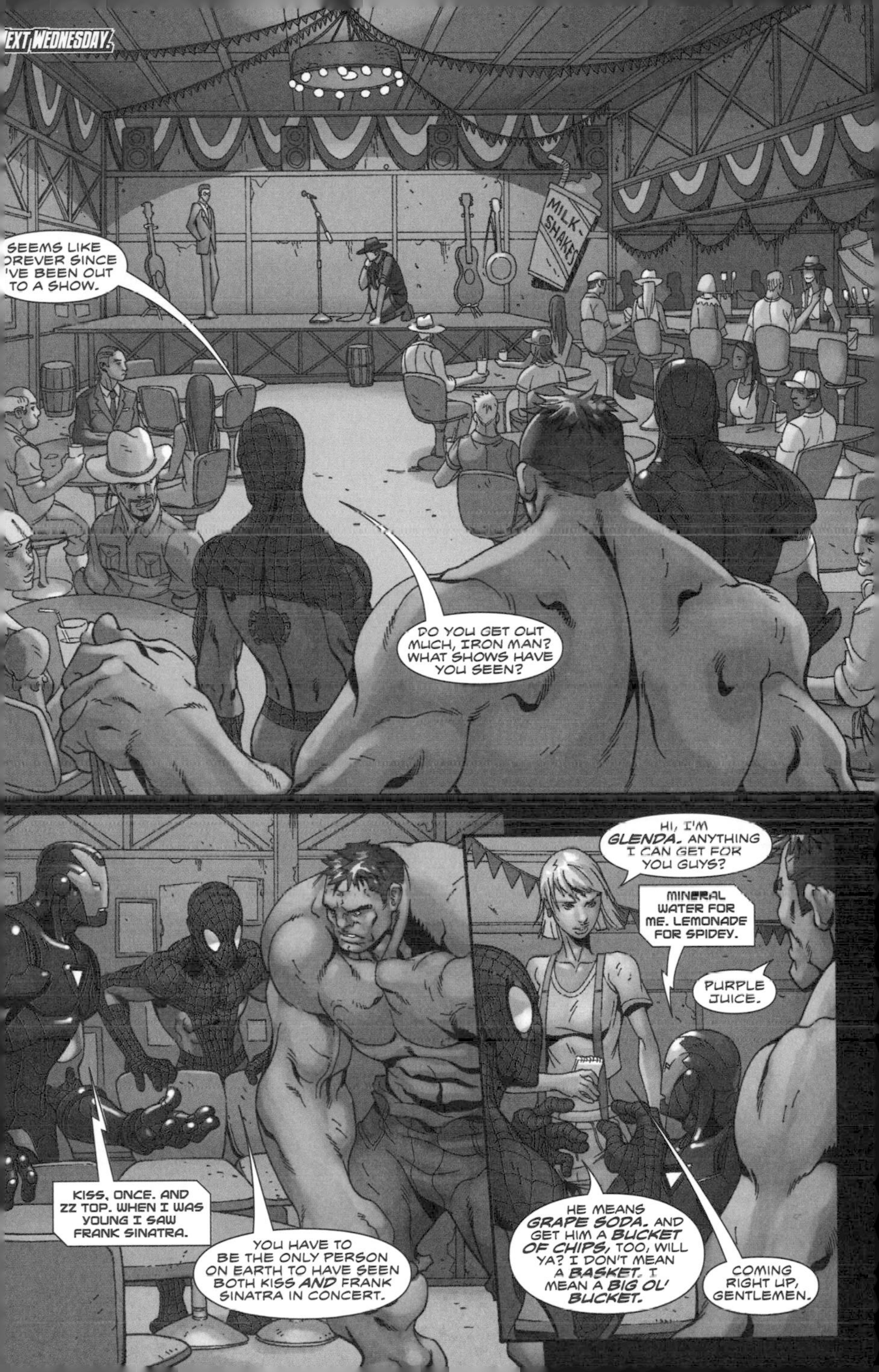
EXT WEDNESDAY!
SEEMS LIKE OREVER SINCE 'VE BEEN OUT TO A SHOW.
MILK-SHAKES
DO YOU GET OUT MUCH, IRON MAN? WHAT SHOWS HAVE YOU SEEN?
KISS, ONCE. AND ZZ TOP. WHEN I WAS YOUNG I SAW FRANK SINATRA.
YOU HAVE TO BE THE ONLY PERSON ON EARTH TO HAVE SEEN BOTH KISS AND FRANK SINATRA IN CONCERT.
HI, I'M GLENDA. ANYTHING I CAN GET FOR YOU GUYS?
MINERAL WATER FOR ME. LEMONADE FOR SPIDEY.
PURPLE JUICE.
HE MEANS GRAPE SODA. AND GET HIM A BUCKET OF CHIPS, TOO, WILL YA? I DON'T MEAN A BASKET. I MEAN A BIG OL' BUCKET.
COMING RIGHT UP, GENTLEMEN.

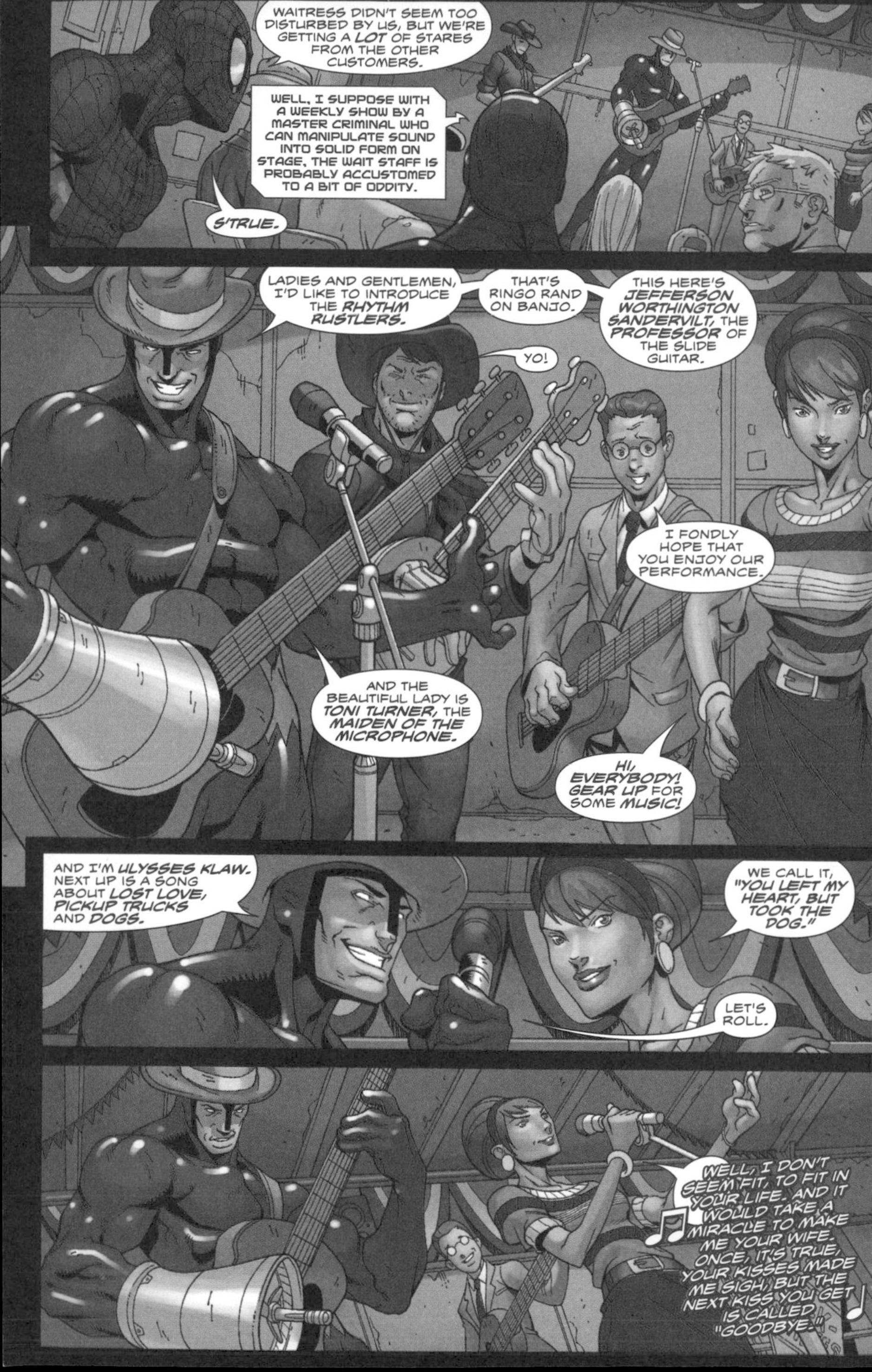
WAITRESS DIDN'T SEEM TOO DISTURBED BY US, BUT WE'RE GETTING A LOT OF STARES FROM THE OTHER CUSTOMERS.
WELL, I SUPPOSE WITH A WEEKLY SHOW BY A MASTER CRIMINAL WHO CAN MANIPULATE SOUND INTO SOLID FORM ON STAGE, THE WAIT STAFF IS PROBABLY ACCUSTOMED TO A BIT OF ODDITY.
S'TRUE.
LADIES AND GENTLEMEN, I'D LIKE TO INTRODUCE THE RHYTHM RUSTLERS.
THAT'S RINGO RAND ON BANJO.
YO!
THIS HERE'S JEFFERSON WORTHINGTON SANDERVILT, THE PROFESSOR OF THE SLIDE GUITAR.
I FONDLY HOPE THAT YOU ENJOY OUR PERFORMANCE.
AND THE BEAUTIFUL LADY IS TONI TURNER, THE MAIDEN OF THE MICROPHONE.
HI, EVERYBODY! GEAR UP FOR SOME MUSIC!
AND I'M ULYSSES KLAW. NEXT UP IS A SONG ABOUT LOST LOVE, PICKUP TRUCKS AND DOGS.
WE CALL IT, "YOU LEFT MY HEART, BUT TOOK THE DOG."
LET'S ROLL.
WELL, I DON'T SEEM FIT, TO FIT IN YOUR LIFE. AND IT WOULD TAKE A MIRACLE TO MAKE ME YOUR WIFE. ONCE, IT'S TRUE, YOUR KISSES MADE ME SIGH, BUT THE NEXT KISS YOU GET IS CALLED "GOODBYE."

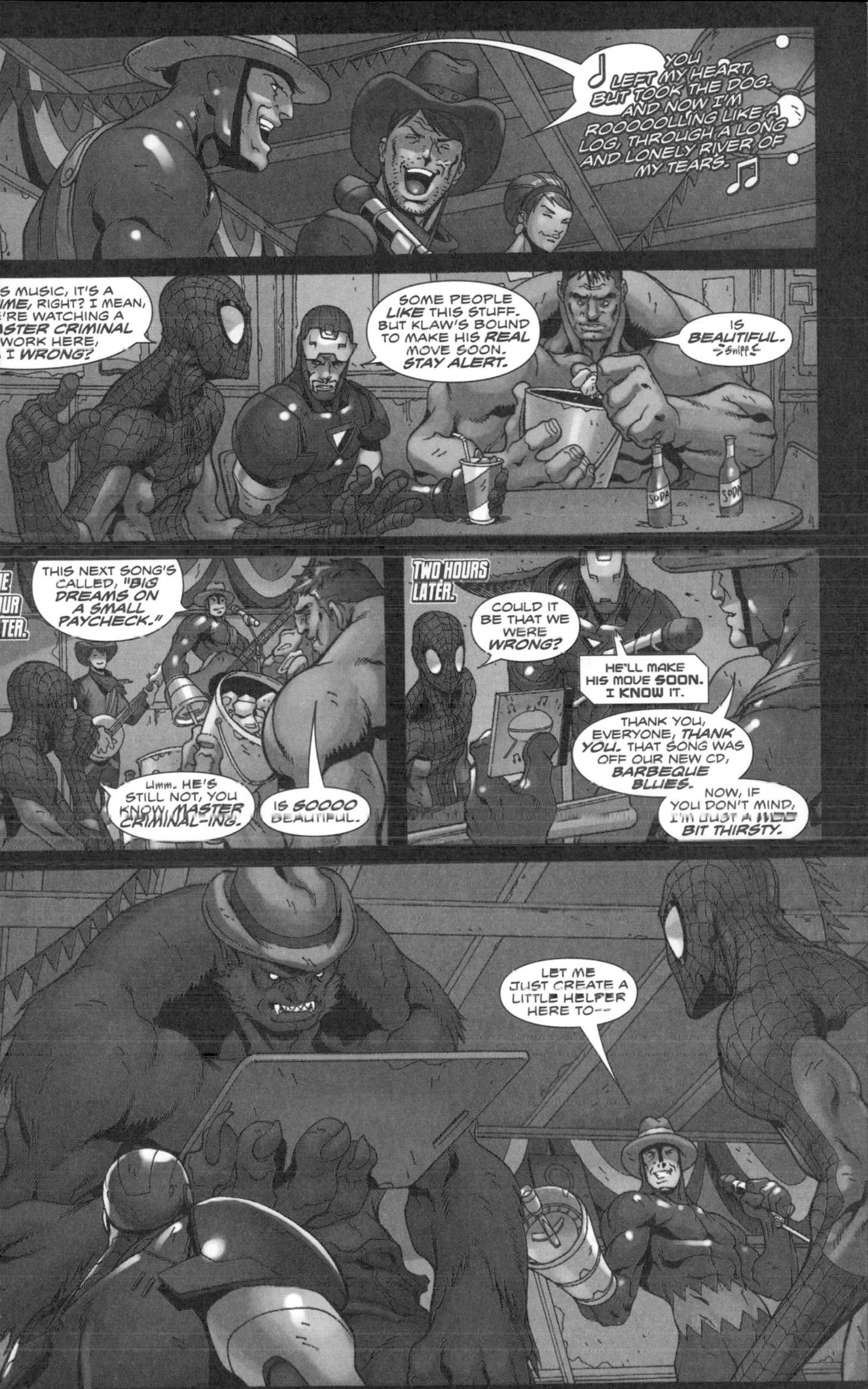
YOU LEFT MY HEART, BUT TOOK THE DOG. AND NOW I'M ROOOOOLLING LIKE A LOG, THROUGH A LONG AND LONELY RIVER OF MY TEARS.
S MUSIC, IT'S A IME, RIGHT? I MEAN, E'RE WATCHING A ASTER CRIMINAL WORK HERE, I WRONG?
SOME PEOPLE LIKE THIS STUFF. BUT KLAW'S BOUND TO MAKE HIS REAL MOVE SOON. STAY ALERT.
IS BEAUTIFUL.
SNIFF
THIS NEXT SONG'S CALLED, "BIG DREAMS ON A SMALL PAYCHECK."
UMM. HE'S STILL NOT, YOU KNOW, MASTER CRIMINAL-ING.
IS SOOOO BEAUTIFUL.
TWO HOURS LATER.
COULD IT BE THAT WE WERE WRONG?
HE'LL MAKE HIS MOVE SOON. I KNOW IT.
THANK YOU, EVERYONE, THANK YOU. THAT SONG WAS OFF OUR NEW CD, BARBEQUE BLUES.
NOW, IF YOU DON'T MIND, I'M JUST A BIT THIRSTY.
LET ME JUST CREATE A LITTLE HELPER HERE TO--

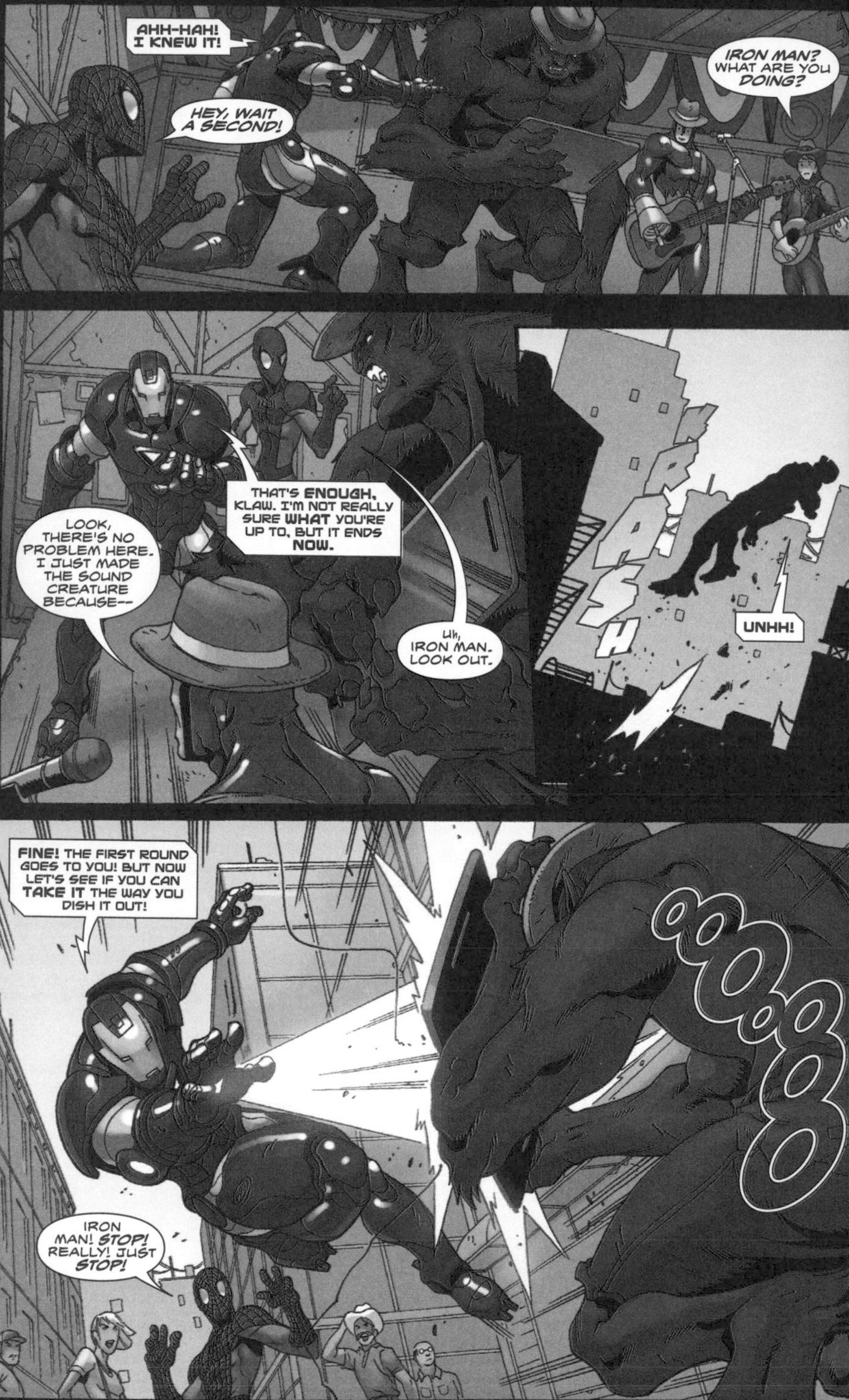
AHH-HAH! I KNEW IT!
HEY, WAIT A SECOND!
IRON MAN? WHAT ARE YOU DOING?
THAT'S ENOUGH, KLAW. I'M NOT REALLY SURE WHAT YOU'RE UP TO, BUT IT ENDS NOW.
LOOK, THERE'S NO PROBLEM HERE. I JUST MADE THE SOUND CREATURE BECAUSE--
UH, IRON MAN. LOOK OUT.
UNHH!
FINE! THE FIRST ROUND GOES TO YOU! BUT NOW LET'S SEE IF YOU CAN TAKE IT THE WAY YOU DISH IT OUT!
IRON MAN! STOP! REALLY! JUST STOP!

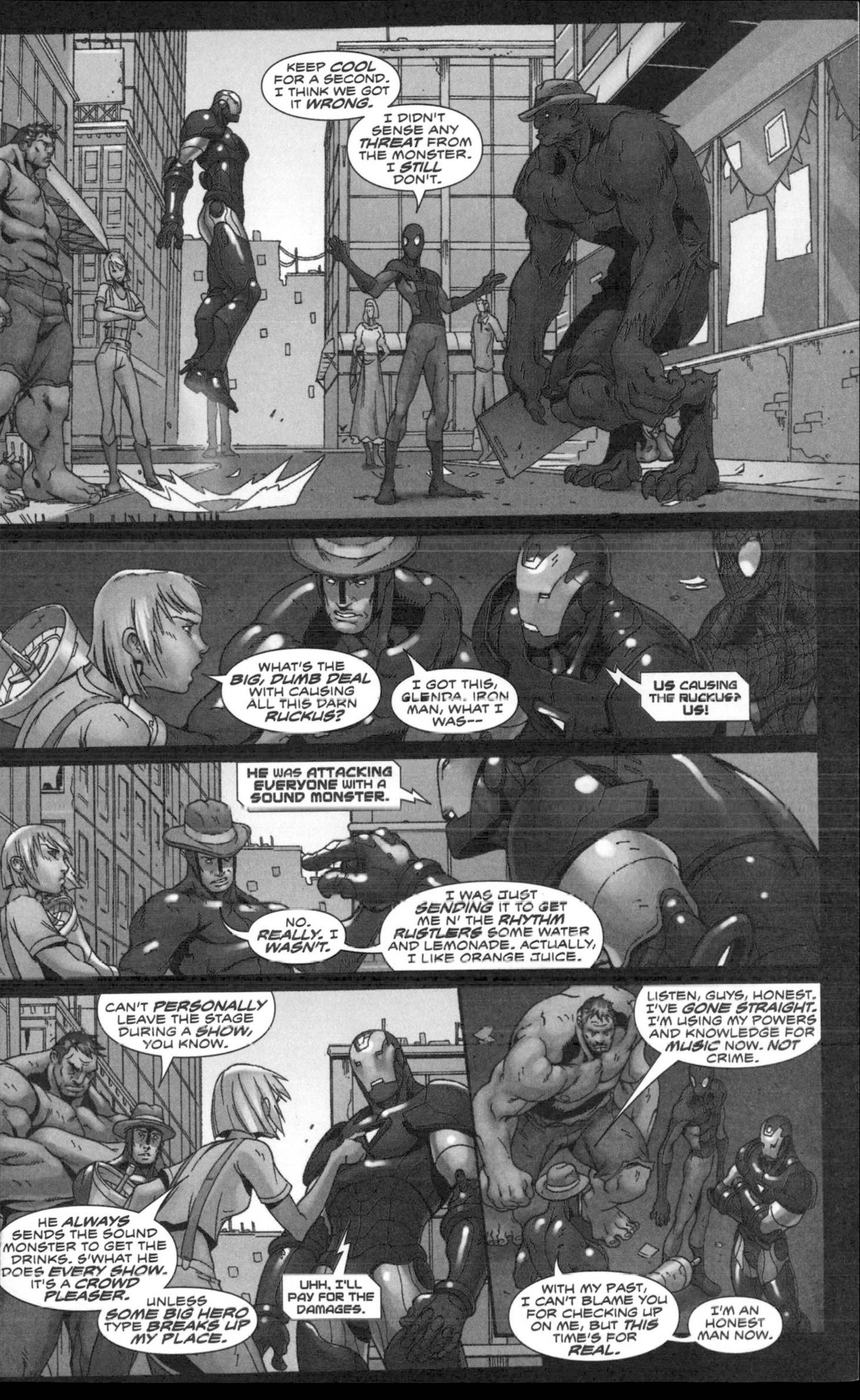
KEEP COOL FOR A SECOND. I THINK WE GOT IT WRONG.
I DIDN'T SENSE ANY THREAT FROM THE MONSTER. I STILL DON'T.
WHAT'S THE BIG, DUMB DEAL WITH CAUSING ALL THIS DARN RUCKUS?
I GOT THIS, GLENDA. IRON MAN, WHAT I WAS--
US CAUSING THE RUCKUS? US!
HE WAS ATTACKING EVERYONE WITH A SOUND MONSTER.
NO. REALLY. I WASN'T.
I WAS JUST SENDING IT TO GET ME N' THE RHYTHM RUSTLERS SOME WATER AND LEMONADE. ACTUALLY, I LIKE ORANGE JUICE.
CAN'T PERSONALLY LEAVE THE STAGE DURING A SHOW, YOU KNOW.
HE ALWAYS SENDS THE SOUND MONSTER TO GET THE DRINKS. S'WHAT HE DOES EVERY SHOW. IT'S A CROWD PLEASER.
UNLESS SOME BIG HERO TYPE BREAKS UP MY PLACE.
UHH, I'LL PAY FOR THE DAMAGES.
LISTEN, GUYS, HONEST. I'VE GONE STRAIGHT. I'M USING MY POWERS AND KNOWLEDGE FOR MUSIC NOW. NOT CRIME.
WITH MY PAST, I CAN'T BLAME YOU FOR CHECKING UP ON ME, BUT THIS TIME'S FOR REAL.
I'M AN HONEST MAN NOW.

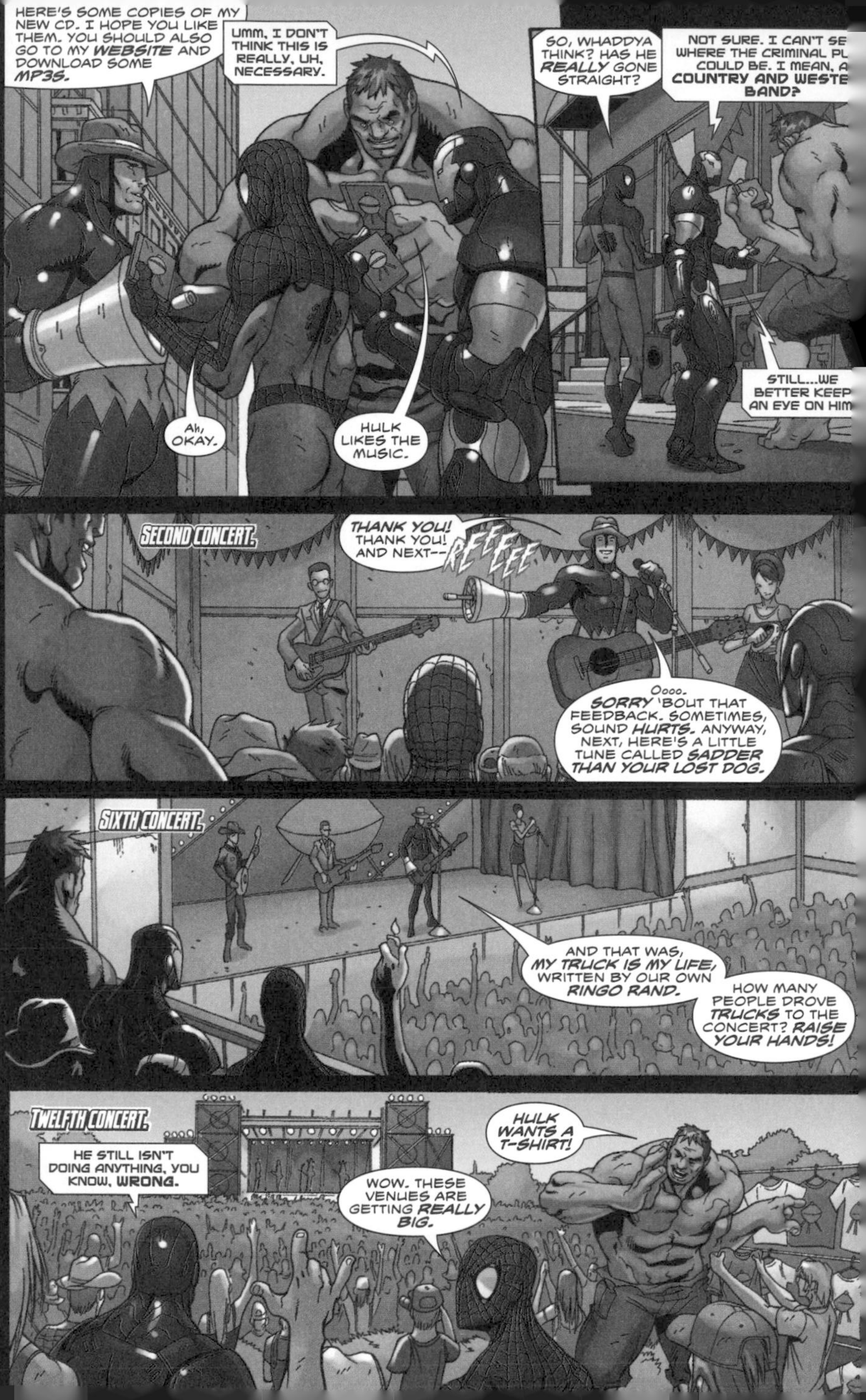
HERE'S SOME COPIES OF MY NEW CD. I HOPE YOU LIKE THEM. YOU SHOULD ALSO GO TO MY WEBSITE AND DOWNLOAD SOME MP3S.
UMM, I DON'T THINK THIS IS REALLY, UH, NECESSARY.
Ah, OKAY.
HULK LIKES THE MUSIC.
SO, WHADDYA THINK? HAS HE REALLY GONE STRAIGHT?
NOT SURE. I CAN'T SE WHERE THE CRIMINAL PL COULD BE. I MEAN, A COUNTRY AND WESTE BAND?
STILL...WE BETTER KEEP AN EYE ON HIM
SECOND CONCERT.
THANK YOU! THANK YOU! AND NEXT--
REEEEEE
Oooo. SORRY 'BOUT THAT FEEDBACK. SOMETIMES, SOUND HURTS. ANYWAY, NEXT, HERE'S A LITTLE TUNE CALLED SADDER THAN YOUR LOST DOG.
SIXTH CONCERT.
AND THAT WAS, MY TRUCK IS MY LIFE, WRITTEN BY OUR OWN RINGO RAND.
HOW MANY PEOPLE DROVE TRUCKS TO THE CONCERT? RAISE YOUR HANDS!
TWELFTH CONCERT.
HE STILL ISN'T DOING ANYTHING, YOU KNOW, WRONG.
HULK WANTS A T-SHIRT!
WOW. THESE VENUES ARE GETTING REALLY BIG.

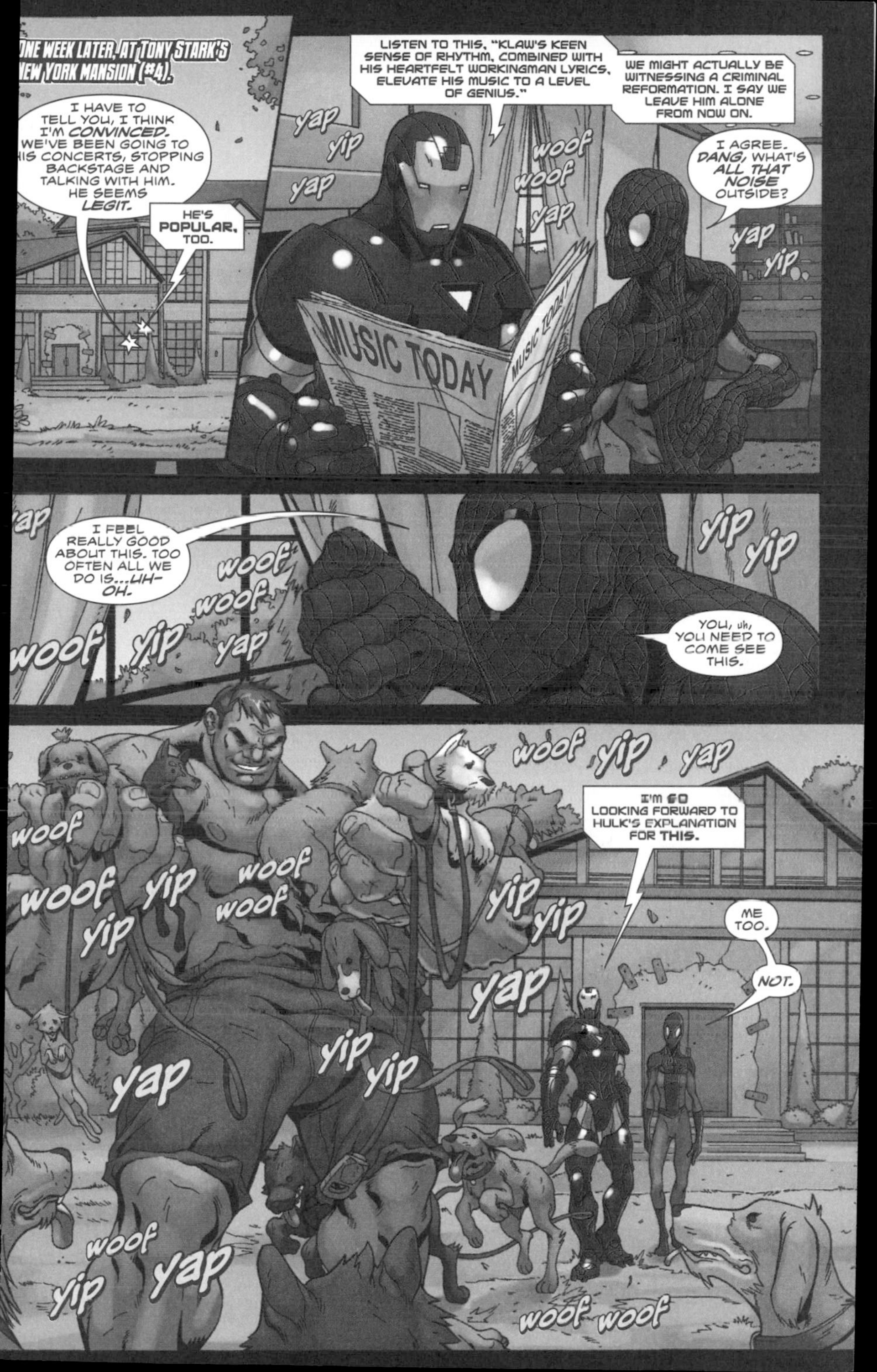
ONE WEEK LATER, AT TONY STARK'S NEW YORK MANSION (#4).
I HAVE TO TELL YOU, I THINK I'M CONVINCED. WE'VE BEEN GOING TO HIS CONCERTS, STOPPING BACKSTAGE AND TALKING WITH HIM. HE SEEMS LEGIT.
HE'S POPULAR, TOO.
LISTEN TO THIS, "KLAW'S KEEN SENSE OF RHYTHM, COMBINED WITH HIS HEARTFELT WORKINGMAN LYRICS, ELEVATE HIS MUSIC TO A LEVEL OF GENIUS."
WE MIGHT ACTUALLY BE WITNESSING A CRIMINAL REFORMATION. I SAY WE LEAVE HIM ALONE FROM NOW ON.
I AGREE. DANG, WHAT'S ALL THAT NOISE OUTSIDE?
MUSIC TODAY
yap yip yap woof woof yap yap yip
I FEEL REALLY GOOD ABOUT THIS. TOO OFTEN ALL WE DO IS...UH-OH.
YOU, uh, YOU NEED TO COME SEE THIS.
yap woof woof woof yip yap yip yip
woof yip, yap
I'M SO LOOKING FORWARD TO HULK'S EXPLANATION FOR THIS.
ME TOO.
NOT.
woof woof yip woof woof yip yip yip yap yip yip yap woof yip yap woof woof

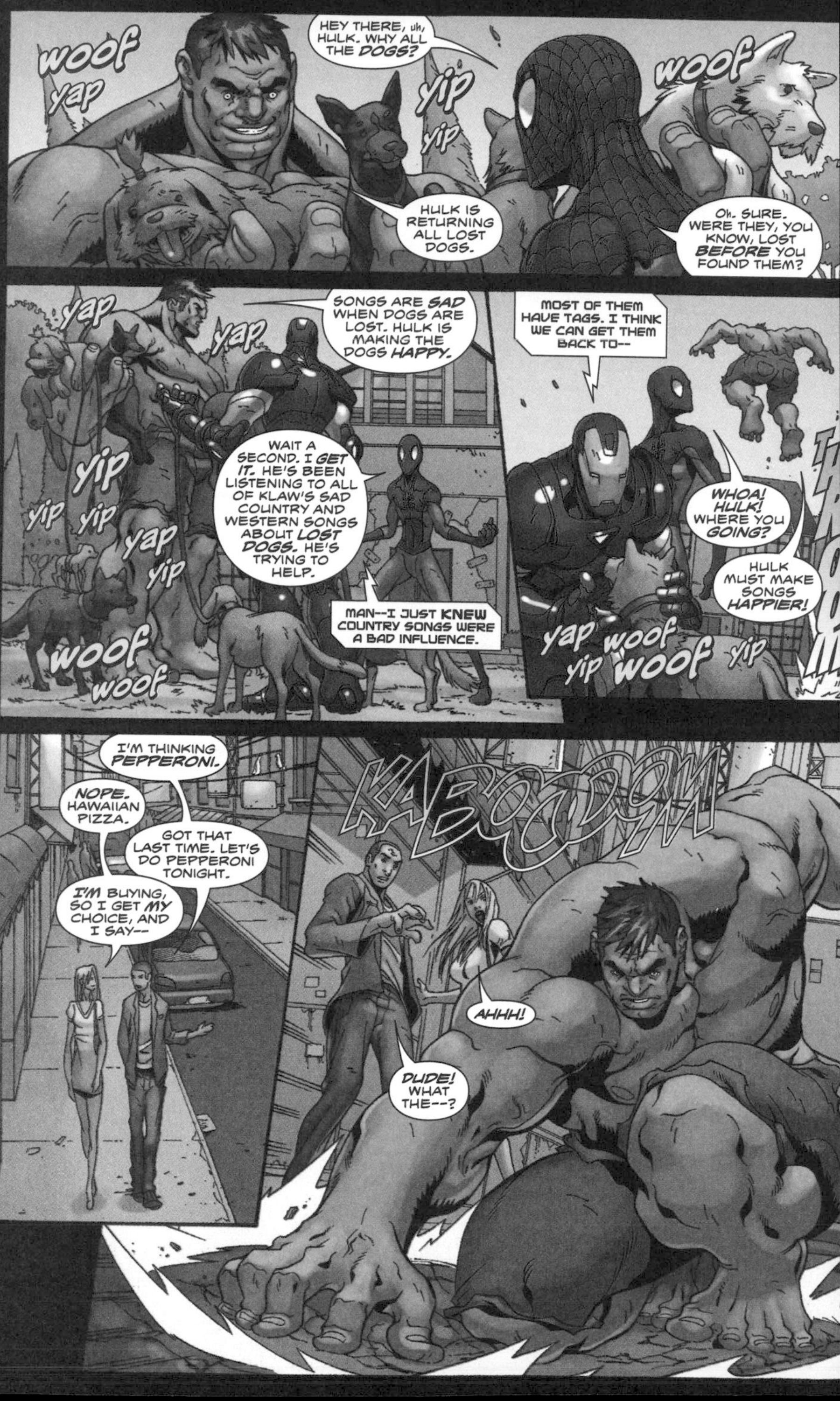
woof
yap
HEY THERE, uh, HULK. WHY ALL THE DOGS?
yip
yip
woof
HULK IS RETURNING ALL LOST DOGS.
Oh. SURE. WERE THEY, YOU KNOW, LOST BEFORE YOU FOUND THEM?
yap
yap
SONGS ARE SAD WHEN DOGS ARE LOST. HULK IS MAKING THE DOGS HAPPY.
WAIT A SECOND. I GET IT. HE'S BEEN LISTENING TO ALL OF KLAW'S SAD COUNTRY AND WESTERN SONGS ABOUT LOST DOGS. HE'S TRYING TO HELP.
MAN--I JUST KNEW COUNTRY SONGS WERE A BAD INFLUENCE.
yip
yip yip
yap
yip
woof
woof
MOST OF THEM HAVE TAGS. I THINK WE CAN GET THEM BACK TO--
WHOA! HULK! WHERE YOU GOING?
HULK MUST MAKE SONGS HAPPIER!
yap woof
yip WOOF yip
I'M THINKING PEPPERONI.
NOPE. HAWAIIAN PIZZA.
GOT THAT LAST TIME. LET'S DO PEPPERONI TONIGHT.
I'M BUYING, SO I GET MY CHOICE, AND I SAY--
KABOOOOM
AHHH!
DUDE! WHAT THE--?

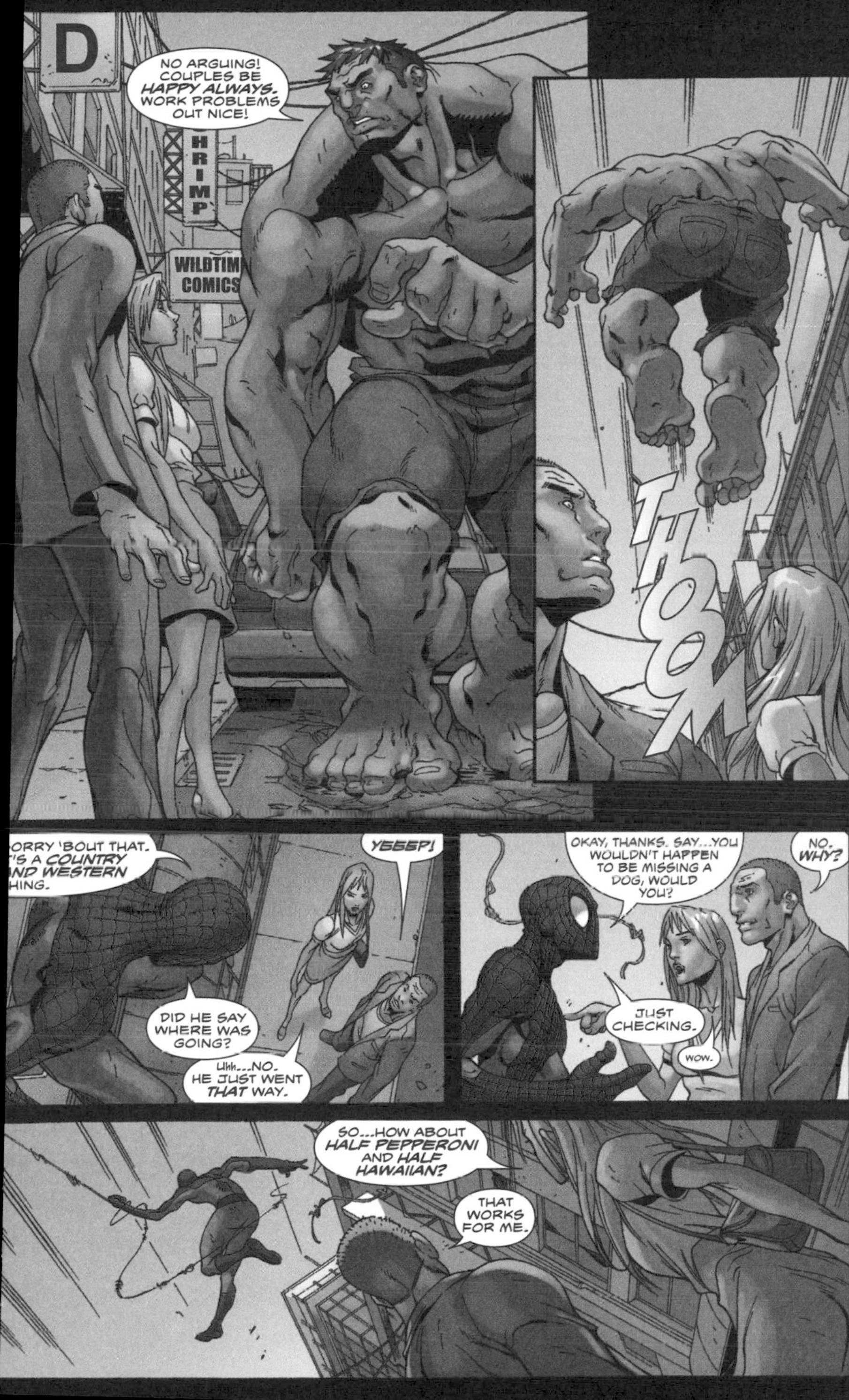

D
NO ARGUING! COUPLES BE *HAPPY ALWAYS.* WORK PROBLEMS OUT NICE!
SHRIMP
WILDTIM
COMICS
THOOM
ORRY 'BOUT THAT. T'S A *COUNTRY AND WESTERN* HING.
YEEEP!
DID HE SAY WHERE WAS GOING?
UHH...NO. HE JUST WENT *THAT* WAY.
OKAY, THANKS. SAY...YOU WOULDN'T HAPPEN TO BE MISSING A DOG, WOULD YOU?
NO. *WHY?*
JUST CHECKING.
WOW.
SO...HOW ABOUT *HALF PEPPERONI* AND *HALF HAWAIIAN?*
THAT WORKS FOR ME.

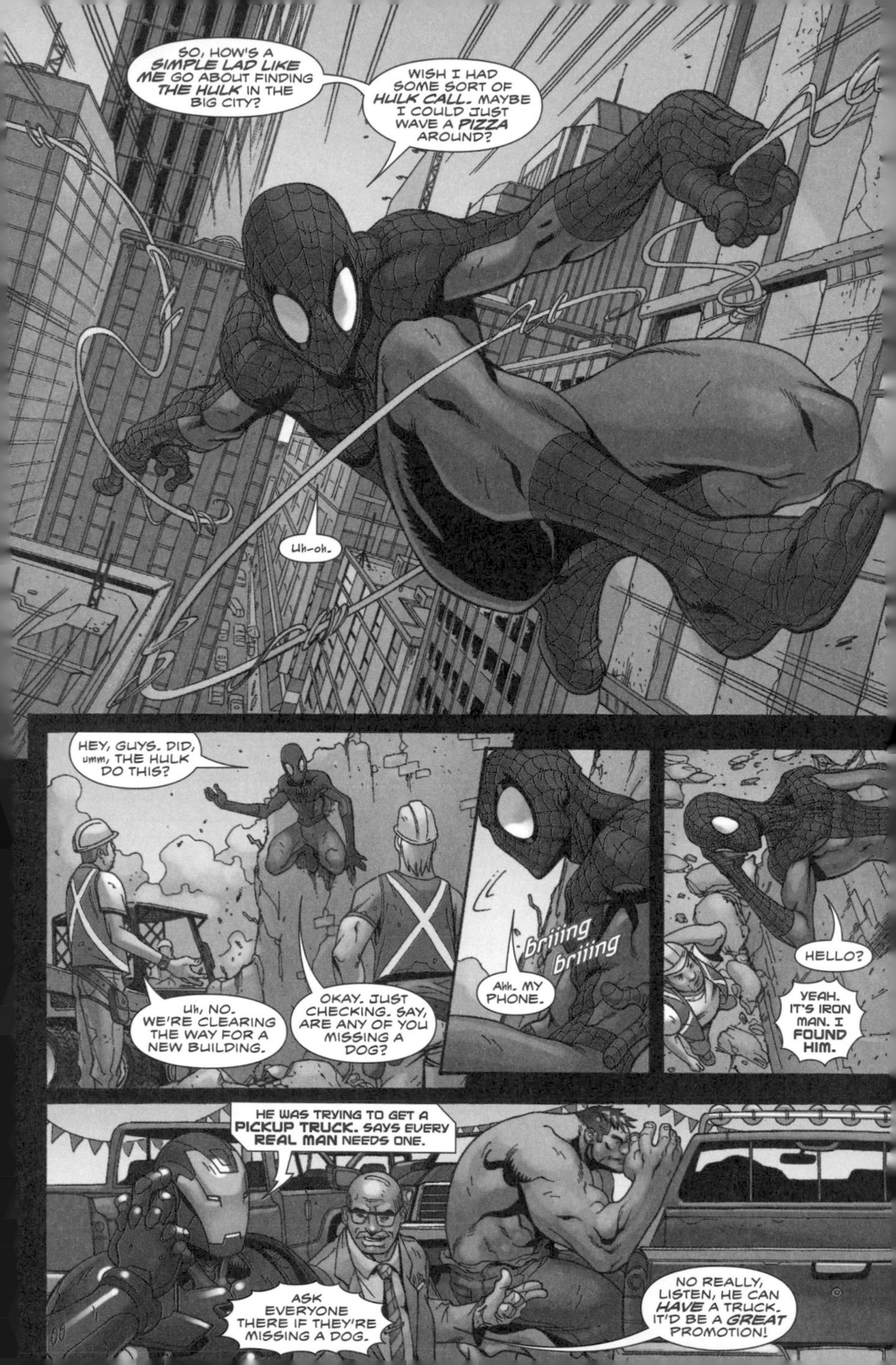
SO, HOW'S A SIMPLE LAD LIKE ME GO ABOUT FINDING THE HULK IN THE BIG CITY?
WISH I HAD SOME SORT OF HULK CALL. MAYBE I COULD JUST WAVE A PIZZA AROUND?
Uh-oh.
HEY, GUYS. DID, umm, THE HULK DO THIS?
Uh, NO. WE'RE CLEARING THE WAY FOR A NEW BUILDING.
OKAY. JUST CHECKING. SAY, ARE ANY OF YOU MISSING A DOG?
briiing briiing
Ahh. MY PHONE.
HELLO?
YEAH. IT'S IRON MAN. I FOUND HIM.
HE WAS TRYING TO GET A PICKUP TRUCK. SAYS EVERY REAL MAN NEEDS ONE.
ASK EVERYONE THERE IF THEY'RE MISSING A DOG.
NO REALLY, LISTEN, HE CAN HAVE A TRUCK. IT'D BE A GREAT PROMOTION!

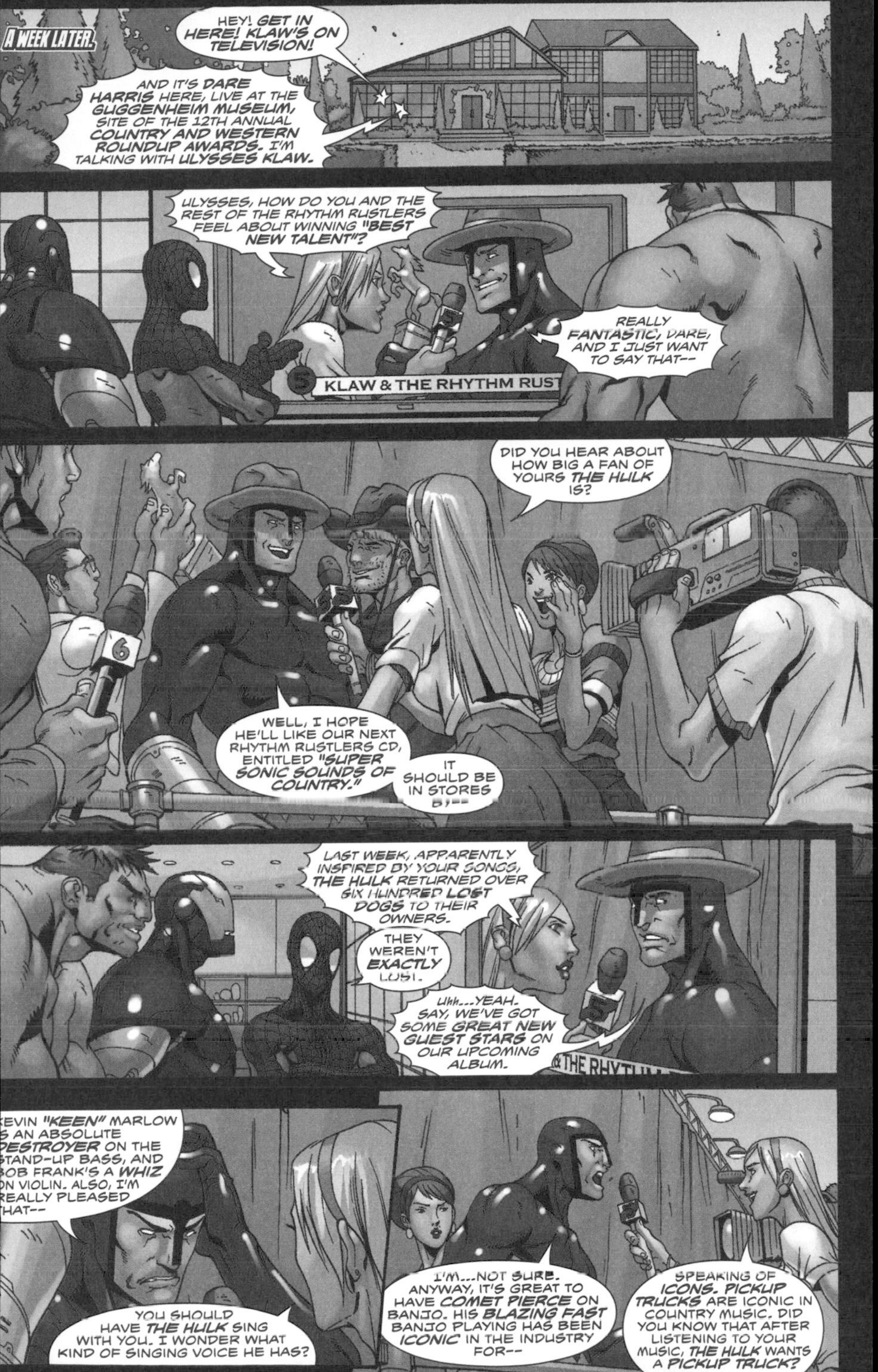
A WEEK LATER.
HEY! GET IN HERE! KLAW'S ON TELEVISION!
AND IT'S DARE HARRIS HERE, LIVE AT THE GUGGENHEIM MUSEUM, SITE OF THE 12TH ANNUAL COUNTRY AND WESTERN ROUNDUP AWARDS. I'M TALKING WITH ULYSSES KLAW.
ULYSSES, HOW DO YOU AND THE REST OF THE RHYTHM RUSTLERS FEEL ABOUT WINNING "BEST NEW TALENT"?
REALLY FANTASTIC, DARE, AND I JUST WANT TO SAY THAT--
KLAW & THE RHYTHM RUST
DID YOU HEAR ABOUT HOW BIG A FAN OF YOURS THE HULK IS?
WELL, I HOPE HE'LL LIKE OUR NEXT RHYTHM RUSTLERS CD, ENTITLED "SUPER SONIC SOUNDS OF COUNTRY."
IT SHOULD BE IN STORES BY--
LAST WEEK, APPARENTLY INSPIRED BY YOUR SONGS, THE HULK RETURNED OVER SIX HUNDRED LOST DOGS TO THEIR OWNERS.
THEY WEREN'T EXACTLY LOST.
UHH...YEAH. SAY, WE'VE GOT SOME GREAT NEW GUEST STARS ON OUR UPCOMING ALBUM.
& THE RHYTHM
KEVIN "KEEN" MARLOW IS AN ABSOLUTE DESTROYER ON THE STAND-UP BASS, AND BOB FRANK'S A WHIZ ON VIOLIN. ALSO, I'M REALLY PLEASED THAT--
YOU SHOULD HAVE THE HULK SING WITH YOU. I WONDER WHAT KIND OF SINGING VOICE HE HAS?
I'M...NOT SURE. ANYWAY, IT'S GREAT TO HAVE COMET PIERCE ON BANJO. HIS BLAZING FAST BANJO PLAYING HAS BEEN ICONIC IN THE INDUSTRY FOR--
SPEAKING OF ICONS. PICKUP TRUCKS ARE ICONIC IN COUNTRY MUSIC. DID YOU KNOW THAT AFTER LISTENING TO YOUR MUSIC, THE HULK WANTS A PICKUP TRUCK?

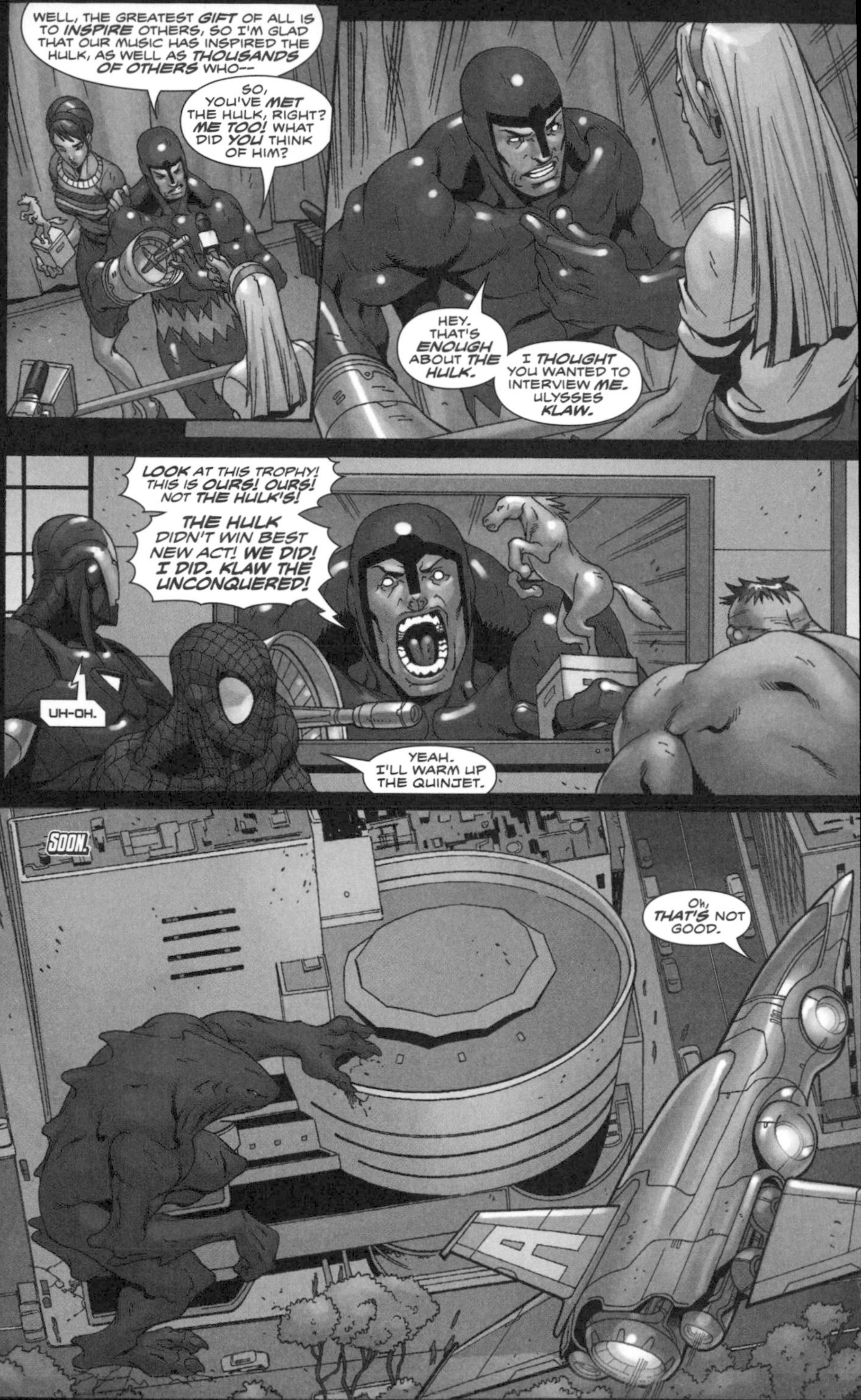
WELL, THE GREATEST GIFT OF ALL IS TO INSPIRE OTHERS, SO I'M GLAD THAT OUR MUSIC HAS INSPIRED THE HULK, AS WELL AS THOUSANDS OF OTHERS WHO--
SO, YOU'VE MET THE HULK, RIGHT? ME TOO! WHAT DID YOU THINK OF HIM?
HEY. THAT'S ENOUGH ABOUT THE HULK.
I THOUGHT YOU WANTED TO INTERVIEW ME. ULYSSES KLAW.
LOOK AT THIS TROPHY! THIS IS OURS! OURS! NOT THE HULK'S!
THE HULK DIDN'T WIN BEST NEW ACT! WE DID! I DID. KLAW THE UNCONQUERED!
UH-OH.
YEAH. I'LL WARM UP THE QUINJET.
SOON.
Oh, THAT'S NOT GOOD.

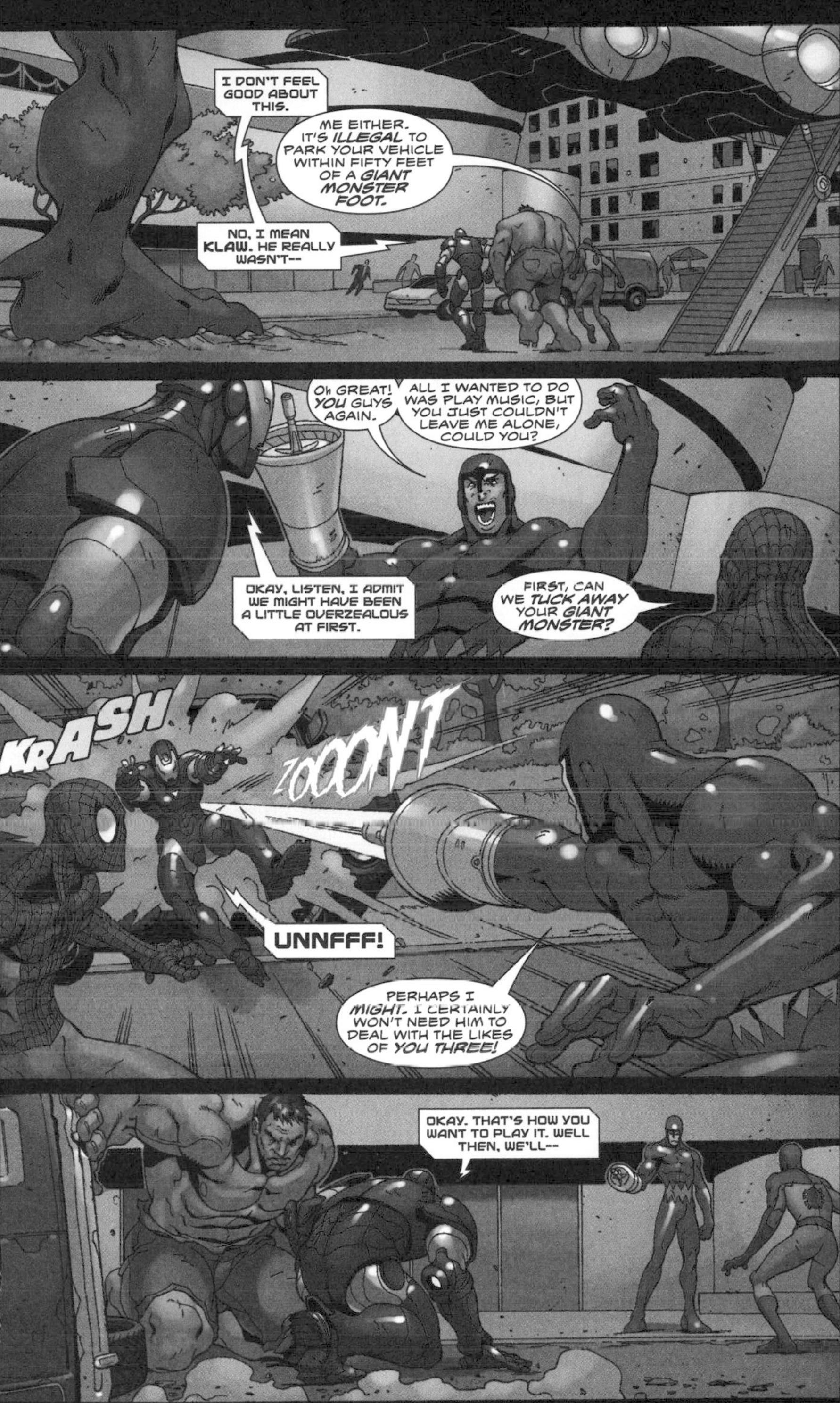
I DON'T FEEL GOOD ABOUT THIS.
ME EITHER. IT'S ILLEGAL TO PARK YOUR VEHICLE WITHIN FIFTY FEET OF A GIANT MONSTER FOOT.
NO, I MEAN KLAW. HE REALLY WASN'T--
Oh GREAT! YOU GUYS AGAIN.
ALL I WANTED TO DO WAS PLAY MUSIC, BUT YOU JUST COULDN'T LEAVE ME ALONE, COULD YOU?
OKAY, LISTEN, I ADMIT WE MIGHT HAVE BEEN A LITTLE OVERZEALOUS AT FIRST.
FIRST, CAN WE TUCK AWAY YOUR GIANT MONSTER?
KRASH
ZOOONT
UNNFFF!
PERHAPS I MIGHT. I CERTAINLY WON'T NEED HIM TO DEAL WITH THE LIKES OF YOU THREE!
OKAY. THAT'S HOW YOU WANT TO PLAY IT. WELL THEN, WE'LL--

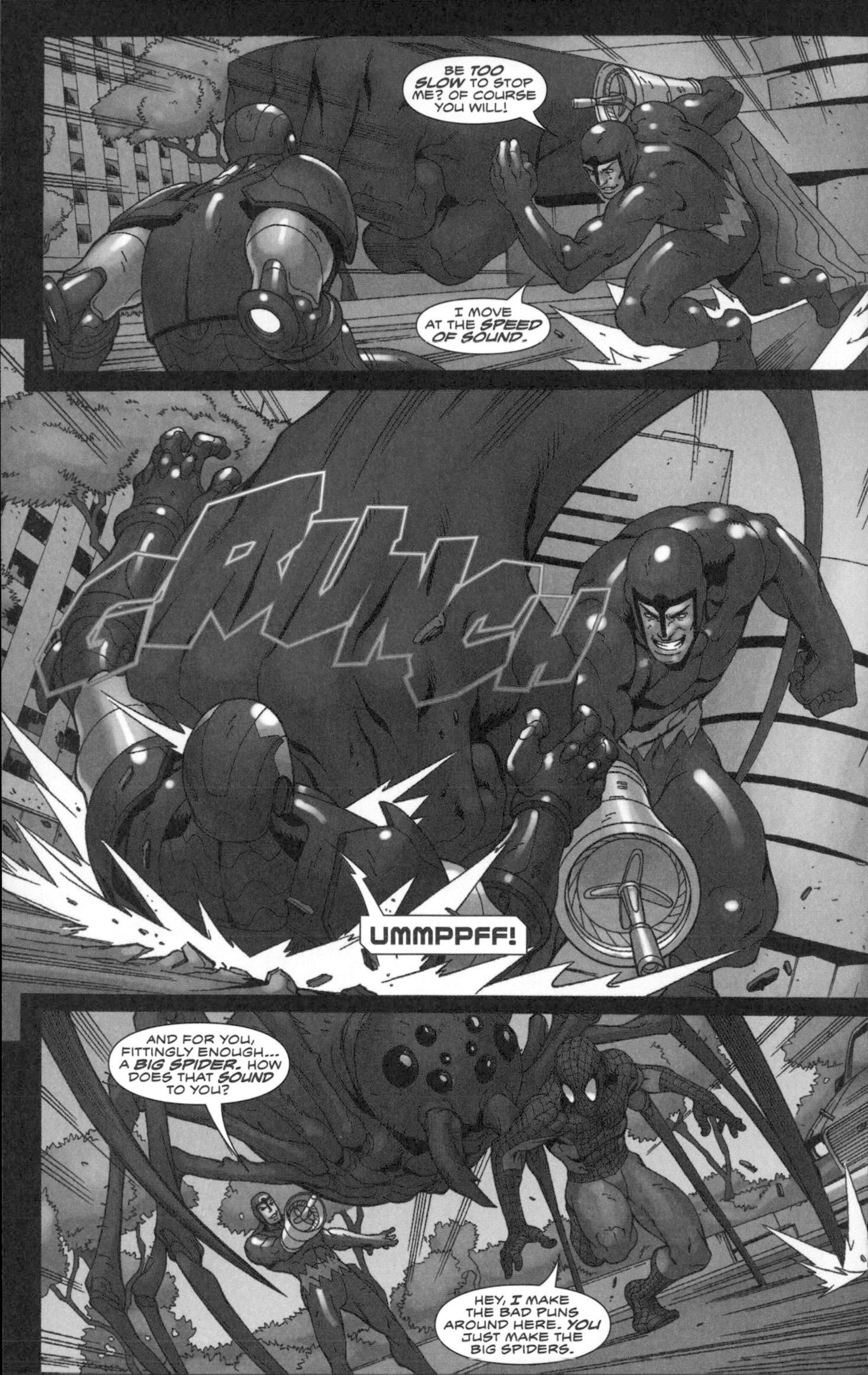
BE TOO SLOW TO STOP ME? OF COURSE YOU WILL!
I MOVE AT THE SPEED OF SOUND.
CRUNCH
UMMPPFF!
AND FOR YOU, FITTINGLY ENOUGH... A BIG SPIDER. HOW DOES THAT SOUND TO YOU?
HEY, I MAKE THE BAD PUNS AROUND HERE. YOU JUST MAKE THE BIG SPIDERS.

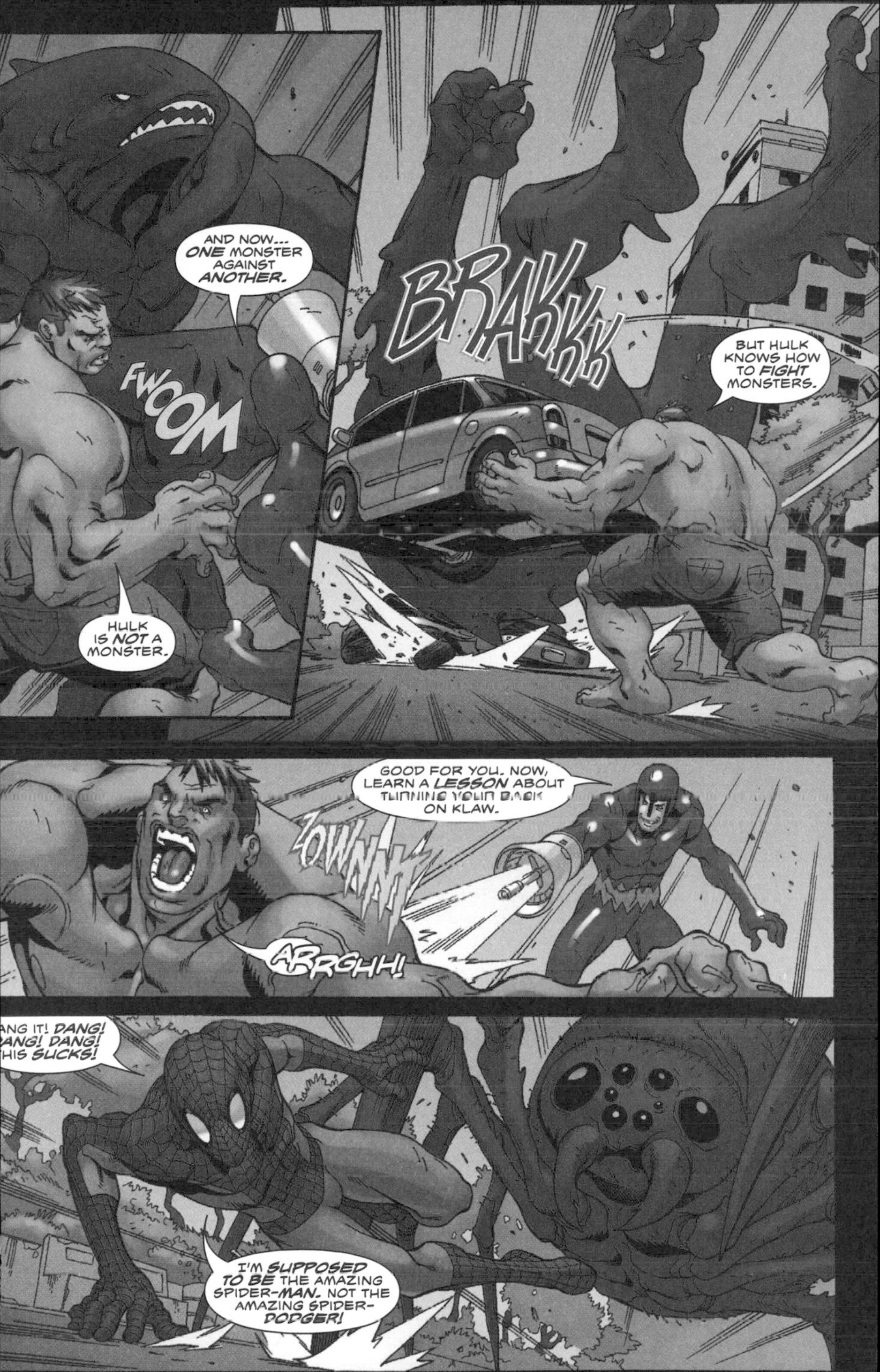
AND NOW... ONE MONSTER AGAINST ANOTHER.
FWOOM
HULK IS NOT A MONSTER.
BRAKKK
BUT HULK KNOWS HOW TO FIGHT MONSTERS.
GOOD FOR YOU. NOW, LEARN A LESSON ABOUT TURNING YOUR BACK ON KLAW.
ZOWNNN
ARRGHH!
I'M SUPPOSED TO BE THE AMAZING SPIDER-MAN. NOT THE AMAZING SPIDER-DODGER!

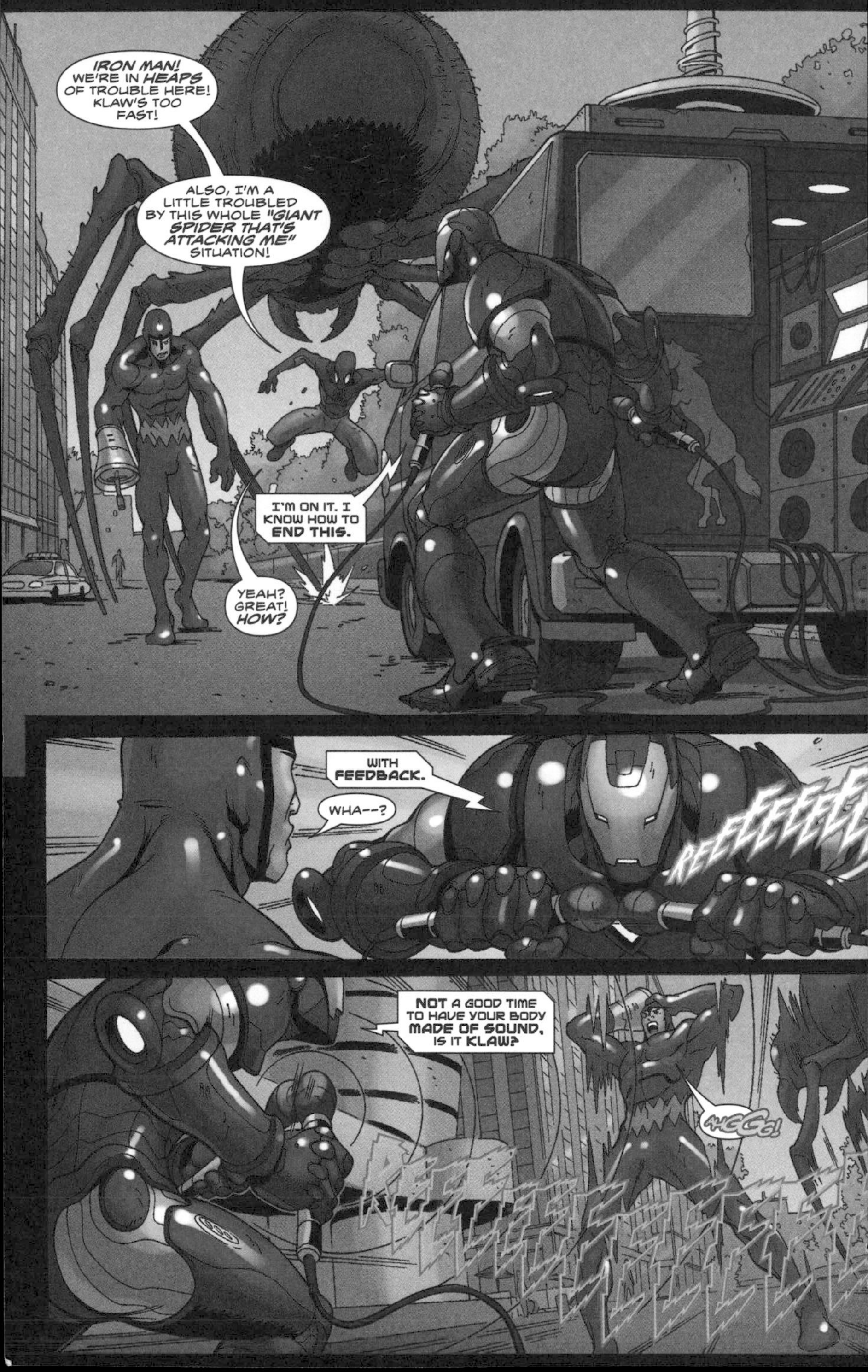
IRON MAN! WE'RE IN HEAPS OF TROUBLE HERE! KLAW'S TOO FAST!
ALSO, I'M A LITTLE TROUBLED BY THIS WHOLE "GIANT SPIDER THAT'S ATTACKING ME" SITUATION!
I'M ON IT. I KNOW HOW TO END THIS.
YEAH? GREAT! HOW?
WITH FEEDBACK.
WHA--?
REEEEEEEE
NOT A GOOD TIME TO HAVE YOUR BODY MADE OF SOUND, IS IT KLAW?
AHGGG!

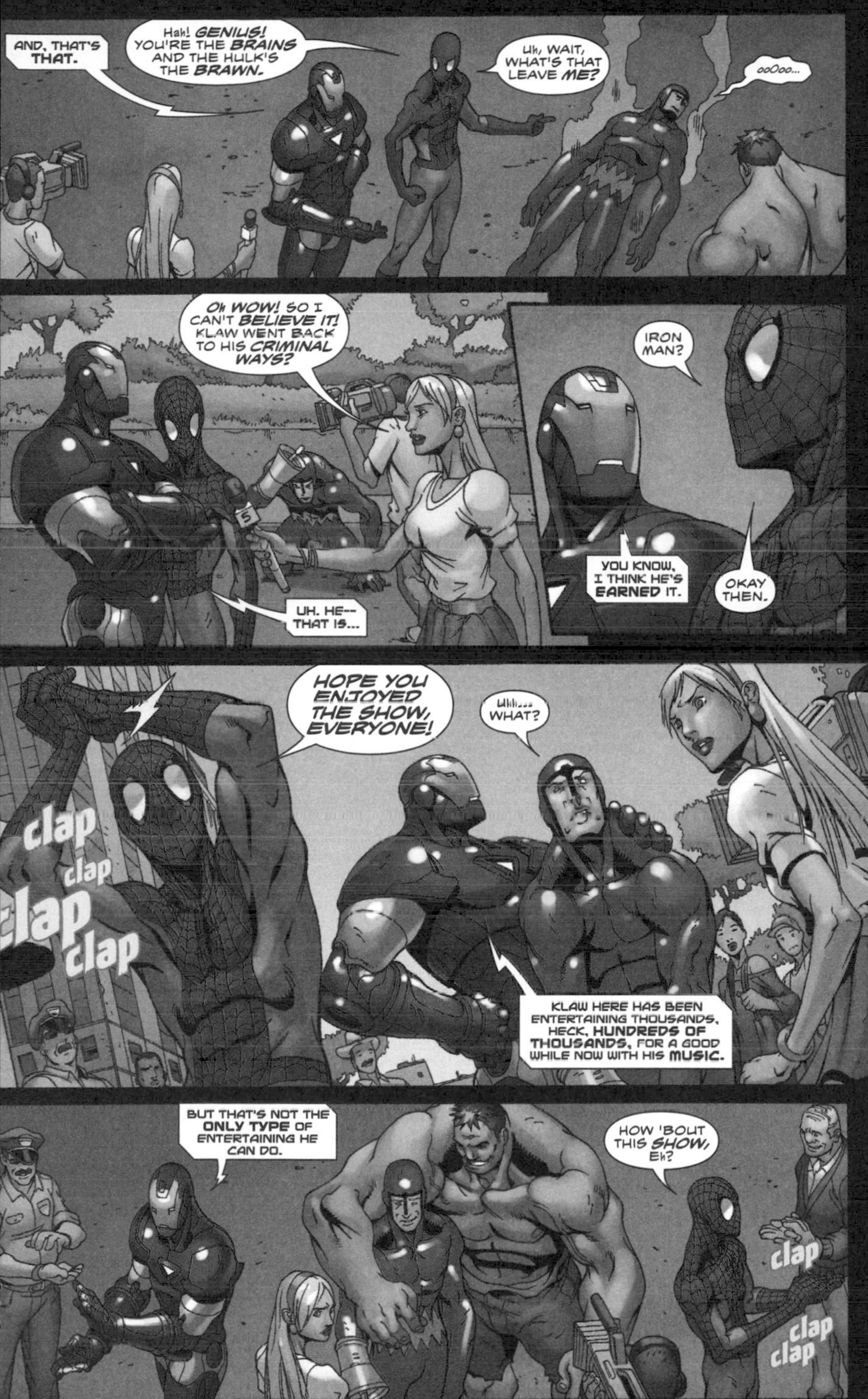
AND, THAT'S THAT.
Hah! GENIUS! YOU'RE THE BRAINS AND THE HULK'S THE BRAWN.
Uh, WAIT, WHAT'S THAT LEAVE ME?
ooOoo...
Oh WOW! SO I CAN'T BELIEVE IT! KLAW WENT BACK TO HIS CRIMINAL WAYS?
UH. HE-- THAT IS...
IRON MAN?
YOU KNOW, I THINK HE'S EARNED IT.
OKAY THEN.
HOPE YOU ENJOYED THE SHOW, EVERYONE!
Uhh.... WHAT?
clap
clap
clap
clap
KLAW HERE HAS BEEN ENTERTAINING THOUSANDS, HECK, HUNDREDS OF THOUSANDS, FOR A GOOD WHILE NOW WITH HIS MUSIC.
BUT THAT'S NOT THE ONLY TYPE OF ENTERTAINING HE CAN DO.
HOW 'BOUT THIS SHOW, Eh?
clap
clap
clap

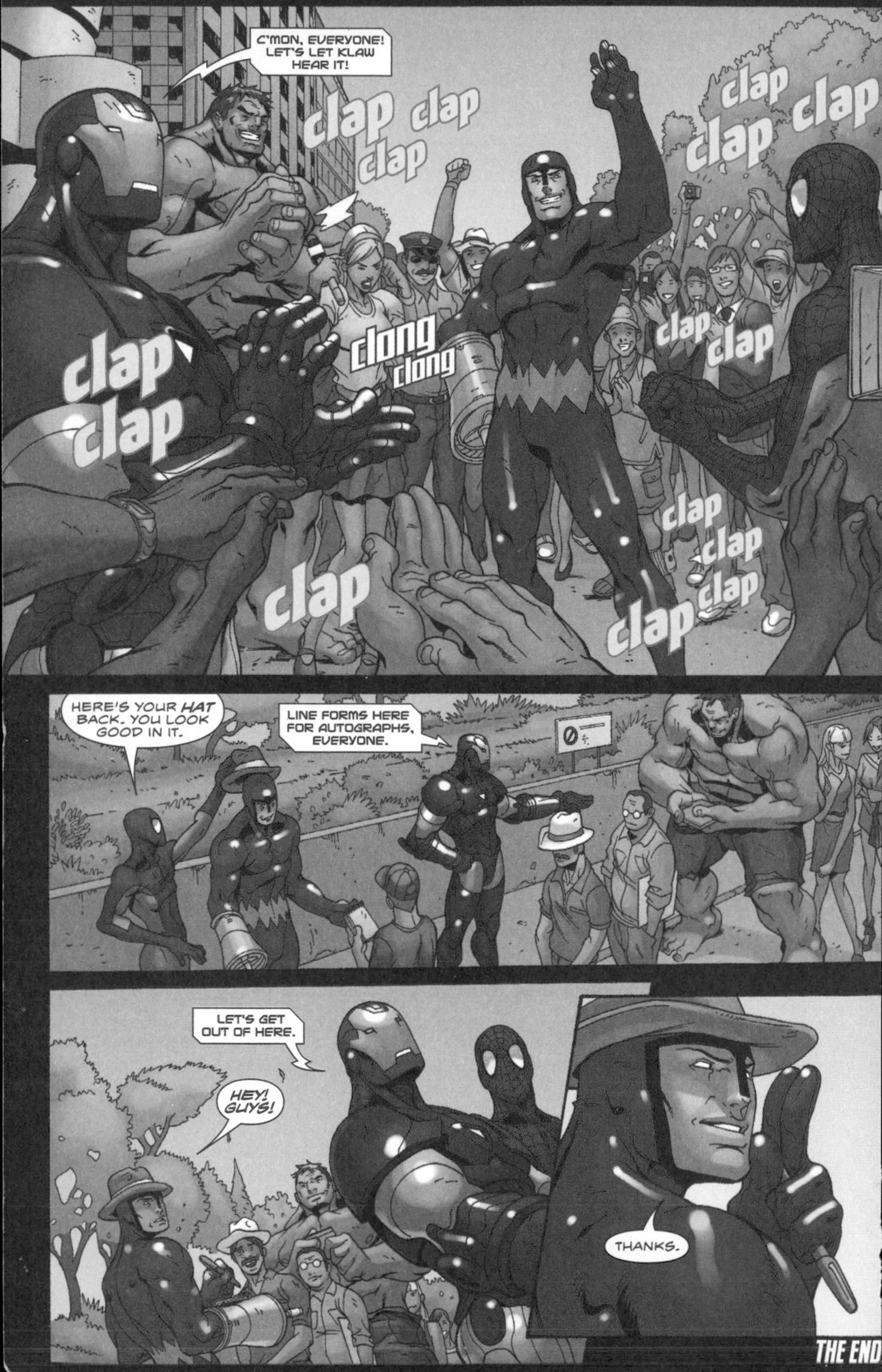
C'MON, EVERYONE! LET'S LET KLAW HEAR IT!
clap clap
clap
clap
clap clap clap
clap
clap
clong
clong
clap clap
clap
clap
clap
clap clap
HERE'S YOUR HAT BACK. YOU LOOK GOOD IN IT.
LINE FORMS HERE FOR AUTOGRAPHS, EVERYONE.
LET'S GET OUT OF HERE.
HEY! GUYS!
THANKS.
THE END